"I don't need you to complicate everything."

"You can fire me. I'll be off this property before morning."

To his surprise, her voice shook. "If I fired you, Jesse would try to take your place. Prove himself the better choice." She lightened her tone. "No, I do appreciate your help. I'll stick with what I have. Thank you for your faith in me."

Cooper reached out to frame Nell's face in his hands, and she didn't jerk free. Her chin tilted up and her gaze held his. "I'm not your enemy, Nell. Remember that."

He expected her to challenge him, to remind him that because he wanted what she did, too, they were indeed enemies. Instead, Nell closed the short distance between them, and in the same instant Cooper drew her to him, relishing the feel of Nell against him. Cooper lowered his head and kissed her, soft and light and warm, telling himself this wasn't good for him, or his plans.

But it was exactly what he wanted...

Dear Reader,

I'm so pleased to be able to tell you about this month's release in my Kansas Cowboys series.

I can certainly relate to the hero, Cooper Ransom. Moving all my belongings across the country to Arizona helped me understand Cooper and his quest to reclaim the Kansas ranch he lost years ago. Could he also have another chance with Nell Sutherland?

Readers of the series might remember Nell—she appeared in *Her Cowboy Sheriff* as Annabelle Foster's friend...and one real tough cookie. Cooper is also in that book. He was Finn Donovan's friend and ex-partner in Chicago. The more I wrote about Cooper and Nell, the more I wanted to bring them together in their own story.

A born cowgirl, and fiercely independent, Nell is determined to fulfill her lifelong dream to inherit the vast NLS ranch. But Nell's family has different ideas. Cooper seems to be the one person on her side. Or is he just trying to take away his former land?

These two will run into a lot of trouble before they straighten things out. In the meantime, I've settled into my new house and am feeling, like Cooper, that I've really come home. It's a good place to be!

I hope you enjoy your "ride" through the NLS under that big blue Kansas sky (Nell and Cooper will be glad to lend you a horse). And if you haven't read the rest of the series, check out the other books in the Kansas Cowboys series.

Happy reading, my friends!

Leigh

HEARTWARMING

The Rancher's Second Chance

———

Leigh Riker

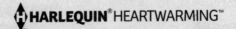

Recycling programs
for this product may
not exist in your area.

ISBN-13: 978-1-335-51067-9

The Rancher's Second Chance

Copyright © 2019 by Leigh Riker

Printed in U.S.A.

® HARLEQUIN®

™ www.Harlequin.com

Leigh Riker, like so many dedicated readers, grew up with her nose in a book, and weekly trips to the local library for a new stack of stories were a favorite thing to do. This award-winning, *USA TODAY* bestselling author still can't imagine a better way to spend her time than to curl up with a good romance novel—unless it is to write one! She is a member of The Authors Guild, Novelists, Inc. and Romance Writers of America. When not at the computer, she's out on the patio tending flowers, watching hummingbirds, spending time with family and friends or, perhaps, traveling (for research purposes, of course). She loves to hear from readers. You can find Leigh on her website, leighriker.com, on Facebook at leighrikerauthor and on Twitter, @lbrwriter.

Books by Leigh Riker

Harlequin Heartwarming

Kansas Cowboys

The Reluctant Rancher
Last Chance Cowboy
Cowboy on Call
Her Cowboy Sheriff

A Heartwarming Thanksgiving
"Her Thanksgiving Soldier"
Lost and Found Family
Man of the Family
If I Loved You

Visit the Author Profile page
at Harlequin.com for more titles.

For the loyal readers of Heartwarming,
a big thanks to all of you!

And another to my editor, Adrienne Macintosh,
and everyone else at Harlequin who helps to
create such truly heartwarming books.

CHAPTER ONE

THE LAST THING he'd expected today was a visitor. This one, in particular.

"I see you're still alive," she said, as if she couldn't quite believe it.

Cooper Ransom shifted in the recliner where he'd been watching TV. Months ago, the movement would have made him groan from his injuries. He still wasn't 100 percent, but Cooper refused to show Nell Sutherland any kind of weakness.

He hadn't seen her in fourteen years, but without warning Nell had shown up at the old Moran farm, where he was staying with friends till he was fully recovered. He shouldn't have been surprised Nell had appeared; she still lived outside Barren, and sooner or later they were bound to run into each other. But there'd been a time when he believed he'd never see Nell again. And he couldn't find a reason for her to be here now.

"Did you think I was dying, or what?"

Barely glancing at him, she strolled over to the living room window. Her voice shook. "I left a bunch of wandering cows to see for myself that you're not about to *cash in your chips*—as my grandfather might say. Don't make me regret my charitable impulse."

Nell looked through the window at the April day, slightly warmer in Kansas than it was in still-frigid Illinois. But he'd left that all behind now, thanks to a spray of bullets during a gang ambush there.

He studied her. In her scuffed boots, well-worn jeans and blue-plaid Western shirt, she still exemplified what she was—a born cowgirl. Nell looked taller than he remembered but she continued to stand with a proud set to her shoulders and the familiar tilt of her head as she gazed out at the horses in the nearby pasture. Her glossy sheet of hair, the same lighter brown it had always been but with newer streaks of blond running through like fingers of sun, tumbled in a waterfall down her back. Cooper couldn't see her eyes, but he knew them well—the clear green of emeralds. He'd once given her a necklace with a tiny chip of the gem nestled in gold, all he could afford then. The last time he saw her, Nell had thrown the necklace back in his face.

She must still hate him, if that wasn't too strong a word. "You were worried about me," he said anyway.

Nell turned and, to his surprise, he saw in her eyes—were those tears? That was more like the Nell he knew. She'd always acted tough, but it masked her vulnerable heart. Long ago, she'd been willing to share it with him.

"Worried I'd never get another chance to tell you what I think of you," she said, "that's all."

"And what do you think?"

He saw a well-remembered glint in her eyes, but her expression had softened. "For now, I'm just glad you're still breathing."

The largest, still-raw scar across his abdomen proved he had, indeed, almost died, and that high-caliber bullet—not the only one to hit him—had plowed through his stomach, then ricocheted inside all over the place, causing more havoc as it spun. Cooper wouldn't say so, but he wondered if he'd ever be whole again. Most of the damage, covered by a white T-shirt and black sweat pants, wouldn't show now. But did she feel sorry for him?

He repeated her earlier words. "So you had to come see for yourself."

Their history wasn't one he cared to dwell on. As teenagers, they'd been inseparable—until his dad had been forced to sell his adjoining ranch to Nell's grandfather, yet another episode in a generations-long feud between their two families over land. Nell had taken her grandfather's side, and Cooper had vowed to get his family's ranch back, destroying their relationship in the process.

She worried her bottom lip. "I heard from Finn you were here," she said, then glanced away. "*He's* still worried about you."

Maybe she'd only wanted to see him brought low again. Cooper followed her glance at the shabby living room with its worn furniture, the old kitchen sink under the far window and the clean but cracked linoleum floor. Other than the fresh paint on the walls, and his friend Finn's new sofa, the place needed work. But Finn was proud to be the owner of these five original acres, plus the hundreds more he'd recently bought, and he seemed happy to belong in the local ranching community, as well as being sheriff. Barren was the county seat.

"Got to love small towns," Cooper said, where news certainly traveled fast. Here, he'd already lost the anonymity of living in a big city, and he didn't appreciate Finn, his former partner in Chicago, spreading the word.

"Your hometown too," Nell pointed out and Cooper flinched.

Instead of one day taking over his family's spread, at nineteen he had been torn out by his roots, deep ones that went back five generations. The Ransom ranch, with the very house where he'd grown up, sat between the towns of Barren and Farrier, its acreage now part of the NLS, the Sutherland ranch.

In the hospital, Cooper had had plenty of time to think. Life, he already knew as a cop, could be short, but now that included *his* life. He wouldn't wait any longer.

He didn't suppose Nell wanted to hear what he had in mind—he was here for his ranch.

WHY HAD SHE mentioned their hometown? Cooper's eyes had closed, his lashes like dark fans above his cheekbones. Was it a cue for her to leave? Seeing him now as if no time had passed—those gray eyes, his sunny hair still the same—threatened to be her undoing. Cooper reminded Nell of two things: his obvious resentment over losing the ranch and her long-ago wish that their version of puppy love might lead to something forever.

He was still the most attractive male she'd ever seen, but he wasn't the boy who'd once broken her heart. Their relationship—her first real star-crossed romance—had ended when that moving van pulled away and headed north for Chicago. If they couldn't talk without disagreeing, she should leave. Frankly, she wished she *hadn't* come.

"How long were you in the hospital?" she asked.

"Too long," he said but with a faint smile. "People poking me day and night. Nurses waking me every five minutes to do the same things all over again. And have you ever seen daytime TV?" He shot a glance at the set across the room. "Torture. It's a wonder anyone makes it out alive."

"But you did *make it out*."

"Yeah." A silence grew between them as if neither of them knew of a safer topic. "How's the NLS?" he asked.

"Couldn't be better." Considering his long-ago quarrel with her grandfather, he'd probably be happy to learn she was in over her head with the ranch, which she told herself, and mentally crossed her fingers, she was not.

"Ned's away?" he asked. "Finn mentioned him going to visit his brother."

Nell fought the urge to roll her eyes. Talk about a worse subject. "If those two manage to survive, I'll be amazed." In spite of her current irritation with her grandfather, her fears for him were never far from her mind. "PawPaw's health isn't that good."

Cooper's gaze sharpened. "I heard about his stroke."

"And let's not forget the car wreck he got into last October. He spent another week in Farrier General then, but there's more to that story." Nell cleared her throat. "Anyway. I was mostly in charge of the NLS while he was laid up, but he was at least able to make decisions with me then. Now it's all me. Unfortunately, he and his foreman don't agree that I should be *el jefe* now."

"La jefa," Cooper murmured as if to remind Nell she was a woman.

"Hadley Smith and I have been tangling ever since PawPaw left for Montana. And really, few of the NLS cowhands are more enlightened." Nell did roll her eyes then. "Feminism and the women's movement haven't reached the NLS."

It had taken her less than a week after her grandfather left to realize she was wasting precious time over Hadley, the NLS's foreman. This could be the chance she'd been waiting for. All her life, Nell's dream had been to inherit the vast ranch, and while PawPaw was gone, she intended to prove she could oversee it. No matter what Hadley might say.

"They don't believe you can do the job," Cooper said for her.

Nell flicked a strand of hair from her eyes. "Even my mother thinks the NLS is too hard a life for a woman—considering the outdated macho attitudes there." Her parents had never liked the ranch, and although her dad had tried to fit in and help his father, when Nell was twelve they'd given up, moved to the city with her brother and never looked back. Nell, who loved the ranch, had stayed to finish growing up with her widowed grandfather.

But if she didn't pull this off now, she could lose her right to the NLS for good. She knew PawPaw intended to redo his estate plan when he got home.

Cooper said, "So you're having trouble with…Smith?"

"Hadley Smith." His very name made her cringe. Normally, he was conscientious and did his job well when he wasn't trying to test or irritate Nell, but he still rubbed her the wrong way. "He reports everything to my grandfather. It's as if he wants me to fail." Hoping to change the subject again, Nell looked at Cooper. "Being a cop in Chicago must be hard too." *Even harder than ranching*, but she wouldn't say that. "And certainly more dangerous."

"It was never boring," he agreed, "but since I couldn't take over Dad's place…"

Nell had never understood his decision to join law enforcement. Just as she didn't want to be anything but a cowgirl, Cooper on a horse had been poetry in motion. He could ride even the meanest of the mean and make it look easy. Why hadn't he come back after he finished college, bought some land in the area and started over? But a light bulb glimmered in her head. "You said *was*," she reminded him.

His gaze flickered. "Yeah. Before I came to Barren, I quit the force."

Her pulse pounded. So far, she'd avoided firing Hadley, but Cooper knew their land as well as she did. "Then you'll need a job soon," she said, "and I may need a foreman. If I had a replacement, I'd fire Hadley in a heartbeat." She looked at him pointedly.

"Me? You serious?" Cooper said. "Does Smith know about this?"

"Not yet." And she'd worry about her grandfather's reaction later too.

She watched the emotions play across his face. Surprise, then temptation and even yearning? Her instincts had been right. Whether or not he'd admit it, she sensed Cooper was still a cowboy at heart.

Then he finally said, "No. Sorry."

His flat statement set her back on her boot heels. Disappointment ran through her like water down a drain. Had she asked simply because she needed a foreman who wouldn't undermine her at every turn? Or because she'd never gotten Cooper out of her system? *Don't go there.*

"Anyway, I have other plans," he said. "I need to tell you—warn you, maybe—" he took a breath "—the reason I'm here isn't just to finish healing, or because I quit my job or to visit Finn." He paused and Nell's pulse kicked into a higher gear. "You said it yourself. This is my hometown too, and when Ned gets back, I'm going to make your grandfather an offer he can't refuse."

"What offer?" She had a bad feeling she knew what he would say though.

"To buy the land my father lost to him."

"That's almost half of the NLS now!"

His mouth set. "Which should belong to me. I'm taking it back, Nell—like I promised. I've had plenty of time to save up the money, to invest what my dad left me when he died… It's the least I owe him."

"And you let me rattle on when all along you meant to start another range war—"

"That's not how it has to be."

"Oh, yes, it does," she said, and turned on her heel.

Nell was out the door before Cooper opened his mouth to say anything more.

And to even think of picking up where they'd left off. That would only show her grandfather she wasn't capable of taking over the NLS, that she needed a man. Long ago, she'd decided to put her focus where it belonged. Nell prided herself on being independent, even tough, and most of the time the facade hid her vulnerability, but all her life people had underestimated her. A romance would only get in the way of proving herself as boss of the NLS. *La jefa.*

She'd given up on love years ago when Cooper Ransom left the state. And now that he'd come home, nothing had changed.

CHAPTER TWO

NELL DROVE HOME with a heavy heart. Although she'd had nothing to do with the sale of Cooper's family ranch to her grandfather, she could see Cooper held her partly to blame for the loss. *Since I couldn't take over Dad's place*, he'd said, and she'd seen the lingering sorrow in his eyes. It didn't help that she understood. But to blindside her like that with his vow to actually take back the land?

She climbed down from her grandfather's pickup to open the gates to the NLS, still shaking. The tension began to drain from her though as she shut the gates. Home. This was where she belonged, and over the years, even the acreage acquired from the Ransoms had become part of her. Without the NLS—all of it—who would she be?

Nell whizzed along the driveway toward the barns, surveying with a practiced eye part of the herd on either side that was pastured there. Through the truck's half-open window, she heard an Angus calf bleat for its mother. All across both enclosures, under the clear blue Kansas sky, cows bent their heads to nibble the rich spring-green grass, and the constant lowing of the herd—as if they were talking among themselves— sounded like music to her ears.

On the other side of the lane, some of the ranch cow ponies, off duty for the day, munched grass too. A frisky colt, delivered into Nell's hands last winter on a cold, snowy night, lifted its head to nicker in greeting. "Hey, handsome," she called out.

At the barn, she brought the truck to a stop in front of the open doors. Her pulse sped up—as it had the instant she'd seen Cooper, if not in the same way. He wasn't here now—thank goodness—but, too bad for her, Hadley Smith was.

Alerted by the sound of the truck's engine, which knocked as if someone were banging on a door, PawPaw's foreman appeared, leading a dark gelding. With one thumb, he pushed back his battered hat, and a hunk of nearly black hair slipped across his forehead. As she climbed out of the pickup, a familiar scowl appeared on Hadley's face, and his cold blue eyes chilled her to the core.

She wished PawPaw had fired Hadley before he went to Montana. She was tired of his insubordination, which threatened her already tenuous authority.

"Wondered where you'd disappeared to," Hadley said in the lazy, exaggerated drawl he seemed to use only with her. Nell felt sure it was meant to put her in her place— the place *he'd* chosen for her.

All hard edges and sinewy strength, Hadley towered over Nell by a head. Everything about him seemed meant to intimidate, from the black hat on his head to his ebony shirt, dark jeans and boots. Even the horse he'd chosen from the NLS string was the color of polished onyx.

"I had errands in town," she said, then clamped her mouth shut. Hadley had a way of making her want to explain herself as if she was his employee rather than the other way around. When her grandfather was here, his foreman didn't dare step over a line, but with Nell on her own, he went out of his way to do so.

"You missed all the action," he muttered.

"What action?" But Hadley didn't enlighten her. Nell propped both hands on her hips. She'd gone over the day's schedule with him before she left to see Cooper, drawn by curiosity once more into his orbit. Compelled by a concern she didn't want to feel. Then he'd made her feel like a fool. One day, being so impulsive would get her into real trouble.

Hadley jerked the lead rope in his hand, and the gelding reared back against his too-tight hold. "Careful how you handle that horse," she said.

"He knows who's *boss*." His dismissive gaze ran down her form, taking in her aggressive stance. "You let an animal get the better of you once, you've already lost control."

Nell doubted he was talking about the horse. In her experience, Hadley was all about using raw power, beginning with her. She was determined to hold her own with him—and everyone else, including Cooper.

"I won't tolerate abuse of that horse or any other. Did you fix that fence on the Ransom side like I asked?" Saying the name aloud only reminded her of her unwise visit to Finn's house. She hardened her tone. "And the feed room's short of grain. That order should have been placed days ago." It wasn't like Hadley to overlook such a basic task.

He scowled. "I know how to do my job."

He didn't tell her whether he'd done it though, just as he hadn't explained whatever *action* she'd missed.

Her mouth tightened. "Then don't forget to call the vet. My grandfather's mare needs her teeth floated." The routine dental procedure filed the molars down to avoid sore spots from a horse's ever-growing teeth. PawPaw's horse was like another child to him. When he came home, his sleek roan would be waiting in perfect condition. Like the whole ranch. "She needs shoes again too. I won't see Beauty come up lame or founder just so you can prove a point."

"What point?" Hadley asked as if he didn't know what she was talking about.

Nell fought an urge to press the matter, but she'd made herself clear. If the work wasn't finished by sundown, he would hear from her. "Just do it."

She turned on her heel, glanced pointedly into the feed room on her way past, then stepped out into the sun, its warmth almost overcoming the chill she felt inside. She sensed Hadley standing there, staring after her. If she spun around, she'd surely catch a knowing smirk on his face, as if he saw right through her shaky confidence.

COOPER REACHED FOR his mug of cold coffee on the end table by the recliner. He took one sip, then with a grimace, set the cup aside. Holding the remote control that was becoming welded to his hand, he changed channels again. He'd seen today's depressing news half a dozen times this afternoon on every station since Nell had left but nothing could remove her from his thoughts.

He couldn't seem to suppress the image: the tilt of her lips when she smiled, the clean line of her jaw, the graceful arch of her neck, her naturally husky voice or the fierce spirit that had first drawn him to her. In the years since he'd last seen her, she'd become a beautiful woman... One who wanted nothing to do with him, Cooper guessed, because Nell all but wore an imaginary sign that said Keep Away.

So what was the foreman thing about? Was that why she'd really come to see him? Nell herself had implied that, most likely, Ned Sutherland wouldn't be able to manage the NLS much longer. What would happen when Cooper made his offer to her grandfather? Once she realized his vow to get his land back was no empty threat, how would she react then?

The front door opened, and he straightened in the chair, half expecting Nell to be there, her eyes shooting sparks and ready for battle. Instead, Finn Donovan walked in, loosening the top buttons of his white dress shirt and running a hand through his dark hair. As the sheriff of Stewart County, Kansas, Finn rarely wore his uniform or badge and almost never a suit. He preferred jeans.

"A day in court, wearing a jacket and shiny shoes. My favorite part of the job," he said, watching Cooper shut off the television.

Cooper shifted again. "My day wasn't that much better. Thanks, by the way, for telling Nell Sutherland I was here."

"She came by?" When Cooper nodded, Finn raised his brows above earnest hazel eyes. "Huh."

"What's that supposed to mean?"

"Nothing." But Finn couldn't hold back a smile. He tossed his navy tie on a chair. In their time together as cops, Cooper had sometimes talked about Nell, a confidence he regretted at the moment. "Hope neither of you drew blood."

"Not much," he said, then told Finn about Nell's job offer. "I told her no."

"Then what happened?"

"Nell walked out."

Finn frowned. "Doesn't sound like Nell to me. What else did you say?"

Cooper squirmed in his seat. "Nothing," he said as Finn had a moment ago.

"I know you better than that. I also know Nell's having a rough time right now with her granddad away. It must be hard to penetrate the old cowboy culture on the NLS."

"Which Hadley Smith is a part of, she told me."

"He's a tough customer, but Nell's a good woman. Capable. She's just as skilled at riding, roping, birthing calves, all that as… Oh, wait. Did you make her feel like less than the cowgirl she is?"

Cooper looked away. "No, but I told her

why I'm here. I appreciated her stopping in to see how I was, but after she asked me to take the foreman's job, I had to come clean with her about my intentions."

"In your usual tactful manner, I'm sure," Finn said. Diplomacy wasn't one of Cooper's best traits, but then neither was his tendency to be outspoken or prone to using sarcasm as a defense, as he'd done with Nell.

Finn started to say something more, then cocked his head. Cooper heard the sound of an engine just before it cut off. His internal alert system was already getting rusty; he hadn't heard the car pull up. "Annabelle's home," Finn said. "You won't want to miss her cooking tonight."

Cooper didn't, that was true. Finn's girl-friend had been feeding him like a goose being stuffed for Christmas, and where else would he eat? She had recently sold her diner, which wasn't open under new management yet, and in Barren there weren't many other restaurant choices. Besides, beyond her being a great cook, he'd always liked Annabelle. That was good, because she'd sold her house in town and, with her young daughter, moved in with Finn.

Soon, Finn, Annabelle and Cooper were inside for the night, and the air smelled of chicken and dumplings. While Annabelle fixed a salad, Finn poured wine for her, then opened two beers for the men. Cooper watched them move about the small kitchen, bumping into each other on purpose. "I booked a new client today," she said to Finn. "I'll be leading a tour of the art museum in Kansas City for a senior high school class."

Finn glanced at Cooper. "Annabelle's building her new business faster than we even hoped—" His gaze faltered and he put a hand on her shoulder. "You don't miss not traveling as much as you wanted?"

She shook her head. "When I was in Phoenix for that class to become a tour guide, I missed you and Emmie too much. Especially while she's so little, I like being home at night, not on the road as a tour director staying in some hotel room."

Finn kissed her cheek. "I like having you home."

Cooper wondered where Annabelle's little girl was tonight, but before he could ask, she said, "Emmie's eating with a friend. She won't be sorry to miss my dumplings. She calls them *soggy doughnuts*."

She and Finn laughed. Apparently, that was some private joke Cooper wasn't in on, and he half wished Emmie was here. She'd taken to him right away, and he'd have been happy to read her little book about a cowgirl with her before bed. Cooper had never married, and he didn't often get the chance to be charmed by a child. Maybe he'd never have kids of his own, but in all sorts of ways, he envied Finn and Annabelle. Their light touches and secret smiles spoke of their sheer newfound happiness.

Annabelle, brown-haired, brown-eyed and plain all her life, had a fresh glow about her now, but Cooper didn't see a ring on her hand.

Finn caught him checking. "We're waiting," he said. "The jewelry store's definitely in our future, but before that, we need to finish redoing this house."

Annabelle waved a cooking fork. "We painted and washed windows before you got here. You're our first guest." She pointed at the sink in front of the window. "But this kitchen needs a makeover."

Her comments made Cooper think of the house where he'd grown up. He looked out the window at the pasture where Finn kept a bay horse and its companion pony and felt a wave of yearning go through him.

"I think you should do it," Finn said now as if he'd read Cooper's mind.

"What?"

"Talk to Nell again about the job. You're almost well again after that shooting, and I see you're getting bored. Might be the best thing for you to be more active, get on a horse again, pitch in with the work at the NLS."

The flash of memory pierced him like another bullet. This *should* have been his place in the world still, but it wasn't. Yet. On the other hand, at the NLS he'd be close to his land again, even before the deed was in his hand. He'd have a chance to assess things. It wasn't as if he'd be deceiving Nell. She was already aware of his intentions.

Annabelle gave Finn a slight nod to encourage him to go on. "I do know you," he said. "You're just itching to cowboy again."

"I'M DOING FINE, PawPaw," Nell told her grandfather that night during one of their way too regular phone calls. She sat in the ranch office at his big polished desk in front of the computer and near the old shelves lined with books, among them PawPaw's handwritten cattle breeding registers and his favorite Louis L'Amour novels. On a long table against one wall stood a genuine Remington bronze figure of a cowboy on a bucking horse. As a girl, Nell had run her fingers over its smooth warm surface so many times PawPaw had told her it would one day melt into a puddle. She suppressed any thought of Cooper or her run-in that afternoon with Hadley. "Please don't worry about me."

"I don't understand why you're so hell-bent on running the NLS. You could take it easy while I'm gone. Hadley's been with me for years."

Nell blew out a breath. She and her grandfather remained close, and she always worried about his fragile health, but now that she was grown up, his antiquated views also tended to make her crazy. Ned Sutherland was a traditional Western male, determined to provide for and protect the women he loved. "Don't be so nineteenth century, Paw-

Paw. I'm not some hothouse flower, some maiden on a Victorian fainting couch. I can take care of things—anything," she said. "Hadley's getting in my way."

She could hear the indulgent smile in his voice. "He seems to believe you're in *his*." Her grandfather hesitated before going on. "Nell, you know what I think."

She'd recited the words too many times. "Like Mom, you'd have me leave ranching to the men, marry a cowboy, then have a family of my own."

"And once you fall in love, which I pray you do, you won't be able to concentrate on the NLS. I've seen it happen." Frustration roughened his tone. "What's old-fashioned about that?"

"If you don't know, I can't explain it." Nell could have mentioned several other ranches now run by the owners' daughters, but Paw-Paw was well aware of their names.

In the background, she heard his older brother chime in. "By the time you go back, Ned, there won't be a ranch. I know Hadley Smith. He'll make mincemeat of you, Nelly."

"Don't call me Nelly," she said in a voice loud enough for her uncle to hear.

But Will could be relentless. "You're no match for him. How much do you weigh?" he asked, as if she and Hadley were prize-fighters about to compete in the ring for some heavyweight championship.

Nell glanced down at her dirty boots, her muddy jeans and the sweatshirt she'd pulled on when the late-day air had cooled. Except for her brief trip to the Moran farm, she'd worked from before sunup to sundown as hard as any man. "What is this, Uncle Will—*Jeopardy*? Don't answer, then ask your own question. We're not on TV." She took a breath. "I'm heavier and taller than you are."

Unlike her grandfather, he wasn't a big man and had shrunk over the years. Nell envisioned him now, appearing almost frail, but with the towering pride he'd always displayed and a poor attitude, in her opinion, toward the females of the species. To Nell, that seemed more memorable than his shock of white hair or the piercing dark eyes he and PawPaw shared. Well, not the hair anymore; after he recovered from his stroke, PawPaw had dyed his to what he thought was its more normal brown. And he'd put on some weight again.

"Haven't you heard?" she said. "Women are running the world."

Will made a harsh sound. "I won't see your *grandfather's* world run into the ground without saying my piece."

Nell dug her boot heels into the carpet under the desk. Why was her grandfather ceding this conversation to his brother? "PawPaw, don't listen to Will," she said, not caring if her uncle heard. "As for Hadley Smith, I can handle him."

"Maybe so, but give him a chance. Hadley's a good man. If I catch the least whiff of trouble between you two, I'll be home."

Nell's pulse stuttered. If he came home now, he'd take over again. "I thought you two were leaving tomorrow on a road trip into Canada. Didn't I hear something about fishing?" Like deer hunting in the fall, it was her grandfather's passion, other than the NLS. Until this spring, he'd mostly fished in the small lake outside Barren, but he hadn't gone since his stroke and then his accident with the truck last October. This time away was his first vacation in years and, in Nell's mind, maybe her one chance to prove her worth.

"We are going," he said. "But if you need me—"

"I told you, I'm fine." *Don't undermine me. Like Hadley does.*

A brief silence told Nell she'd made her point. Possibly. For a few more minutes, they chatted about the new calves born since PawPaw had left the ranch, the tagging and branding that were going well. She didn't mention Hadley's failure to order grain. By the time they hung up, Nell had almost relaxed in her grandfather's wide leather desk chair.

Until he said, "Thanks for the update, Nelly. Think I'll check in with Hadley."

CHAPTER THREE

NELL PULLED HER horse to a halt. She'd been riding fence, a chore she usually loved. The big open sky of blue this morning with a few white puffy clouds, the breeze blowing through her hair and the expanse of lush grassland spreading out before her to the horizon should have calmed her spirit. But as she'd ridden, stopping now and then to inspect a section of barbed wire, she'd had to work to overcome her sense of pending failure after her talk with her grandfather.

Suddenly, Bear, her big teddy of a horse, pricked up his ears and his muscles bunched beneath her. Sitting deeper in her saddle, Nell took a tighter grip on the reins. As dependable as he was, Bear was still a herd animal whose first instinct was to flee. Whatever had alerted him, she wouldn't let him bolt.

At first, she didn't believe her ears, but then the howling sound came again.

"Did you hear that?" she called out to the two cowboys who were trailing behind her.

Were they keeping a respectful distance or were they trying to avoid her supervision?

Several other men of the crew tended to keep away or respond to her requests, like Hadley, with deliberate slowness.

Clete, the more experienced hand who'd worked for PawPaw since Nell could remember, closed the gap between them. Small and stocky, Clete had fine pale hair and light gray-blue eyes. His muscular piebald quarter horse kept fighting the bit in its mouth, clearly frightened like Bear.

From farther off, along what had once been the boundary with the Ransom ranch, she picked up the panicked bellowing of the herd, then another long high-pitched howling cry.

"Dogs," Clete said under his breath, but there were no dogs now on the Ransom property, unless they were feral ones. Clete must know that.

Nell remembered something from long ago. Once, on a spring day like this, she and

Cooper had ridden to this same area for his father, searching for a lost calf, its mama frantic without him. They'd heard similar howls and yips that had curdled Nell's blood. In a gully, they'd finally found the calf—half eaten by a coyote. Over the years since then, there'd been occasional, sporadic trouble, but not for a while.

"Sounds more like coyotes to me," she said, a shiver running down her spine. She didn't wait for Clete's answer. "Just in case, we'd better move the rest of the herd closer to keep watch on them. At least half a dozen cows still have to drop their calves."

"Easy pickings for coyotes," Clete agreed.

His kindly tone didn't quite reassure Nell. He'd tacked up her first pony long ago, a birthday gift from PawPaw and, years later, watched her ride her palomino mare when she'd graduated to a full-size horse. Clete had seen her turn from a chubby toddler to a thin girl, all legs and arms, to a young woman in her high school cap and gown. He'd been here when Nell returned from the agriculture college in Manhattan, the ink not yet dry on her brand-new degree in animal husbandry. She imagined he still thought of her as that little girl though. A hard role for her to outgrow, apparently.

And if she was wrong about this, Nell would be viewed as incompetent, out of her depth.

"You may be right," Clete muttered, his gaze avoiding hers. "Hadley claims he spied a small pack a few days ago on the ridge."

Nell dug her heels into the stirrups. "You didn't see them?"

"He was alone."

"He should have said something to me then."

She nudged Bear's sides. The other cowhand, Dex, had sharp bladelike cheekbones and blank dark eyes. He rode toward them on a loose rein as if he had all the time in the world.

Nell gave him a curt nod. "Head back to the barn. Tell Hadley to send some men over to the Ransom side." Nell still referred to the far reaches of the NLS that way. "See if there are any injured cows, then round up the herd. Before sundown." After dark, if there were coyotes, as she feared, they would begin circling the herd, hoping to pick off the weak and newborns. Predators were always a concern on the ranch.

I have some of my own on the NLS, the two-legged kind, thought Nell.

Clete hesitated. "Hadley's not at the ranch."

Nell looked at him, now riding beside her, their bridles jangling. "Not at the ranch," she repeated. In fact, she hadn't seen him this morning. "Where is he?"

Another pause. "In town, Miss Nell. On business."

She took a breath. "His *business* should be right here. That's what we—what I—pay him for." If he'd gone into Barren to buy grain, he could have phoned in the order as usual.

"Court or something," Clete muttered like a man condemned to the gallows.

"For what?"

"He didn't say why."

Several possibilities raced through her mind. Speeding. A DUI after some bar fight at Rowdy's on Main Street. She didn't think Hadley was a drinker, and Finn Donovan, the sheriff, hadn't mentioned his getting into trouble, but there was always a first time.

She remembered their confrontation at the barn. Lately, Hadley's work hadn't been up to par. Had being charged with some crime distracted him?

Nell said, "Okay, Dex, you go get the men to round up the herd." The cowboys had their code of honor, which included not pressing a man about his personal life or spreading gossip, and Nell wasn't about to break through that. She'd seen the motto more than once. *If it's not yours, don't take it. If it's not true, don't say it. If it is not right, don't do it. Honor God, family and country.*

She watched Dex head back down the fence line at a lope toward the ranch buildings. His tight mouth had told her—if she'd had any doubts—he didn't like taking orders from her either.

A few weeks ago, she'd had some daydream of running the NLS with one hand tied behind her. It wouldn't be that easy, as last night's conversation with PawPaw reminded her, and ever since she'd learned Cooper was home again, Nell had felt unsettled. Everyone, it seemed, must be watching, expecting her to fail in this definitely man's world. Was that why Cooper had turned her down about becoming her foreman?

Think I'll check in with Hadley, PawPaw had said.

Nell planned to prove them all wrong.

SHE RODE INTO the barnyard just as Hadley's truck turned off the main road, then started up the long drive from the NLS gates. Staying on her horse, she watched him come from a vantage point that for a change let her look down on him as he climbed out of the pickup. Clete, who'd been beside her, went on by into the dark recesses of the barn where she heard him say a word to Dex, who was brushing his mount in the cross ties. The low murmur of their voices and an occasional whicker from a hungry horse drifted on the air. "I need to talk to you, Hadley."

That familiar smile spread across his face as he tipped his hat. "Yes, ma'am." He leaned a shoulder against the driver's door of his truck. The cooling engine ticked, sounding loud in the sudden silence. The men inside had stopped talking. Even the horses went quiet.

"You had some trouble in town today?"

"Trouble?" he repeated, as if he didn't understand.

"A court appearance. Please don't insult us both by pretending you had—"

"Business," he said, shoving the hat back farther on his head.

"Hadley, this ranch needs a foreman who does his job. Someone I can rely on, and lately that's not you."

His long body uncoiled from his stance against the door. "Now, look here—"

Nell leaned on her saddle horn, meeting his eyes. "The NLS is my responsibility while my grandfather is gone and I won't let him down. Whether or not you agree with how things are, I'm in charge—not you. I was born on this ranch and there's not a thing I don't know about the land I love."

He smiled. "Now you sound like a song. 'America the Beautiful' or something. Maybe a country ballad. Patriotic."

"You think this is a joke? It's not."

His mouth tightened. "I don't work for you. I work for Ned. I answer to him, no one else. If you're unhappy with my work, take it up with him. I doubt that will do you any good though. Ned trusts me."

"Until you got in trouble with the law," she said before she stopped to consider her words. "He won't like hearing that."

Hadley made a sound of disgust. "The trouble is with my wife. We're getting a divorce and I had an appointment with my lawyer, that's all."

Nell straightened in her saddle. "I'm sorry you're having personal issues."

"I'll work it out. If you want, I'll be in this barn tomorrow morning before sunup, which I usually am anyway."

"No," Nell said, having made up her mind. The threat of coyotes on the ranch so near the herd had hardened her resolve.

Shading his eyes from the sun with one hand, Hadley blinked up at her.

"What's sticking in your craw exactly? My not ordering some grain quick enough? I have calls in to the vet and the farrier, waiting for them to schedule. One of the boys will fix that section of fence—"

"Already done. We checked the lines while you were otherwise occupied," she said, remembering the animal cries she'd heard earlier on the range. Was she supposed to wait until an attack happened?

He scowled. "But I—"

"Did you or did you not come across coyotes on Ransom land?"

"Didn't actually *see* them." Hadley hesitated. "I told Clete I heard something that sounded like—"

"And failed to tell me."

"I didn't want to stir you up," he said, and Nell saw red. Bear shifted beneath her, muscles tight as he sensed danger again. "You know how you've been with Ned away."

Nell ignored that. She didn't have to think any longer. "The coyotes were the last straw, Hadley. I won't jeopardize the herd, the NLS or my chance to inherit the place I love more than anything else in this world by trying to work with you one more minute. You're fired." She pointed toward the ranch-owned bungalow in the distance where Hadley lived. "Get your things and be out of that house by sundown."

Which left Nell without a foreman. Had she acted rashly? Twice in two days? Well, it was done, and she wouldn't take back what she'd said.

His frown even darker, Hadley took a step toward her. "This is the thanks I get for keeping this ranch running while Ned was laid up from his stroke, and again after the accident?"

Nell turned Bear, putting the gelding between her and Hadley. Her horse was about to shy when, to her surprise, Clete appeared in the barn doorway. "Miss Nell, you all right?"

"Right as rain." She glanced at Hadley. "But we're going to need a foreman."

FOR THE FIRST time in fourteen years, Cooper drove through the open gates onto NLS land. His grip on the wheel of his rental car tensed. Seeing it become part of Ned Sutherland's spread hadn't been easy then, and it wasn't easier now. But Cooper thought he'd found a way. He'd waited overnight in case he changed his mind, but Finn had been right.

He'd just reached the barn when a dark-haired man burst out into the sunlight carrying a saddle. Cooper heard a few words that sounded far from complimentary. About Nell? Cooper heard her name and got out of the car.

"Whoa," he said, getting pushed aside as

the cowboy headed for a nearby truck. He shouldn't say anything but if this was about her… "What's going on?"

"None of your business, whoever you are. But take my advice. Turn around and get off the NLS before that b—"

Cooper cut him off. "Watch it. Nell is a… friend of mine."

He eyed Cooper for a long moment. "Didn't think that woman had any friends." He started toward the pickup again, heaved the saddle into the rear bed, then headed back to the barn. "I should call myself lucky to be out of here."

Ah. So that was it. "Hadley Smith?" Cooper asked.

He shrugged. "Ned's foreman, or I was until now. If I were you, I wouldn't believe a word she says. Soon as I talk to her grandfather," Hadley said, "he'll set her straight. In the meantime, she's bitten off more than she can chew with this ranch."

Cooper doubted that. His mouth set but he didn't correct Hadley Smith. His rant came from anger, justified or not, and now Cooper's purpose seemed even clearer. He almost empathized with Smith; whether or not he was a good ranch manager, losing the job had obviously rattled him. Like Cooper, when he'd had to leave the place where he'd grown up. A sudden smile crossed his face. Now he was back, and this might be easier, his decision more right, than he'd first thought.

Hadley hopped into his truck, slammed the door and sped off down the driveway, leaving a rising cloud of dust behind. At the end, he braked, red lights glowing through the dust storm he'd created, then fishtailed onto the two-lane road that led into Barren.

Cooper heard approaching footsteps. Nell crossed the yard, smoke practically steaming from her ears. Her green eyes flashed. "He's gone. Thank heaven."

"You fired him," he said.

She propped both hands on her hips. "Which should have happened long ago. He may have PawPaw bamboozled but not me. Those coyotes only clinched my decision."

"Coyotes?"

"The boys and I heard them this morning. Clete—you remember him—admitted Hadley encountered them too a few days ago. Seems he *forgot* to tell me."

"So did Clete then, apparently."

"True," she agreed, "and I've had words with him. But Hadley? He's now a thing of the past—along with his attitude." Her shoulders visibly relaxed. "I just have to convince Clete and the others this was a wise choice for me to make. Before PawPaw gets home, I *will* have their respect."

"I admire your grit, Nell, but your grandfather won't be happy to learn you got rid of his foreman."

"I'll deal with him."

"And you're going to be spread pretty thin."

"I realize that." She cocked an eyebrow, assessing him as if she were thinking about their quarrel. "What brings you here?"

"Figured I'd apply for the job."

"I don't think so," she said. "I appreciated your honesty the other day, but there's no way I'd hire you now. Knowing what I know," she added.

He shot a look toward the eastern boundary of the NLS. "I won't lie to you. I haven't changed my plan." A part of his soul seemed to settle at the view of the blue sky, the land that rolled away to the horizon, the familiar scents of grass and cowhide that drifted on the breeze. "That doesn't mean I couldn't do a good job for you."

"I don't doubt your abilities, though they must be rusty. I doubt your intentions."

"You said yourself. I've been upfront with you, Nell."

"Then let me be just as plain. My grandfather will never sell that land. I'll never let him—because the NLS, all of it, is going to be mine one day. You can buy as many acres as you want elsewhere."

"Preferably—for you—in a different state," he said under his breath.

"Anywhere you like. Just not here."

But his family's land was the only land he wanted, and not only for himself.

Cooper shook his head. "When my father lost our ranch, he lost more than that. It broke his health and killed him in the end, as far as I'm concerned."

"I'm sorry but—"

"I won't have it kill my mother too. Since he died, I worry about her as you do Ned. I'd hoped she was getting past the worst part of her grief, but then I got shot and she nearly lost me too. She hasn't been herself."

"Of course not. You're her only child," she said.

"The ambush certainly set her back. Her *fondest wish*, she keeps saying, is to spend her days in the place where she lived with my dad, where she raised me, where she could wake up each morning in that house— which I understand has been standing empty all this time—and watch the sun rise again over their land. She never dreamed they would lose that. I'm going to make her wish come true."

Nell blinked. She followed Cooper's gaze. "When PawPaw had his stroke, it was so hard to see him in the hospital, then later in rehab. He was like a shell of himself until he got home again. I would have done anything to make that happen."

So. She understood that much, even when she probably didn't want to, and Cooper saw his opening. "Then we have a deal?"

Nell hesitated. "I always liked your mother and so did PawPaw. I'd want her to be happy too." Yet, he could sense her thinking, was that a good enough reason to hire Cooper? To have him right here on the ranch every day?

Finally, she took a breath. "I may regret this but…yes. We do." She paused again. "But be warned, I will protect PawPaw. I won't have him stressed out and risk another stroke," she said, then offered her hand. "Deal. As long as we stick to business."

He grinned. "Then I guess you've got yourself a new foreman."

CHAPTER FOUR

AMY SMITH COULD see that Hadley was not a happy cowboy. Her husband was not only out of a job—one he'd performed well for Ned Sutherland without a single complaint—but he had no immediate prospects for another, and very little cash to support them for the short-term until he spoke to Ned.

Amy preferred having nice things and Hadley had worked hard to provide what he could. She didn't want to be a thorn in his side, especially right now, but that seemed inevitable. Fully aware that he'd also met with his lawyer today, she was going to have to make things even worse for him.

"You'd think Nell would give me notice," he was saying, "or allow me to stay in the foreman's house until I got hold of Ned. But no. She's never liked me and vice versa. She was sure in a hurry to kick me off the NLS." He sank down onto a chair in the living room of Amy's small apartment and ran a hand through his hair. "I enjoy working for Ned. I like that house you and I shared when I still thought we could make things work. Go figure."

"Why don't you call Ned now?" It was equally important to Amy that he get his job back, but she liked Nell. She considered them to be casual friends, although there'd always been that line drawn between her as Ned's granddaughter and Amy as an employee's wife. But friendship wasn't her reason for urging him to call.

Hadley reached into his pocket for his cell phone.

After a long moment, he left a message, then hung up. "Ned must be out in the wilderness somewhere," he said.

But what if he didn't return to his brother's place for weeks? Ned wasn't in the habit of sharing his plans with Hadley other than the business of the NLS. It wasn't as if *they* were friends, really, although Hadley liked to think they were. But Hadley's employment as foreman concerned the ranch, so it qualified. "Keep trying," she said.

"Yeah—unless I win the lottery, which

would sure please your parents. Then I wouldn't need a job and you'd be set for life too."

"*We* would," she said, then regretted the words. She had a habit of still saying *we* when they weren't a couple anymore. Hadley didn't have a great track record at relationships, but there'd been a time when she thought—hoped—their marriage would last forever. Amy came from a close-knit clan, and was her parents' only child. She'd hoped that if she waited him out, he'd realize their separation had been a mistake. But she didn't have the luxury of waiting anymore. "I can't dream about winning some lottery," she said. "You have to get your job back, Hadley."

"I'm trying. Don't get all worked up. I know you've been sick with that virus, and things look bad right now, but you already feel better. Don't you?"

Amy didn't answer. She wrapped her arms around her middle, trying to hold on to herself.

He cleared his throat. "I just stopped in to give you the heads-up. If I'm late with the money this month, I'll make it up to you as soon as I can. Okay? But that's the worst-case scenario. Ned will see things my way."

"Not okay." She'd started with a firm tone, but hesitated. There was no telling how he'd take this news. She softened her voice. "About my feeling sick… I went to see my doctor, as you suggested, and it's not a virus."

"Then…what?" Hadley's face had paled.

"It's all your fault," she said, her lower lip quivering.

He raked a hand through his hair again. "How can I be responsible for you getting sick? Just spill it. If it's something serious, which I hope it's not, I want to know. I'm not in a good place, but I'll do what I can to help."

"You do still care for me," she murmured.

He sighed. "We were married for seven years. Of course I care, just not in the same way now."

Her tone wavered. "Maybe *you* need to rethink that."

Hadley frowned. "Amy, we've been through this before. It's time you got your own life in order. I know I'm a fine one to talk right now and, sure, we had some good times. I'm okay with remembering them—"

"Like our night together in this apartment?"

A muscle ticked in his jaw. "That was a mistake." After they'd separated, he'd helped her move in to the apartment, ordered pizza later for their dinner and all at once, they'd been back in their early days together when everything seemed new and possible, and they loved each other. After their nostalgic conversation, he'd ended up spending the night, something Hadley told her the next morning he regretted. He didn't want her getting more ideas, he'd said. He was done and should have let it stay that way.

"I don't see it as a mistake," she said. This time she didn't hesitate. "I'm pregnant."

THE NEXT MORNING, Olivia Wilson hailed Nell on the street. Olivia owned a pair of antiques shops, one here in Barren, the other in Farrier, the next town over in the county. With the NLS between the two, Nell could do her shopping in either place. With an answering wave, she waited while Olivia crossed the street from the diner that used to be their friend Annabelle Foster's and would soon become the Bon Appetit. She felt tempted to turn the other way, even though she'd known Olivia all her life. She could also guess why Olivia wanted to see her.

In recent months, the pressure to join her Girls' Night Out group had intensified. Nell had gone once or twice, though before their meetings began she was usually ready for bed, exhausted from the day's work. She got up by 4:00 a.m. each morning and had too much on her mind to socialize. Besides, she didn't fit in with the others, all of whom were girlie girls.

Her blond hair flying, Olivia rushed over to her. "Morning, stranger. Do you have time for a cup of tea?" She held up a paper bag. Steam flowed from its top.

"I'm a coffee person," Nell said, "but I've had mine."

Olivia patted her pregnant stomach. "Baby and I had a yen for cinnamon rolls too. So, of course—" she laughed "—I had to buy several. I'm happy to share."

Nell's taste buds went into overdrive. "Sounds delicious but—"

Olivia had already taken her arm. "I

haven't seen you in weeks—none of us have—and I'm dying to hear what's been going on with you." She steered Nell toward her store, went inside, then flipped the closed sign around to open. She led Nell into her office and gestured at a comfy chair.

Nell didn't sit. "Really, Libby. I'm in town on ranch errands, not to chat."

First on her list had been the Ag store to put through the grain order Hadley had neglected to place. Nell had been headed there when Olivia called out to her.

Olivia's blue eyes darkened. "We all have businesses to run." She pushed a stack of papers aside on her desk, then laid out the pastries. "By the way, how's Ned? Is he still away?"

"He called the other night from Montana, but his check-ins always make me feel like he's looking over my shoulder. My uncle Will has been feeding him poison." At Olivia's startled expression, Nell said, "Figuratively, I mean. Will has put doubts in PawPaw's mind about my ability to run the NLS."

"Oh, Nell." Olivia reached out to touch

her hand. "Pay no attention. Maybe they'll find some new mischief to get into."

"They were planning to leave on a fishing expedition. I'm already worried one of them will step into a deep pool in some rushing wild river, swamp his waders and drown in the middle of nowhere."

Olivia sipped her tea. "I'm sure they can take care of themselves. You can too. If anyone other than Ned can manage the NLS, it's you." She picked up a cinnamon bun and caught Nell looking at her. "Don't tell anyone about the sugar load I'm about to eat."

Nell had to smile. She took the chair Olivia had offered. She could spare a few moments. After firing Hadley yesterday, then hiring Cooper, she needed some time with another woman. "You're bad. What will you do for cinnamon rolls when you're in Kedar?" The small country in the Himalayas where Sawyer McCord, Olivia's fiancé, had a medical clinic, as well as his practice here in town, couldn't be further from the life Nell knew and loved.

Olivia's hand rested on her stomach. "Bake some."

Nell had helped more than one calf and

foal into the world, and she was well aware it wasn't always easy. "Are you sure you want to fly more than halfway around the world this spring? What if you give birth there?"

"I may and Sawyer's worried about that, but we have to consider the weather in the Himalayas. I'd worry more about getting stuck in those mountains for the winter, which will end before we go."

Nell stirred sugar into her tea. "But the baby…"

"Will come in good time, and Sawyer's clinic has the equipment for a birth. Since the terrible earthquake and landslide there, it's been rebuilt and resupplied." She paused. "After all, the first time I went there last summer I helped him deliver his partner's son. The boy even has Sawyer's name. We'll manage."

"I can't imagine," she said, taking a bite of her cinnamon roll. Nell groaned at how good it tasted. "Yum." She relaxed into her chair. It was a rare treat for her to enjoy a break. She didn't envy Olivia, however, except for the love she and Sawyer shared; Nell didn't want to go anywhere. The NLS was all she cared about. At least Hadley was out of her way. Had she lost her mind though in hiring Cooper? Still. With him near at hand, she could look for any sign that he was about to make that offer. Nell had been amazed to see him on the NLS yesterday, much less asking for a job.

Olivia brushed crumbs from her hands onto the plastic wrap on her desk. "You do know Finn and Annabelle are coming with us?"

Nell wrinkled her nose. "Yes, and I can't understand them either, but she's always wanted to travel."

Olivia leaned closer as if anyone would hear them. "This is a secret, but Finn told Sawyer he's going to propose to her there."

"Oh, how lovely." Annabelle had spent most of her life bound to the family diner she'd hated. Now she had Finn. "It's good she's happy at last." But Nell pressed her lips together and wished she hadn't spoken. She should have expected Olivia to seize this opportunity.

"She'd be even happier if you came to our next meeting. Really, it's going to be a farewell party for the two of us. Don't miss it."

"I would come, but I—"

Olivia clamped both hands over her ears. "No excuses. I'll text you where and when." Since Annabelle had sold the diner, they no longer met there. Then, lowering her hands, she studied Nell. "I hear—from Annabelle— that Cooper Ransom's back in town."

Ah, now they were getting to the other reason Olivia had invited her to tea this morning. "Did the grapevine also tell you I've hired him as my foreman?"

"No." Olivia arched an eyebrow. "I didn't hear that part but, Nell, are you sure that's wise? From what Finn says, Cooper would still rather work his family's land."

"Which doesn't belong to him." With a twinge of guilt she shouldn't feel, Nell set her empty cup on the desk.

"I'm afraid you're getting into a situation that can only end badly."

"Nothing new," Nell said. "But it's time Cooper realizes he lost that land a long time ago—and he's not getting it back."

"I doubt it's that simple." Olivia finished her tea. "Now you *have* to come to our meeting. The group can offer their input."

"I really can't, Libby. Besides, this is my

situation, not theirs. Or yours," she pointed out, trying to soften her tone.

"Yes, but more heads are better than one. You and Cooper were pretty tight years ago. I remember when his family left town." She eyed Nell again. "You sure you're over him? If not, things could get dicey."

"I'm aware of that, but there's a saying. Keep your friends close and your enemies closer." She took a last bite of her roll, then rose. "I need to go. I'm holding up your business this morning, and I have a ranch to see to."

One that included thousands of acres of former Ransom land—and now had a Ransom as foreman.

COOPER UNLOADED HIS bags from the rental car, then carried them into the foreman's house. Two furnished bedrooms, a modest bathroom, a square living room and an adjoining kitchen. It wasn't a third the size of the house in which he'd grown up, but for now, not bad.

At Finn's farm, Cooper had indeed become quickly bored out of his mind. But was he crazy? Seeking out Nell to ask for the job as her foreman after all? Yet, he felt energized by his decision. No more hospitals for him, no more rehab…no more staying in Finn's house all day, or doing light tasks for Annabelle. Now, here he was on the NLS, ready to take action and in charge of Nell's cowhands.

A quick double rap on the front door frame brought his head up. Recognition dawned, although the man standing there had aged. "Clete. Good to see you again."

A man of few words, if Cooper remembered right, Clete Warner nodded. "Came to say welcome aboard."

"Appreciate it."

"I was surprised to hear you'd quit the police force up north. Think you're still able to stay in a saddle?"

"On a good horse, I can." His riding skills might be rusty, but he wouldn't let that on to Clete. To be effective as foreman of the NLS, he had to establish his right to the job and his authority. If he showed weakness now, he had no doubt that Clete would spread the word to the other cowboys who might want to test him too.

The older man wandered into the main

room. "I ought to give you a word of warning. Hadley Smith didn't take to being fired."

"Who would?" It had been hard enough for Cooper to leave the Chicago PD, and he'd resigned voluntarily.

Clete shook his hand. "Hadley's got a temper. Part nature, part whatever life has handed him. Of late, that hasn't been good. I advise you to watch your back."

"He doesn't worry me. If he shows up here again, he'll be trespassing."

"He's also got Ned's ear. The boss relied on him."

Cooper frowned. "Nell hired me. She'll have to break the news to Ned."

"Fly on the wall," Clete said with a half smile. "Wish I could be there."

"You say her grandfather depended on Hadley Smith. As his foreman, did Smith hope to make her fail? Nell believes so, and she also told me he never mentioned some coyotes that were seen on the range near—" He'd almost said *my land*. No sense alerting Clete to his future plans. "—the eastern boundary of the old NLS. Why do you think that was?"

"No idea," Clete muttered.

Cooper opened a kitchen cabinet. Plates and mugs, half a dozen glasses and bowls. "You didn't tell her either." He waited, but Clete didn't respond. "I understand she already spoke to you, but don't let something like that happen again."

Clete shifted from one foot to the other. "I told her I was sorry. Guess it slipped my mind 'cause I hadn't actually seen those coyotes—still haven't—and wasn't sure of what I'd heard."

Cooper didn't quite believe him. Clete was an experienced hand. He'd been around when other predators had threatened the herd, one of them near the same spot years ago. If he was so fond of Nell, why would he risk alienating her? Destroying her trust?

Clete wandered toward the door but Cooper hadn't finished. "Speaking of Nell. You've known her for a long time. You're aware she wants to take over the NLS when Ned's done. What's your take on that?"

Clete's gaze softened. "Miss Nell's like my own daughter. I love that girl, but it's still a man's world out here and the other men don't see her in the boss's place."

"Then it's my job—and yours—to help change their minds. I'll be counting on you, Clete."

"That all it is?" he asked, his eyes keen. "Just a job?"

Cooper gave him an honest answer. "All I can let it be."

"You had a real eye for that girl last time I saw you."

And he still did, but to allow his attraction to Nell to derail his own agenda? Not going to happen. Too many years had passed; there was too much at stake.

"She had an eye for you too, as I recall." Clete scuffed at the floor with the toe of his battered boot.

Cooper studied his own running shoes. He was in danger of being seen as a greenhorn on this ranch, a man who couldn't do the job he'd been hired for, and Clete, at least, also saw him as a threat to Nell.

Maybe they'd all be keeping their eyes on each other.

CHAPTER FIVE

KEEP YOUR ENEMIES CLOSER.

"Truer words were never said," Nell murmured, remembering her talk with Olivia a few days ago. She and Cooper were riding toward the western boundary of his former land—the eastern edge of the original NLS. At dusk, the light was beginning to fail, turning the grass to burnished gold beneath a reddening sky on the horizon. His profile was in shadow, and he hadn't said much since they left the barn. Nell mistrusted the silence. Was he brooding about the Ransom land he'd lost?

"What words?" he finally asked.

Nell didn't realize she'd spoken aloud. She eyed Cooper, watching his light touch with the reins, the easy way he sat the dark horse that had been Hadley's ride as foreman, his boots set just right in the stirrups. Never mind the years he'd lived in Chicago; Cooper looked like a born cowboy. But could he really do the job? His success here would be her success, and so would his failure. He also had plans, she reminded herself.

"Clete's had several calls from Hadley, who's been trying to get hold of my grandfather. Hadley wants his job back, and he hopes PawPaw will give it to him—thus overruling me. I told Clete that will never happen."

"Stay tough, Nell," Cooper said. He turned in the saddle and smiled, but Nell stiffened. She'd finally gotten rid of Hadley. She wouldn't let Cooper disrespect her as some of the ranch hands did. Because he was foreman, they would look to him for guidance in how to treat Nell.

"Don't mock me. I can fire you too."

He frowned. "I wasn't mocking. I'm on your side. Try to remember that. And about remembering, maybe first, we need to do just that." Cooper's gaze stayed on Nell. "About how we were together, you and I, years ago before I had to move to Chicago. And you actually liked me then, liked being with me—as often as we could." His eyes had darkened, but Nell didn't want to remember their closeness as kids or that first teenage romance.

"Nell."

"Don't get all sappy about something that's over." She hitched her chin toward what passed for a ridge in the otherwise flat landscape. "Let's try to find those coyotes instead. We have a better chance with the sun going down." Coyotes tended to be most active at dawn and dusk, though they could sometimes be seen during the day too.

"Have it your way. For now," Cooper said. He straightened in his saddle. "Hear that?"

Nell listened. A far-off cow bellowed once, then again, and a shiver fell down her spine. Several others in the herd joined in a chorus. The cattle were always edgy and could panic, then stampede in a heartbeat. The Angus alarm system was going off. "Could be coyotes but I don't hear them."

Cooper took up the slack in his reins, then spurred his horse into a canter before Nell could gather her determination even closer. He'd noticed that one cow before she did, and the oversight didn't sit well. Neither did his attempt to bring up their past, the closeness they'd shared, a love that had died. Could she really trust that he was on her side now?

Nudging Bear from his slow trot, she caught up to Cooper, who'd already slowed and raised a hand as she reined in her horse. "Easy," he said. "No rush."

Nell briefly pressed her lips tight. "I give the orders here."

Cooper returned her glare. "And I carry them out. You really want to spook the herd—and any predators closing in?"

"No, and I wasn't, but the next time you go over my head will be the last."

"Chill out, Nell. We work together or we don't work at all."

Nell needed his support, but for generations there had been a war between their families over the land. "And you don't own a single acre of this ranch anymore. Remember that—"

Nell was still talking when Cooper rode on, up and over the small ridge, leaving her behind again. As she topped the slight hill, the herd, black hides gleaming in the lowering sun, milled around, eyes rolling so the whites showed.

Cooper scanned the area once, then twice.

"No coyotes that I can see. Let's ride into the herd. Maybe one of the cows is sick and has gone down somewhere."

Nell found herself in a dilemma. Cooper was right, but she didn't care for his taking the lead. Born cowboy or not, he hadn't ridden probably since the day he left Kansas, and he also hadn't herded cattle, fixed fences or even ordered grain. Like his boots, his saddle was brand-new. Rather than use NLS tack, Cooper had bought his own gear. While she admired his independence, even his take-charge attitude, she wouldn't play second fiddle in this band. He hadn't proven himself yet.

Nell rode ahead of him, weaving her way through the cattle, soothing them here and there with a soft word or two. "It's okay, girls. No worries, Babe," she said when she recognized an individual cow. "Nothing here to—" She was almost at the far edge of the shifting mass of cows and calves when she recognized the problem. "Cooper! Over here!"

In danger of being trampled, a calf lay on its side, thrashing, and Nell bit back a curse. The calf, with its mother hovering nearby as if to shield it, had plunged through the fence and caught one leg in the shredded wire.

Cooper slid off his horse and so did she. He knelt down, ran a hand over the calf's side, then looked up at Nell. "No telling how long he's been here like this."

"Any amount of time is bad, but the calf's beginning to go into shock." Its leg was bleeding badly and the poor thing was clearly terrified.

"You bring wire cutters?" Cooper asked. "If we don't do something, he'll die."

Their gazes met over the calf that couldn't be more than a few days old. Losing a valuable animal wouldn't please PawPaw either, but at the moment all Nell cared about was the calf's survival. Nell and Cooper were its only chance.

Cooper was on his feet again, searching through a saddlebag, while Nell tried to calm the injured calf with gentle strokes on its head and body. "We don't have much time. He's giving up, Cooper." Nell had watched more than one cow do just that, lie down in a field with an expression that said, *I'm done*, then simply die on the spot.

Cooper laid a hand on her shoulder. The

rest of the herd had clustered nearby as if to lend support, but she barely heard their mournful calls or the stamping of hooves. "Move aside." He held up a pair of wire cutters. "Hadley must have forgotten them. He didn't stick around long after you fired him."

"Thank God." Nell meant for the wire cutters.

She rose to her feet, wiping her bloody hands on her jeans. She stood back to let Cooper cut the calf free of the fence, but it didn't even try to get up. Nell's lip quivered. The calf's leg was in bad shape. She doubted he would last the night.

"Hey," Cooper murmured, noting her expression as he looked over his shoulder.

Nell shuddered. "I hate this! I should have sent Clete out to survey the herd this morning. We usually keep a close watch this time of year. Maybe he could have found this baby and brought him to the barn then."

Cooper rose and drew her into his arms before Nell could resist. She was shaking. "And maybe this accident didn't occur until just before we found him. It happens."

"Not on my watch." Briefly, she thought of pulling away but didn't move. She wanted to lean against his solid chest and press her cheek against his strongly beating heart, and Nell only gave a shaky sigh. "Sorry, I'm not helping."

"We have to get this little guy home," he agreed, easing her from their short embrace. "I wish working together this first time had gone better."

Reaching Bear, she mounted up. But what if she'd gone looking for coyotes by herself? And come upon this very calf far from the barn? Alone, she couldn't lift its limp weight onto her saddle, but Cooper easily picked it up, then laid it across Nell's lap. "I'm still the boss," she told him, but her voice trembled.

"Got it," he said after he'd swung onto the bay's saddle. "We used to be a pretty good pair though. I'd like to think we still are."

They started toward the barn, the calf silent, its mother following close behind, making sounds of distress. Nell was in danger of liking Cooper too much for her own good. She'd certainly been grateful he was here today. "As long as you don't start another range war between the Ransoms and the Sutherlands," she said.

THE NEXT MORNING, another range war was the last thing on Nell's mind. She had another looming battle at the foot of the front porch steps. She gritted her teeth as her brother got out of his car, tipped his obviously new straw cowboy hat, then sauntered toward her.

"What are you doing here?" she couldn't keep from asking.

"That's some greeting," Jesse said, glancing around the yard, then toward the barn. She hadn't seen him since last Christmas when, as holiday gatherings often do, the family tensions escalated until he finally left in a huff.

"PawPaw's away. I don't know when he'll be home. You should have called before you came." She and Jesse didn't have much in common.

"I already talked to him." He grinned like a hungry wolf—or a coyote. "Didn't realize I had to make an appointment with my own family. I came to see you." He winked. "I've missed my baby sister."

Her pulse thumped. "Jesse, I haven't heard from you since New Year's." When he'd called to apologize for Christmas. "Why show up now?"

He took off his hat, turning it in both hands. His hair, a darker brown than Nell's, looked mussed. "I've got a proposition for you."

Nell rolled her eyes. She'd heard his offers before. Like Cooper's, she could bet she knew what this one was. It felt as if the NLS was under siege.

"And I have this ranch to run." She started down the steps, intent upon checking again on the injured calf's condition and its mother in an adjoining stall. As far as its injuries were concerned, to Nell's relief the calf had survived the night. "Breakfast is over but you're welcome to fix your own. Today, I'm vaccinating calves."

"Let me unload my bags. Then I'll help."

Nell propped her hands on her hips. How long did he intend to stay? She didn't want his help. "No," she said, "you won't. An inexperienced hand would only get in the way."

"Inexperienced? I was on this ranch before you were a gleam in Dad's eye."

"Too bad you've never done a thing to keep the NLS going. If I remember right, cattle and horses aren't your *thing*." Jesse was a city boy and proud of it. He was also a serial entrepreneur who'd recently sold his latest company, some kind of tech or software operation. He was the family success. "I'm wondering what changed your mind."

"You."

"Ah. PawPaw phoned you, didn't he?" More than once her grandfather had sung Jesse's praises, as he did Hadley's, not so subtly suggesting to Nell it might be better for her to let her brother take over the NLS. "Well, doesn't that beat all? I'm working myself half to death while he's gone, you're clear across the state amusing yourself while making gobs of money and now I'm supposed to let you inherit this ranch? I've told you, Jesse. This is where I belong—you don't, and that was your choice."

"PawPaw doesn't agree."

Apparently so, and Nell wanted badly to talk to him, but she had no way of reaching her grandfather until he chose to come back to civilization.

She said, "You spent your first fourteen years telling everybody who would listen that you couldn't stand this place. Couldn't wait to get off this land." Unlike Cooper, who'd wanted to stay but couldn't. "You always said you never wanted to see another cow or horse again."

"I'm a new person now," he said, propping one foot on the bottom step. "Whether you like it or not, I'm here. With PawPaw's blessing."

"I can't believe this." Or was he lying? She wouldn't put that past him. With their grandfather out of cell phone range for now, she couldn't question Ned, complain or defend herself. Jesse must have known it would be open season on Nell until PawPaw came home. He could tell her anything he liked. Despite her best effort to steady herself, her voice shook. "My heart belongs to the NLS."

"It's a business, Nell."

"More than that," she insisted. "Yesterday, Cooper and I rescued a newborn calf. Seeing that baby injured hurt me—as it ought to. I won't have this ranch in the hands of a man who never showed any interest, who doesn't even like the animals I care so much for—"

"Assets," he said. "That's what they are." He paused. "You and *Cooper*?"

Nell nodded, trying to swallow around

the growing lump in her throat. "Yes. I fired Hadley. Cooper's his replacement."

"Does PawPaw know?"

"He doesn't, but he will. I'll tell him as soon as I can."

Jesse laughed. "Wait till he hears this. Weren't you around when Cooper Ransom threatened to show up some day and take back his family's land? Now he's *your* foreman? He pulled the wool over your eyes once, Nell. I'm surprised you'd fall for that again."

"I haven't, and I won't. He's been plain about wanting the old Ransom ranch, and he's a good manager so far. That works for me." As did his being on the NLS so Nell could pick up on any implementation of his plans.

"He'll take over—if he can. I don't mean to let that happen either." He climbed the steps, brushing past Nell. On his way by, he ruffled her hair, a lifelong habit that seemed to tell Nell she was still his *baby sister* but also his inferior, and Jesse meant to manage things properly. *When pigs fly*, she thought. He opened the screen door. Over his shoulder, he said, "You lost your head over Cooper years ago. With the NLS at stake, I'm on the job now."

"REALLY, NELL?" her mother said by phone later that day. "When Jesse told me you'd hired Cooper, I wondered what you were thinking."

"About the NLS. Nothing more." Nell studied her boots, ankles crossed on her grandfather's desk. "Jesse's only concern is a balance sheet."

"You're thirty-one, Nell." Mom gentled her tone. "Maybe it's time to stop playing cowgirl. Being a grown-up can be fun too."

Playing cowgirl? She bristled. "What are you saying? I am an adult. I happen to love working this ranch. You sound worse than Jesse." In contrast, Nell's father had always wanted her to do whatever made *her* happy, but he mostly kept that opinion to himself to avoid setting off her mom or Jesse.

Her mother took a different tack. "Good grief. And why did you fire Hadley?"

Nell briefly explained. "He'll find something on another spread and the NLS was overdue for a change. I can be more effective for PawPaw if I don't have Hadley breathing down my neck. With Cooper here—"

"Nell. Jesse's right—you're not only risking the ranch by hiring Cooper, you're risking more heartache."

Nell took her legs off the desk. "I thought you liked him."

"I did until that wrangle he had with your grandfather. Be careful, sweetheart. I worry about you."

"I know, I know, but Cooper and I are both fourteen years older, not teenagers anymore. This is a business arrangement, which Jesse should understand." Nell didn't mention keeping Cooper close for another reason. That would only harden her mother's heart against him now as foreman. "I wish you'd have more faith that I can take care of myself."

"You're still my baby," her mom said, sounding teary. "I only want the best for you, and if you try to tell me the men on that ranch are fine with you as their boss, I know better."

"I'm working on that, Mom. Trust me."

"I do trust you," she agreed. "Cooper is another matter."

When Nell hung up, she sat there, her gaze on the top of her grandfather's desk, her mind in a whirl. Had she made the right decision?

It seemed she'd put the whole family in an uproar.

CHAPTER SIX

COOPER WAS WORKING in the barn when Jesse Sutherland strolled in. "Huh," he said, glancing in through the bars where Cooper had been mucking an empty stall. "This place looks the same. It's like a time warp."

"What did you expect?" Cooper resumed tossing soiled bedding into the wheelbarrow in the aisle. He wasn't surprised to see Jesse. Clete had given him a heads-up earlier, and Nell's brother appeared much the same as Cooper remembered, only older. A spray of fine laugh lines around his keen eyes, and he'd gained a few pounds, filled out just as Cooper had, but the similarity ended there. He and Jesse had once been friends but, as with Ned Sutherland and even Nell at the moment, that was over. "The ranches in this area have been working spreads for at least a hundred and fifty years. I imagine Ned's made a few renovations to the place over the years, but otherwise…"

"I meant you. Being here. Hanging around Nell again."

Cooper straightened, the pitchfork in his hand. The still-healing scar on his stomach sent a slow rolling ache through him, and Cooper guessed his muscles would hurt later from the work he'd been doing. "Don't start, Jesse." Although, he had expected the subject to come up. His shoulders had stiffened the instant he'd seen Nell's brother. "I'm her foreman. That's all." Jesse didn't have to know how good it had felt to have Nell so briefly in his arms yesterday. Cooper needed to process that reaction himself, but his relationship with Nell, whatever it might be, should be none of Jesse's concern. "What's the occasion?" he asked instead. "Seems odd you decided to pay a rare visit to the NLS."

"Nell's not thrilled but she's also wrong. She isn't the person to run this ranch," Jesse went on. "Which makes me all the more glad I came, but I didn't realize the full extent of the situation. As for you…"

Cooper simply raised his eyebrows. There'd been a time during their teens when Jesse could size him up with uncanny accuracy where Nell was concerned. "You know she has her heart set on this place." Which Cooper certainly understood. He didn't want Jesse to see that in him though. "Aren't you still living in KC?"

His chest puffed out with apparent pride. "Yeah, I've founded and sold half a dozen companies since I graduated from KU. Business degree," he informed Cooper.

Six businesses in, what, eleven or so years? He and Jesse were the same age. That wasn't much time to develop whatever enterprises he chose to set up. "So the NLS is to be your next project?"

Jesse leaned against the frame of the open stall door. "Just claiming my rightful heritage. I'm the oldest, not Nell, and the only son. Our mother worries about her, so—"

"You're stepping up to the plate at last. I don't buy that, Jesse." Cooper paused. He'd spent a lot of time with Nell's brother as kids, and he'd never seen Jesse display any devotion to his family's spread. He wondered if he felt any more allegiance to the businesses he'd sold in such short order. "After selling all those companies, you must be loaded now. Or is the ranch some kind of early retirement plan?"

Jesse smiled but it didn't reach his eyes. "I don't have to explain. If you want to keep your job as *foreman*, finish cleaning that stall."

Cooper dropped the pitchfork and got right in Jesse's face. "We were friends once so I'll give you the benefit of the doubt and forget I heard what you just said. But to make things clear, I work for Nell—not you. And as *her* foreman, I do what has to be done on my own schedule unless she says otherwise."

Jesse's gaze wandered over him. Another pain went through Cooper's abdomen and Jesse saw him flinch. "You sure you're up to the job? I mean, after getting shot in Chicago? Right now, you look like a horse just kicked you. Or are you really here for some other reason? And being her *foreman* is only an excuse?"

Cooper fought another twinge of discomfort, his weakened muscles protesting work he hadn't done in a while, but Jesse's question hit even harder than the pain. Cooper picked up the pitchfork again. "I'm up to this job. Not sure you are—or why. Maybe you should go back to Kansas City, buy up another business, since you're such an almighty success."

Jesse scoffed. "The ex-cop does Barren, Kansas. Might make a good movie." He straightened from the doorway. "Watch yourself. You think you work for Nell, but the NLS will be mine—and I'm only going to tell *you* this once." Jesse sauntered along the barn aisle to the doors. "Keep your nose out of my business. And except for work, keep away from my sister."

Cooper didn't need the warning. He already told himself that at least ten times a day. His attraction to Nell could be problematic in such close proximity, but he could manage that. It was the prospect of having her hate him all over again for eventually buying back his land that troubled him. He knew that would hurt her, and that kept Cooper awake at night.

"YOU'RE FINE, LITTLE ONE," Nell crooned a few days later to the Angus calf lying across her lap, spindly legs sprawled. She nudged the plastic bottle into his mouth again, but the wounded baby refused to nurse, and his pink tongue pushed out the nipple that contained life-saving milk. Hour by hour, she could see his strength fading. "Come on, now. Take a sip. You'll like it, I promise."

"Problem?" Cooper said from somewhere nearby.

Nell glanced up at the sound of his deep voice. She could feel her cheeks heat. She hadn't forgotten how she'd fallen into his arms on the range after they'd found the calf and its mother, or how Cooper had taken over. "He won't drink, not even water, and he's dehydrated."

"Where's his mama?"

Nell sighed. "She rejected him. After following us all the way home—" Nell broke off, regretting that she'd referred to the NLS as Cooper's home too "—so I finally released her to the herd." Keeping her downward gaze focused on the calf, she heard her tone quaver. "I'm going to lose him after all."

Cooper hunkered down in front of them, his gaze seeing right through Nell.

"You're not a quitter. Keep trying."

"I hate to give up but there's nothing more to be done. I can hydrate him through an IV line, but if he won't eat, he'll die. I know," she said before Cooper could speak, "that's part of ranch life. I get that, but I'll never be used to it." She stroked the calf's velvety head. "Losing a newborn like this one, having to put down a horse, a barn kitten getting stomped, sending a steer to slaughter…" Her voice caught on the last word.

Cooper started to cover her hand with his, then drew it back as if he too remembered holding her that other day and wouldn't risk repeating the experience. Not that he probably wanted to. "Yes, you do know that. So do Ned, Logan Hunter and Sawyer McCord, Grey Wilson…and Hadley Smith, I imagine." He half smiled. The other ranchers in the area had been his friends too long ago. "The natural cycle of life isn't any easier to face for them either." He hesitated. "How are the calf's wounds?"

Nell couldn't show him. All the cuts and scratches, and the real damage were on its other side, cushioned by the soft blanket she'd laid across her lap. "The stitches are good. No sign of infection. He seems comfortable enough. The vet says he'll do okay if we can get him eating."

Cooper moved closer. "Then let's do that."

Nell stiffened. She'd said *we*. She hadn't meant to include Cooper. There was nothing he could do that she hadn't already tried, and his closeness now was worse than letting him hold her on the range had been.

"I'll manage," she said, the bottle in her hand.

Losing the calf to a barbed-wire incident would have been awful, but she couldn't bear to see him fail day by day. Nell still hoped to save him by the sheer force of her own will. "As if the calf's decline isn't bad enough, I've had a dozen calls from Hadley," she said, hoping to redirect her own thoughts.

"Smith's harassing you?"

"I wouldn't say that, but according to the messages he left me, his *situation* has changed."

"Maybe you should answer. Tell him there's no chance about the job."

Nell frowned. She shouldn't have said anything, even to change the subject. Cooper laid a hand on her arm, and she jerked back from his warm touch. She wouldn't give in to even that small comfort. "Maybe you should leave me to manage Hadley Smith—and this calf—and go do whatever it was you were doing." Instantly, she regretted the sharp words. "Sorry, I'm a bit on edge today."

He stayed silent for a moment. "I don't imagine you're all that happy to have Jesse here right now either. I've talked with him, Nell. I have to wonder. Why is he here now, exactly? It's not as if Ned is on his death-bed."

"Sibling rivalry, and he probably knows PawPaw's planning to update his estate plan."

"More than that, I'd guess. What do you know about his business dealings?"

"Very little, except he does seem to delve into one thing after another."

"I think so too. I always thought Jesse had a short attention span. That fits, but he'd have me believe he's practically Bill Gates—or some corporate raider. Something else must have brought him to the NLS. The question is, what?"

"I'll get it out of him," she said, her attention directed at the calf.

Cooper rose. "Let me know if you change your mind and want my help."

He stood gazing down at her. "Am I supposed to apologize for the other day? For holding you? Because if we're going to work together, Nell, and since you won't talk about the past, we need to establish a few boundaries."

"I said I was sorry I snapped at you. I am. You don't need to apologize. I know why that happened." Idly, she stroked the calf again. He'd drifted off to sleep, one ear twitching as if in a dream.

"It won't happen again," Cooper promised, then dropped back onto his haunches. "Let me give this a try." But he didn't reach for the bottle of formula. He teased the calf's mouth open, then slipped his index finger inside, moved it across the baby's tongue— and all at once the calf began to suck.

"I never thought of that," Nell said, her gaze meeting his.

His gray eyes warmed. "My dad's maneuver. It's like offering a human baby a pacifier, he always said. Now see if he'll take the nipple."

Nell's first attempt didn't work, but to her

relief the second succeeded. Cooper watched the calf latch onto the bottle, then eased his finger from the calf's mouth, his touch grazing Nell's hand, making her skin tingle. He stood again. "Guess I should get back to *whatever I was doing.*"

She froze, listening to the sounds from along the aisle, the whinny of a horse, the hiss of a barn cat that had come too close to a lethal hoof, the suckling calf.

"I think he may be okay now." At least she had hope. "Thank you."

"No problem," he said. "Later this morning, we'll get that delivery of grain. Then it's branding, vaccinations, worming for the rest of my day. What do you want me to do about the farrier? He said he'd come this afternoon, then canceled, and Ned's horse really does need shoes. If we wait much longer—"

"I'll contact him myself."

His gaze fell. "Whatever you say. Call me if Smith gives you trouble."

She started to say, *I'll straighten him out,* but something stopped her. The look in his eyes, maybe, as if he knew she'd never trust him. Didn't really want him here or wouldn't even let him do the job she'd hired him for.

The look Nell had seen the day he'd left Barren with the moving truck.

"Cooper. I couldn't ask for a better foreman."

At least she would give him that.

COOPER STEPPED OUTSIDE and ran straight into Hadley Smith. Just what he needed. Cooper headed him off before Hadley could enter the barn. He didn't want the ex-foreman to startle Nell or the nursing calf, and after their talk, he was in a mood to assert his authority. "You're trespassing," he said.

Smith shoved his black hat farther off his face. "I need my last two weeks' pay. I'm here to talk to Nell."

"If it's about getting your job back too, that's a no."

"You speak for her now?" Hadley scoffed. "Nobody speaks for Nell Sutherland. She won't answer my calls. I had to come get the money she owes me in person. I'll talk to her, not y—"

"Keep your voice down. She's caring for a sick calf."

To Cooper's surprise, he grinned. "The original bleeding heart, that one. Well, I have to admit with animals, she's tender-hearted. People? That's another thing."

Cooper couldn't disagree. "I'm not going to discuss Nell with you. She fired you and she won't change her mind." He turned away. "I'll let her know you want your pay. Then you're through here, Smith. A ranch can't be run well with the kind of tension you created."

"All in her mind," he said. "Ned won't agree."

"To what?" Nell asked from the open doorway, the bottle still in her hand.

Cooper shot her a look. "Smith's here for his last pay. Go write him his check. We'll wait here. Then he'll get in his truck and drive off the NLS. He won't bother you again."

"What's your stake in this, Ransom—other than taking my job?" Hadley's gaze moved to Nell. "Seems to me you had this guy lined up all along. Ever since Ned left—"

"Whether I did or not, you've been re-placed, Hadley. Live with that."

"Don't think I can," he said, his gaze fall-ing, "and when I get hold of Ned, he'll over-ride you both." Hadley scraped the toe of his boot in the dirt like a defiant horse pawing the ground.

Every muscle in Cooper's body tensed. Smith's blue eyes were like chips off an iceberg. "What's this situation you mentioned in your messages to Nell?"

Hadley looked between them, then back to Nell.

"My wife is pregnant. Yeah," he said when Nell's eyes widened. "Surprise. I never wanted kids, after the way I grew up, but here we are."

"I'm happy for Amy." Nell's cheeks flamed with color. She turned away. "I'll get your check."

Hadley took a step but Cooper blocked him. "Let it be."

"I can't" was all Hadley said again, his face crestfallen. He watched Nell stalk across the barnyard toward the ranch house.

For an instant, Cooper almost felt sorry for him. He'd never lost a job he wanted to keep, but he knew how hard it had been to lose his family's land.

He also knew firsthand how tough it could be to win Nell over.

CHAPTER SEVEN

"COOPER! COOPER!"

Nell's voice.

The pounding at his door woke him from a sound sleep, which wasn't the norm for him these days. Lately, he'd had a hard time falling asleep because of Nell. He couldn't forget that one moment on the range when, for the first time in so many years, he'd held her again, and later Cooper had called himself ten kinds of a fool.

The knock thudded against the door again as he hauled himself out of bed, pulled on the jeans he'd left on the floor, then went to answer. Nell stood there on the scrap of porch that was part of the foreman's bungalow, her eyes wild.

"Coyotes." She was gasping for breath. "I heard them—did you hear them?"

"No," he said. Once he'd stopped pondering that afternoon with Nell, he'd slept like the dead.

Nell avoided looking at his bare chest. "They've attacked the herd—just as I feared they would. The cattle are going crazy. Hurry. Jesse is saddling horses."

As she said the last word, Cooper heard the panicked herd bawling in the distance. Then a series of yips and howls sent a streak of ice down his spine. "Give me a minute." He left Nell standing there while he dressed and grabbed a shotgun from the rack on the wall. By the time he reached the porch again, Nell was halfway to the barn.

In the aisle, Jesse struggled to heave a saddle onto a buckskin horse with a flaxen mane and tail. Cooper's bay and the horse Nell called Bear were already tacked up, their hooves impatiently stomping the floor.

Cooper stepped around Jesse. "You don't tighten these cinches, we'll all end up on our rears in the dirt." Swiftly, he redid them, including Jesse's, checked the bridle fastenings, then mounted up. "Let's ride."

Nell dashed first out of the barn with Cooper right behind. Jesse followed at a distance. Staying safely out of whatever action they might encounter? As they neared the grazing land where Nell and Cooper had found the calf the other day, the sounds of terrified cattle grew ever louder until finally they crossed the old border onto Cooper's ranch. He didn't have time to appreciate being there once more as he'd yearned to do for years, not far from the house where he'd grown up.

The unmistakable howls of a coyote pack grew even louder until Cooper and Nell rode into the near edge of the herd. Then the yips grew gradually fainter as the predators ran off, alarmed by the horsemen. He could only hope they hadn't done any real damage.

The cows and their spring calves milled about, bellowing, ever-moving, shifting as one in the dark, seeming to head by design toward the far side of the big pasture. Cooper gestured to Nell, but before long they came upon a scene of carnage that made Cooper's pulse spike. Even with no light except for that of the half moon, he could see pooled blood on the ground and the still carcass of a cow.

Before Bear even stopped moving, Nell jumped off the horse. "Oh, no," she cried, then knelt beside the body, the sheen of tears on her cheeks. She laid a hand against the cow's side. "Nothing," she said, having checked for a pulse. "She's gone."

Cooper climbed down from the bay, leaving his reins to trail in the grass. He squatted beside Nell, putting a brief hand on her shoulder.

"I'm sorry," he said.

Calling out as if he'd been a part of things, Jesse showed up at last, then pulled his horse to a stop among the herd but didn't come closer. Some of the cattle had ceased moving, were standing in a bunch near their fallen comrade as if they knew what had happened and were in mourning. "Well," Jesse said, peering at the cow, "looks like we'll have prime rib and steak for a while."

Nell gasped. She glanced up at her brother, the tears still coming. "Is that all you can say? That she was just an animal, a lost asset on the NLS balance sheet? I never want to lose a single cow—but this one—" She broke off, then tried again. "I know every head of cattle, their calves too. They're not sides of beef to me or a fancy meal in the making!"

Nell didn't go on. Cooper lightly touched

her shoulder again, offered her the hand-
kerchief his mother had always insisted he
carry for just such an occasion, then stood.
For a long moment, they stared at each other,
Nell still kneeling by the cow.

"We'll give her a good burial tomorrow,"
Cooper said.

She waited, then finished with more tears
in her husky voice, "The little calf we saved?
She was its mama. Her name was Elsie."

Cooper winced. Elsie's baby was doing
better since he and Nell had gotten him nursing, and Cooper made a silent vow to make
sure the calf thrived. Might even make a
good bull one day. He supposed Nell had already named him too as some ranchers did,
including old Sam Hunter, Logan's grandfather, on the Circle H with his bison. He spun
away from the dead cow, approached Jesse's
horse with his blood boiling in his veins—
and hauled Nell's brother from the saddle.

Cooper felt tempted to hit him but dropped
his fist to his side.

While in the hospital months ago, he'd
missed out on the arrests of the Brothers gang
that had shot him to pieces. He'd been itching
for a fight ever since, as if he'd been deprived

of the justice his friend Finn had gotten for him. But he'd settle now for a good tongue lashing for Jesse. "Listen to me and listen good. This ranch means everything to Nell. You hurt her again, in any way—and I mean *any* way—I'm still a cop inside and I know a dozen ways to take you out. Hear me?" For good measure, he shook Jesse hard.

"Cooper." Nell held up a hand. He hadn't heard her approach. "I don't need you to defend me."

"Right then you did," he insisted, his jaw taut.

"Jesse is my brother. I can speak for myself—just like I can run this ranch."

Cooper shook his head. "You're welcome, Nell," he said, then stalked off to tend to the dead cow. A minute later, he heard someone ride away. Glancing up, he spotted Jesse's horse disappear over the ridge. When Cooper looked around, Nell was still there.

"I have half a mind to fire you, Cooper."

He leveled his gaze at her. "Are you?"

"Not this time. I need you to stay here and keep watch on the…herd." She meant the fallen cow too. She walked toward Bear, grazing on the rich spring grass nearby, then back again. "One more thing."

Cooper's mouth set. He was tired of Nell fighting him, making his job here all the harder. He had half a mind to quit. "Yeah?"

"Thank you."

NELL'S MOTHER CAME to visit the next day. The fact that she'd driven from Kansas City to the ranch was a shock; she hadn't been on the NLS in years.

They met on the front steps. "Mom, wow. This is more than a surprise—no, but actually it's not." She groaned. "Jesse must have called you."

Judith Sutherland hugged her. Slim and fit from hours spent in the gym, she had skillfully colored ash-blond hair, which she wore in what she called a lob (or long bob) and the green eyes Nell had inherited. Good genes but not the kind Nell preferred. She glanced down at her dirty clothes. Today, her mother was all decked out in four-inch heels with red soles that had to be Christian Louboutin, formfitting jeans—obviously new—and a stylish coral silk blouse.

Money wasn't a problem for Nell's parents. Her father owned a chain of high-end tack stores in the area, and he also collected a share of the profits from the ranch.

"And why shouldn't Jesse call me? You could have been killed last night. Riding over that rough terrain in the dark—he said there are holes everywhere for a horse to step in. He was right to intervene. You could have broken your neck, and for what? Cattle die all the time—"

Nell shuddered, remembering the calf's mother lying so still, her body already cooling on the blood-soaked ground. "Not on the NLS, they don't. Not like that. And I know that land as well as I know my face in a mirror." As well as Cooper used to know every inch of his family's ranch. "Bear didn't step in a hole and there were no bogeymen lying in wait—"

"Nell," her mom said in that chiding tone she'd heard since childhood.

"Well, you're being just as ridiculous. If you came out here to sway me, I told you I'm fine and so is the NLS." In her work-worn jeans with the hole in one knee and a shapeless gray T-shirt that should be in the ragbag, the contrast between Nell and her mother couldn't have been starker. "I'm always happy to see you, but you changed your schedule today for no reason. What was it, a tennis date this morning?"

"A lunch with friends at The Stockyard." The popular upscale restaurant in the city was her mother's favorite, an irony not lost on Nell. Beef cattle were the business of the ranch, and the Sutherlands were purveyors of meat for many classy restaurants. But not Elsie, never that. Earlier, Nell had watched Cooper ride out to see to the cow, a backhoe for burial following his horse.

"You make me sound shallow, sweetie," Mom said.

"Of course you're not. Are you a chic city girl since you and Dad abandoned the ranch? Yes, and I still love you," Nell said, "but I wish you'd stop expecting me to come live in that spare bedroom—"

"It's your bedroom. Always waiting," she said as if she couldn't resist.

"—so you can introduce me to every eligible male from thirty to forty you think would make a good husband. If I wanted a man, I'd find one." Nell repressed any mental image of Cooper. He'd been her first love, the boy she daydreamed about whenever they weren't together, the one she'd expected to marry and have a family with, the man with whom she'd hoped to grow old. No wonder she wouldn't discuss that with him.

Her mother threw up her hands. "If I want grandchildren before I'm too decrepit to enjoy them, I guess I'll have to work on Jesse."

"I wish you would." Nell put an arm around her mother's shoulders and walked her into the house, where her still-smooth face immediately showed distaste. "Really, why has no one ever updated this relic?" She went from the front hall into the living room on the right, looked at the scarred wooden floor, which in Nell's view gave it character, the walls that hadn't seen fresh paint in decades, the flattened cushions in a faded Western print on the large sofas that flanked the huge stone fireplace. There were cold ashes on the hearth, and the smell of burnt logs hovered in the air. "If you insist upon living here, why not at least hire a decorator?"

"And wipe out generations of history?" To Nell, it was a cozy place. "I love this house the way it is. I can feel PawPaw here, and Gram, and Dad and...you," she finished.

Mom wrinkled her nose. "I was never meant for ranch life. The day your father carried me over this threshold I cried all night. The mattress in our bedroom must have been stuffed with horsehair a hundred years ago. It was rock hard, like trying to sleep in a coffin—and I almost wished I hadn't married your father."

"But you did. And you lived here for how long?"

She didn't hesitate. "Sixteen years, thirty-seven days and nine hours."

Nell sighed. "But who's counting, right?"

Her mother trailed a finger over an end table, checking for dust. Her finger came away coated, and from the designer bag she carried, she drew a tissue to wipe her hands. Grimacing as if she'd stepped in cow manure, she tipped her head toward Nell. "The point is, I never fit in here. I tried because I thought your dad wanted to help PawPaw, which he did, and inherit the NLS, which he didn't. When I found that out, I knew at last where we really belonged."

"I'm glad you're happy where you are," Nell said, "but so am I."

"Working yourself to death twenty-four hours a day? Endangering your life?"

"I wasn't in danger last night, Mom. I had Cooper...and Jesse with me." She didn't mention that her brother hadn't done much—except nearly get his nose bloodied.

"Among a bunch of *coyotes*? I may not be a rancher's wife any longer, but I haven't forgotten the threat those animals pose. We lost several calves and a foal when I lived here. Why didn't you let the men chase after them?"

"The pack was all but gone when we got there, and Cooper and I both had shotguns."

Her mother's gaze sharpened. "Cooper," she echoed.

She'd said his name just like Jesse had. Nell focused her gaze on the fireplace, where a parade of family pictures in old-fashioned frames marched across the heavy marble mantel.

"This is your mother speaking." She turned Nell to face her. "Oh, baby, do you think I've forgotten? Watching you grieve for that boy? Your heart broken in two?"

Boot heels thumped on the porch stairs, and a second later, Cooper walked into the house, pausing only to rap a quick announcement of his presence on the front door frame. He came into the living room and stopped cold, then removed his hat. "Mrs. Sutherland."

"Hello, Cooper," she said coolly, her gaze raking him from head to toe. Her eyes widened. With his grimy hands twisting his battered hat, his jeans smeared with mud and… Nell didn't want to think what else…his shirt unbuttoned halfway, he looked no better than Nell did. Hard work wasn't pretty. Still… "You've grown up," her mother said.

Cooper shifted from one foot to the other. "I hope so, ma'am." He looked at Nell. "Sorry to interrupt, but I got the cow settled. You can go see her spot under that big cottonwood tree whenever you like."

"Thanks." Nell's throat had closed at the mention of Elsie. She didn't want to talk about the cow, but neither did she want to continue the conversation she'd been having with her mother about Cooper. "You have time for a cup of coffee? I was going to make a pot."

"No, the farrier's finally here." He plopped his hat on his head and touched its brim with one finger. "Ma'am. Nell." He walked out the door, escaping before she could find another reason to keep him there.

"Well, my. I must say he's grown up nicely," her mom said, then frowned. "All the more reason for you to be cautious. The worst thing I can imagine would be my daughter marrying the man who nearly destroyed her years ago."

"Don't worry. I'm not going to marry anyone."

Though she guessed that wasn't the answer her mother wanted either.

THE NEXT DAY, Cooper watched Nell dismount from her horse, the sun gleaming on the gold glints in her hair. Holding Bear's reins, she walked over to the cottonwood tree not far from a spring where the cattle liked to drink. Kneeling as she had the other night, she rested a hand on the mound of churned earth where the calf's mother lay buried. "I'll get a stone for her," he said.

"You don't find that silly?"

"Of course not." Cooper understood her

respect and affection for the animals in her care. He was glad he'd suggested marking the spot, as it had brought a half-smile to Nell's face, a softer look to her eyes. "For two animal lovers," he said, "I can't think of a better idea for Elsie's resting place."

Stepping back to give her space, he studied the land around them. The herd had drifted off, tails swishing like flyswatters. They lowed softly, almost resembling a sweet dirge, yet their grieving seemed over. They were moving on.

As they topped the small rise farther off that flowed onto the former Ransom ranch, he heard another sound though. Cooper tensed. *Coyotes*, or at least one. It wasn't like them to be so active during the height of the day, but maybe they'd decided to search for any remains of their feast anyway. "Nell. We should go."

She was already turning from the grave to her horse. "What is it?"

A disturbed murmuring had broken out among the herd, and several cows with their calves picked up their pace. The steers among them followed.

"The pack must be close by." This could be their chance.

"I can come back later," Nell said, stuck her left foot in the stirrup and smoothly swung into her saddle. Before Cooper urged his horse into a lope, she'd reached the ridge. "I don't see any coyotes—"

"—which doesn't mean they aren't here."

Beside her, Cooper listened but didn't hear another howl. Had he been mistaken? In silence, they rode on, gazes sweeping the area before them, taking in each brush and tree that could be used to hide the pack as they passed by. Drawing a pair of binoculars from his saddlebag, he glassed the area. Empty, nothing but the land—*his* land just over there. "Elusive creatures, aren't they?"

"Deadly too," she said, one hand resting on the stock of the shotgun sheathed in a scabbard by her leg. "Nothing would give me more satisfaction than to take revenge for Elsie's…death."

"We'll get 'em, Nell. If not today, then soon."

We, he'd said. But to his relief, she didn't take offense. Just then, a lone coyote burst from the underbrush and started running across the open range between them. Cooper reached for his shotgun at the same instant Nell did hers. Almost simultaneously, they got off two shots before the coyote streaked under a gap in the far fence and, yipping, disappeared.

"Winged him maybe," Cooper said, shoving his shotgun in its sheath. He surveyed the range. "Seems strange it was alone when we've heard a number of them before." Maybe they could flush out more.

By now, without his noticing, they'd passed over the original boundary again from the NLS. He stretched his legs by standing in the stirrups. *Ransom land.* She must realize where they were, but when Nell didn't object he rode on, his pulse pounding, half hunting for another coyote, half enjoying the view and just being here. There was the overgrown trail he'd ridden with his dad, learning to cowboy at his side; the stand of trees where he'd first kissed Nell…and down that slope ahead, he saw the house.

He expected Nell to rein Bear around and head onto the old NLS, tell him he didn't live here anymore and never would again.

But her next words weren't those he'd anticipated.

"Let's take a look," she said, and without glancing his way, cantered down the slope. Maybe she had some idea to tear down the house and barns, use that acreage for extra grazing land. He wondered why she and Ned hadn't done that already or at least rented out the house.

At the front steps, they dismounted. Cooper's pulse kept speeding as if he were on some racetrack, accelerating into the corners. Leaving the two horses ground tied, they walked up onto the porch. Cooper heard a loose board creak and leaves and bits of brush littered the floor. "I don't have a key," he said.

Nell twisted the knob on the front door. It protested at first, the lock badly in need of some oil, but then it gave and the wooden door swung open. "Aha, just as I thought. You know PawPaw doesn't believe in keys. He always says, so far from the road, who would even guess a house was here?" It was true; the former Ransom ranch had a long, winding driveway from the gates, which

Cooper had seen again on his way to the NLS that first day before Nell hired him.

On the threshold, he hesitated. His family's house had dirt and debris scattered over this lower floor. The sight shocked him, yet a tidal wave of memories washed over him.

"At Christmas, there was always a wreath on this door," he said.

Obviously remembering too, Nell added, "The dining room table would also be set with your mother's best china."

Cooper smiled. "Inherited from her mother, and we always used my dad's family's silver carried by a long-ago relative from the east when they headed west in a covered wagon."

Nell blinked. "I wonder how many holidays we all shared here."

Oh, Mom, he thought. Except for the trash, the rooms were empty now—the living room where she'd read to him each night by the fire, the kitchen with all the appliances pulled out and shipped to Chicago. He pointed. "This half bath in the hall that's really a quarter bath, just a toilet in the revamped space of a closet, is still here too," he said, glancing at Nell.

"Sad, isn't it though? The whole house seems sad." She paused. "And yet there are happy memories here too."

She had an odd expression on her face, taking this trip down memory lane with him, that must have mirrored Cooper's expression. Upstairs, the rooms looked cleaner, but the master was also bare. "My parents' vintage brass bed is in my mom's apartment in the city now," he told Nell. "And she still uses that old Singer sewing machine she had here."

Nell rolled her eyes. "She made me such cute little dresses."

"Which you wore now and then to please her," he said with a smile.

Nell wasn't one for skirts. At the end of the hall, they came to the room that had been a nursery after he was born, then a little boy's space, occasionally lonely for the only child he'd been but more often *his* place, and his alone. Cooper's room held even more memories. With Nell. He ran a hand over the door latch.

"In my teens, I installed this small lock for privacy. Remember?"

"We spent a lot of time here," she said, looking around, "doing homework—"

He raised his eyebrows. "Making out…"

Nell's cheeks turned pink. "Until your mother knocked at the door and we sprang apart like guilty thieves. Oh, Cooper." Her expression shifted again, softening, and without another word, Nell slipped her arms around his waist, then laid her head against his pounding heart. He hugged her in return, but the embrace didn't last long. Nell drew away, her gaze downcast in what might have been embarrassment for initiating that touch, and she took a few steps toward his bedroom door. "Well. Hmm." She cleared her throat.

"Nell, thanks for coming with me, but please don't regret it. I'm glad we shared this. I think it helps to revisit who we were then." Even though she hadn't wanted to do so the other day. "And you don't have to act tough all the time. It's okay to show your softer side, to just…be a woman. A woman with a big heart."

"Don't let that go to your head." The throat clearing again. Another glance into the hallway as if she were waiting for rescue. "Let's explore the rest of the house while we're here."

Suppressing a sigh, Cooper clattered down

the steps behind her. He didn't trust himself anyway to be alone with her in this place that held so many memories, especially the better ones that made him wish for their long-ago friendship and that first love. "We should be careful. No telling what shape this structure may be in by now, but it was solidly built at the end of the last century—like Ned's house—so I hope not that bad."

At the bottom of the stairs, Nell faced him. "Meaning you do plan to fix it up. For your mother," she said accusingly.

"I told you what she wants, Nell. What I want."

She squared her shoulders, pressed her lips together as if to keep from saying, *No, you won't get this house, this ranch. I don't care about the past we shared. I don't care about you.*

Yet, the very air in these rooms—his old room—had changed the dynamic between them somehow, and underneath her determination to run the NLS and keep his land as part of it, he sensed she also understood.

CHAPTER EIGHT

EXHAUSTED, NELL TRUDGED from the barn to the house. As soon as she opened the door, she smelled dinner. In the kitchen, her mother bustled around, stirring a pot, setting plates on the table, pausing to take a sip of the coffee she'd poured into a mug. She tossed Nell a grin.

"Wonder how many suppers I've made in this house. I knew just where to find everything—as if I still lived here." She rolled her eyes. "Not that I ever will again. I decided you could use a home-cooked meal."

"Thanks, Mom." Nell reached into the refrigerator for a bottle of water, then took a few sips, reminded of her afternoon jaunt with Cooper to his old home. He hoped to make his mother's wish come true, but that would also give them squatters' rights of a sort on their former land, which wouldn't please Nell or her grandfather at all. "I appreciate that. You don't have to stick around for me though. I'm sorry Jesse made you worry."

Nell supposed Cooper, as a son, felt much the same about his mom. He certainly remembered his old home and the happy memories there. For a short while in his bedroom, she'd felt…close to him again. However, that didn't mean she'd had to put her arms around him.

"Don't frown, baby girl. You'll put lines in that pretty face."

"Was I frowning? Just tired, I guess," she said. When the door opened again and her brother walked in, she was grateful for the interruption. Her mother had a way of getting things out of Nell, and she wasn't about to discuss the afternoon. Or Cooper.

Jesse threw his sweat-stained hat on the table, narrowly missing a place setting at the end seat. "Cooper says you two shot up a coyote today."

"We shot *at* a coyote. Maybe we hit him, but I'm not sure." She took a breath. "Where were you? I thought you were going to brand the last of the calves, then muck stalls at the south side of the barn." When Nell had quit work for the day, she'd noticed none of that had been done. "If you're so set on being part of the NLS after all these years, I'd suggest you pitch in." Nell hadn't forgotten how he'd lagged behind that night when she and Cooper found Elsie.

"Children," their mother murmured, tapping a spoon against a pot.

Jesse's mouth flattened. "I went with Clete to mend that gap in the fence where the calf got caught. Not my favorite part of this business, but I'll pay my dues to get what I want."

Their mother's face set. "Must you two quarrel? If Jesse's willing to take over the NLS, why not let him? You're a young woman with her whole future ahead. Why tie yourself to this place when you could have—"

"A luncheon date with friends at The Stockyard? A tennis lesson?"

"Don't take that tone with me, Nell Marie Sutherland. Instead of riding around with a shotgun, spending the day with Cooper Ransom, you should be worrying about tomorrow, not the past."

Nell flushed. Because that's what she had been doing, especially in Cooper's room, remembering all their happy yesterdays.

Her brother chimed in. "Mom's right, and I'm here, so you can let Cooper go. No sense paying someone when family can help."

"You're not helping, Jesse. I have to follow after you to clean up your mess—or handle whatever you failed to do. The other hands weren't happy to pick up your slack with the calves or the dirty stalls."

He shrugged. "I'm not a cowhand. I'm the future owner of this ranch."

"With an entitlement attitude. There's no place for that here. If you were anything close to a real rancher, you'd know that by now. Everyone does his job, including Cooper—"

"Ah. Leap to his defense, Nell, why don't you?" Jesse glanced at their mother, a clear expression of triumph in his eyes. "See what I mean?"

"Jesse has a point," Mom said, carrying a bowl of steaming spaghetti to the table. She'd made her special sauce that simmered all day, and as she mixed it with the pasta, Nell's mouth watered. While spending her afternoon with Cooper, she'd forgotten to eat lunch. "Sit, please. We won't settle this tonight."

Nell sat, reached for a slice of garlic bread fresh from the oven. She loved her mother, even loved her brother when he wasn't threatening her livelihood, but she'd be darned if she let them win. Two against one. "Outnumbered," she said to her plate, "but no one is going to drive me off the NLS into Kansas City, so I can meet some eligible man and go shopping at the mall every day on his money."

"That's enough, Nell," her mom said, passing the bowl to Jesse.

"Sorry, that was mean." The words had popped out of her mouth, but Nell hadn't finished. "You're entitled to your opinion. You assume you need to protect me, but your view is as outdated as PawPaw's—or Jesse's, for that matter."

"Because we're right," he muttered.

Well, about one issue they could be. Cooper posed an even bigger threat to Nell than she wanted to believe. After she'd impulsively hugged him in his old bedroom in the former Ransom ranch house, she couldn't deny the truth, at least inwardly, that was right in front of her. Her attraction to him was not only still there; in the years they'd been apart, it had gained another dimension. Understanding. Compassion, maybe. Even caring once more.

How could she not understand his love for that house, for the land that would have been his? Certainly, he knew how she felt about the NLS, and Cooper had shown his support for her more than once.

Yet, she couldn't let her feelings deter her. Nell's sole focus now had to be on the NLS, which also meant having to deal with her brother every day, hoping their grandfather didn't show up too soon. Before Cooper made his offer to PawPaw to buy his old land, which she had no doubt he would, she had to nail down her right—not Jesse's—to inherit the ranch.

THE DOORBELL RANG and Amy tensed as if the sound had been a rifle shot. Squaring her shoulders, she went to answer. Her heartbeat kicked up as soon as she saw him, her soon-to-be ex, unless she had her way. "Hadley. Come on in."

"Can't stay," he said. "I'm working for

Grey Wilson this week. He didn't much care for my taking off after you called."

"This is more important." Amy would fight for what she wanted—just as she had tried to settle in at the NLS after she married Hadley against her family's wishes. She'd tried to make the simple foreman's house— a temporary space, as it turned out—into a home. Unused to domestic chores, she'd somehow managed to keep it clean and cook Hadley's favorite meals since she was a better cook than she was a housekeeper. Still, she'd never adjusted to living on a strict budget. Amy glanced around the living room of the apartment she rented in Barren.

Without Hadley, she felt adrift. Didn't he realize how much she missed him? If she didn't, she would have tried to smooth things over with her parents. She steered him into the main room. Big and broad-shouldered, he seemed to dominate the modest area, and Amy left him the sofa, his hat propped on his knee, while she sat in her one uphol-stered chair beside the TV. "Have you spoken to Ned Sutherland?"

"No, but I got my pay. Ned's still in Canada out of cell phone range, as far as I know.

I've left messages. Nothing more I can do." Hadley set his Stetson on his knee. "You said this was urgent."

She smiled a little. His interest again in her well-being was a good start.

"I don't want the divorce," she said, laying a hand on her abdomen.

"Amy, we've worked out most of the details. If you're so worried about my having a job to pay alimony, then I need to get back to work and stop sending every other dime I make to the lawyer."

"Is Grey going to hire you full-time?"

He shook his head. "Grey already has a foreman. I can give him a few hours, lend a hand for a week or two, but I don't want a regular job as a cowpoke. That would be going backward and that's not part of my plan."

"Your plan used to include me. We were doing fine until you decided to cut me loose," she said, hating the way her lower lip had begun to tremble. Her emotions were all over the place these days, and she suffered from nausea. It was no fun being pregnant without Hadley to take care of her. "Why don't we talk about everything? There must be some way for us to…reconcile," she insisted.

"You want to get back together?" He gaped at her. He spun the hat on his knee and focused his gaze on it. "I had enough of all the fighting, the tears whenever I said something you didn't like. I was never what you wanted. I was sure not what your folks had in mind, and you—"

"We loved each other, Hadley. You know we did."

He frowned. "If that was love, I'm not buying."

Amy flinched. He'd always claimed he couldn't love anyone and she'd vowed to change that. This wasn't how she'd expected things to go now. "I realize you had a tough time growing up," she began but he talked over her.

"One big reason why we didn't work. What did I know about marriage? We were two trains on a track heading straight for a crash." But it wasn't her fault she'd been raised in a comfortable home with loving parents. What was wrong with wanting that for their baby too? "What do I know about being a *father*?" he asked.

She blinked. "Now you're being nasty."

Without warning, she burst into tears. Through the screen of her lashes and blurred vision, she watched a look of horror come over his face. Hadley hated tears. She supposed most men did, which could work to her advantage.

He bolted from his chair, then hunkered down in front of her but didn't take her in his arms. He patted her shoulder. "Now, now… don't cry."

"I hate it here," she said, gulping down a sob. "I want to come…home."

"There is no home," he pointed out. "I got thrown out of the foreman's house at the NLS and kicked off the ranch. Someone else is living there now. I've been sleeping in my truck." He shrugged his shoulders as if to ease a knot in his neck. "Is that how you want to live? I bet it's not."

She couldn't deny the statement. She'd always had expensive taste, or rather dreams of buying the best of whatever she wanted. But Hadley couldn't supply that, and her parents had practically disowned her. "Sleeping in your truck? You poor man." With the tears streaking down her face, she gestured at the apartment. "Why not move in with me then? I don't have much room but…" She started to bat her probably tear-starred eyelashes, then thought better of it. She shouldn't overplay her hand. "Why not? You could find work here in town." Amy added, "After all, I need to be near my doctor."

Hadley scowled. "What kind of work would that be? All I understand is cows, and horses, and manure. If you wanted some guy with a fancy college degree, somebody who could get a desk job and make real money, you made a bad choice." He paused. "We're a lousy match, Amy. I can't believe you'd try this a second time."

She jumped up from her chair. She swiped her hands down her cheeks. "Hadley, I loved you—and no matter how we messed up before, I still do."

He stood too. "Amy, if you hadn't walked into Rowdy's bar that night, we never would have met. We shouldn't have," he said. "Your folks are right about us. You could do better."

"But I can help you overcome your bad experiences as a kid. Together we could be happy."

He briefly pressed his lips tight. "They were more than bad," he said, his gaze meeting hers for a second.

Still, she could sense him weakening. "I can help you to…heal." She laid a palm against her stomach again. "If you don't care about me, think of the baby."

Hadley flinched. "You're really going to play that card?"

"I realize you never wanted kids—I understand why. But I am having a baby—*we* are having a baby—and I can't believe you'd abandon us like this."

He swore softly under his breath. "I'm not going to fight about this anymore, or about anything else." He stood, then started for the door. "Unlike my father, I'll own up to my responsibilities. Somehow, I'll find the money to support you and…the kid. Whatever the court says I have to do. But that's all, Amy."

And it wasn't enough. She knew she was good for him. She knew he'd make a wonderful father once he got used to the idea. She knew that, even when he couldn't say so, he still loved her.

"Hadley." But before she could say *please*, he was gone.

"WHAT DO YOU MEAN, you fired Hadley Smith?"

In the ranch office, Nell listened to the tick of the clock on PawPaw's bookshelf, feeling more isolated and alone than she ever had before. She didn't do well with anger, especially from someone she loved with all her heart, and Nell was still reeling from her quarrel with her mom and Jesse earlier. Now—at last—her grandfather was on the phone. She'd been expecting his call ever since she let Hadley go and to say he wasn't happy with her was putting it mildly. "Yes, I did fire him. How did you learn about that?"

"When Will and I got into town up here in Canada, I checked my messages. Most of them from Hadley begging for his job."

Nell propped her boots on the desk and took the offensive. "Why are you surprised I let him go? You knew he wasn't doing his job for me the way he did with you, PawPaw. He didn't respect me and so neither did the cowhands. Hadley did as he pleased. He tried to intimidate me. If I'm to run the NLS while you're not home—" *and in the future*, she silently added, remembering her brother's taunts "—it makes sense I should hire my own people. I decided that was best for the ranch."

PawPaw's familiar voice seemed to blast the airwaves between the NLS and the village where he and Will were apparently staying the night. "Nell, I didn't give you that authority."

"I guess I took it then," she said, trying a cheeky smile he couldn't see. Then she sobered because this was serious business, and if he knew about Hadley, he might also know about his replacement. "I won't be worrying every day and night how Hadley will try to override me. Wondering what he's kept from me. That's not healthy, PawPaw— and now I have Jesse in his place, thank you very much. Which I've been waiting to talk to you about. I never imagined you were so against my taking over the NLS. You were the one who trained me. What's changed your mind?" She hesitated, remembering their previous conversation with Will in the background. "I can't believe you sent Jesse here to watch my every move."

"That isn't why," he said. "The last time I spoke to your brother, I realized this is exactly what Jesse needs." He paused. "You do too."

When he continued, she could hear the growing anger in his tone. "I just talked to him again—and he tells me you've hired a new foreman. Again, without my permission."

Her heart skipped a beat. That was two strikes against her. She should have mentioned that sooner. "Then I suppose he also told you his name."

Her grandfather all but spit the next words. "*Cooper Ransom* is not welcome on that ranch. It's *my* land, Nell, and I still have a more than bad taste in my mouth from fourteen years ago. I regret what happened to his family. I regret how losing their ranch affected his father, his mother too. John Ransom was a good friend of mine, but I did what I had to do—and I don't regret that. Cooper was a hotheaded kid then and I wouldn't normally care about some threats made in the heat of the moment. But he went too far."

"I agreed with you then, remember. I chose family over Cooper. But he's the best man for this job now." Even when he meant to buy back his land.

"I care about you," PawPaw said, and Nell could envision him shaking his head.

"I'm glad you do, but I *don't* need Jesse here. He's no help at all, and his notion to take over the NLS instead of me one day is crazy. My brother is the furthest thing from a cowboy you could get. You know that."

"Yes I do, and no, I haven't lost my mind. I'm certainly not senile. I see this as Jesse's chance to prove himself. If the ranch is really what he wants, it will make a man of him."

But he didn't fool Nell. "You mean may the best man—or woman—win." She could scarcely contain her disappointment in her grandfather. "I don't mean to throw Jesse under the bus, but I don't intend to let him win any competition between us. I will prove to you that *I* can do the job, PawPaw. And to be clear, Cooper is not holding me up so I don't fall down. We work together," she said.

"Is that all? Or did you hire him for another reason?"

Nell groaned. "You see, there's the problem! Right there. Why automatically assume I'm about to fall in love? With any man?"

"Because that's what I want for you, Nell. Except not Cooper."

The clock ticked steadily as if to remind her time was running out. "Well, I'm not about to fulfill your dream with him or anyone else. Why can't you accept me as a rancher, which others have done with their daughters around Barren and Farrier and a lot of other places in this state? As a capable person?"

"Yes, you're a woman, Nell, a fine one, and you love the NLS, but you're not a girl following me around now. Your mother is right. It's too hard a life. I don't want you to learn that lesson as she did and break your heart in the process." This time he didn't add, *with Cooper.*

Nell sniffed. She was outnumbered all over again. "I know you love me." Her voice broke. "I love you too, PawPaw, but please. Give me a chance."

"I'm giving you and Jesse both a chance. Let's see what happens."

He hung up before she could respond.

Nell collapsed in the chair with a groan. And realized she hadn't told him about the coyotes and Elsie.

Yet another point against Nell.

CHAPTER NINE

COOPER RODE OUT with Jesse to check the herd and search for coyotes. The sun felt good on his shoulders, and Cooper was in a fine mood this morning—until he reminded himself that Nell had lost a pair of calves only last night. She hadn't taken that well, but he'd persuaded her to stay behind while he managed Jesse.

Jesse glanced around warily. Cooper noted the tense set of his shoulders and the tight grip on his reins. Jesse had never been a horseman. "You don't think that pack of jackals will be here now, do you?"

Cooper shrugged. "I promised Nell we'd find out. She and I did run into that one near this very spot after that first cow was killed." The day they'd visited his old home, the day he'd sensed a new connection to her. Once he got his land back, he hoped not to deal with Jesse for the rest of his life.

"This is a waste of time," Jesse grumbled. "And so what if we find a bad section of fence somewhere while we're out here? I don't want to fix more fence. You should have sent Clete."

Cooper turned slightly in his saddle toward Jesse, who was lagging a few paces to the rear. "You have something more important to do?"

"Thought I'd drive into town today, pick up my saddle at the tack store."

"That's a personal errand," Cooper said, guessing Jesse had ordered a custom-made, high-end model that must have cost thousands. Nudging his horse up to the old boundary of the Ransom ranch, he left Jesse to trot after him. "Pull your weight. On the NLS there are no prima donnas."

"I do my share." His tone sharpened. "You calling me a girl?"

"I hope you don't mean like Nell." Cooper stopped the new mount he'd chosen from the ranch's string of quarter horses, a big black named Domino with a white star on his face. He'd decided Hadley's bay wasn't for him. "Good thing she didn't hear you say that. Don't do it again."

Jesse trotted up the small hill. He reined in his mare, which stood fifteen hands to Domino's sixteen, and glared up at Cooper. "You may have Nell's ear, but that won't matter, Ransom. I'm the one you should keep on the good side of…and don't forget that."

Cooper's jaw tightened. "Stop pulling rank on me, *Sutherland*."

"Or what?"

Cooper didn't respond. He didn't need a petty argument. "Be quiet for a second, will you? I want to listen for coyotes."

Cooper heard none, which came as no surprise. The animals were, if nothing else, crafty and secretive. The sad damage they'd already wrought on the herd though was obvious. He didn't want to bury or haul any more carcasses away, and the two calves they'd lost had been valuable assets too— something Jesse should understand.

Nell's brother sat his horse with stiff legs and white-knuckled hands as if he expected the mare to bolt any second. If he really wanted to be a rancher, he should seem a lot more comfortable in the saddle. So what was his real motive for wanting the ranch?

Nell, if not Ned Sutherland, had wondered the same thing.

After a long minute of listening and scanning the area, Cooper said, "Nothing. Maybe you'd like to take the first watch tonight out here. Ride among the herd and watch for the pack."

Jesse gritted his teeth. "I don't take orders from you. I can help in other ways. Handling the ranch accounts, for example."

"Nell takes care of that. She has a good head for figures." But so did Jesse, he supposed, as a businessman. Maybe he wasn't being fair. "With your experience running all those companies you've sold, you might work together."

Jesse's gaze slid away from his. "I don't mind desk work, being shut in the office. Nell would rather run around being a cowgirl, I'm sure." He paused. "Maybe you'd rather she came with you today instead of me."

"I only need to get the work done—whoever's free can join me."

Jesse didn't rush to reassure him that he was on board.

Cooper glanced at him. He'd had a hunch

the first day that Jesse was lying. Hiding something. Cooper dropped his reins against Domino's neck and the horse lowered his head to graze on a clump of green grass. "What is it, Jesse? What do you want? You don't really like to ride, you don't like to fix fence, you don't even like the animals you supposedly want to claim along with the NLS's land. Is it more money?"

Jesse shifted in his saddle. The leather creaked, and high overhead an eagle soared in lazy circles through the sky. "Why would I need money? I told you—"

"I remember. You sold a bunch of businesses for a big profit. But maybe—just a hunch here—you're in some kind of trouble anyway."

Jesse's face turned red. "I'm not in trouble."

Cooper only raised one eyebrow.

Jesse wheeled his horse around. "My reason for coming home—which is something you can't do, is it?—is my business. No one else's."

Leaving Cooper to look after him, he rode off down the slope onto level ground, headed for the barn.

GRIEVING OVER THE loss of the two calves last night, Nell decided to talk to Finn Donovan. On one of her rare trips into town, she soon learned at the sheriff's department that he was off duty for the day so she headed out to his farm, hoping to catch him there.

"Nell!" With a wide smile, Annabelle Foster met her at the front door before she had lifted a hand to knock. She ushered Nell into the house. "I recognized your grandfather's truck. I was just making coffee and setting out some doughnuts."

At the last word, a small streak of human lightning shot between them, then skidded to a stop. Nell smiled at Annabelle's little girl who, wearing jeans and a T-shirt that read I Love Horses, gazed up at her. "You like doughnuts?"

"I do," Nell said. "Are you willing to share?"

Emmie, all blond hair and blue eyes, nodded. "I share at my school."

Over her head, Annabelle grinned. "She means day care. She's always ready for doughnuts." They walked into the kitchen, where Annabelle gestured at a chair, then poured two mugs of coffee. She set a plastic glass of milk in front of Emmie, who promptly reached for the plate of glazed doughnuts. Her hand already sticky, she took one, then handed Nell another.

"Thank you."

Emmie didn't sit at the table, and Nell imagined she rarely sat at all. She seemed to be always in motion, and something tugged at Nell's heart. Once, she'd believed she would marry Cooper and have a family with him. She'd never quite worked out in her mind where they might live—on the NLS, or Cooper's ranch or if they'd build a house of their own somewhere in between. Now, she knew that had been only a teenage daydream. She refused to dwell on her ongoing attraction to him or the new bond they'd shared at his former home. She had bigger problems.

Emmie gulped down her milk, snatched a second or third doughnut from the plate, then ran toward the hall. "I eat with Finnie in my room," she called over her shoulder, red lights blinking on her sneakers.

"Oh, no," Annabelle said. "More laundry to do."

"She's adorable," Nell said with a lump in her throat. "Who's Finnie?"

"That's her name for a stuffed lamb Finn gave her when they met—" her smile faded "—at the scene of her mom's accident."

Nell remembered the tragic event last autumn. Emmie's mother, Annabelle's cousin, had died not long after that from her injuries and little Emmie had been left an orphan. Well, not quite...

"It was so good of you to adopt her."

"How could I not?" Annabelle asked. "Her father gave up any claim to Emmie." Nell had heard all the rumors in confidence from several members of the Girls' Night Out group, but so far, the fact that the mayor was Emmie's father hadn't become general knowledge. To protect the mayor's wife and family—and Emmie—she hoped it never would. "I'll sign the final papers soon, then Emmie will be mine," Annabelle said. "Finn will go through the same process after we get married."

Nell had learned from Olivia that his proposal was already planned, and she couldn't be happier for them. She had the NLS—or she would!—to sustain her. Still, that long-ago daydream ran through her mind again.

Even PawPaw had thought she and Cooper had made a good match then.

Nell broke off another piece of her doughnut. "Olivia tells me you two are going with her and Sawyer to Kedar."

"Emmie's going too," she said. "Since she heard there are other kids there and Olivia's son, Nick, is going, she hasn't stopped talking about the trip." Annabelle finished her coffee. "I'm not sure we'll be so excited after such a long flight to get there, but we'll find out. Finn promised me this adventure. Talk about my wish to travel…" she trailed off. "By the way, did you come to see him? Finn had a meeting with the mayor—yes, on a Saturday. He should be back shortly."

"I came to see you both." Nell ate the last bite of the doughnut. "We've been having trouble lately at the NLS with coyotes. I wondered if Finn's had any reports from other ranchers in the area."

"Not that I'm aware of," Annabelle said.

"They can cover a pretty broad range, so I thought I'd ask." She rose from the table. "We've already lost a cow and a pair of calves."

Annabelle shuddered. "How terrible."

"Yes, and I don't want to lose any more." Nell pressed her lips tight. "If Finn has news—"

"I'll have him call you or drop by the ranch. By the way, how's Cooper working out?"

"Fine," she said, hoping Annabelle wouldn't pursue the subject. That wasn't in her nature, unlike Olivia at times, or even their friend Shadow, another reason Nell seldom attended their meetings. Annabelle tended to be less bold where other people were concerned.

"Just fine?" she asked, making Nell question her last notion.

"You've been talking to Olivia. Cooper's not a problem," she said, mentally crossing her fingers. "My grandfather, my brother and my mom are. I'm fighting this fight now so girls like Emmie won't have to. When they're grown, a woman rancher will be common." She thanked Annabelle for the doughnut and coffee, then walked to the front door of the open-plan room. From down the hall, she could hear Emmie giggling at a video that was playing.

Nell stared at the doorknob. "But I have to say, having a close-knit family isn't always a good thing."

THAT NIGHT, COOPER crossed the yard from the foreman's bungalow to the barn where a light was shining through a stall window.

Nell was there, as he sensed she would be, feeding a bottle to the injured, and now orphaned, calf. She was the only one who worked after sundown on the NLS except during emergencies, and in the past few days, she'd avoided him.

She glanced up, a slight flush on her cheekbones. "He's doing really well now. He can probably join the herd soon." Obviously, she wasn't going to mention their ride the other day, the tour of his house or their talk about shared memories.

"You consider my suggestion?" Cooper asked.

"What was that," she said, as if she really didn't care what he thought.

"Not to make him into a steer. Use him instead as a breeding bull."

She perked up a little. "His temperament's calm, though he's still a baby. His conformation's good, and he's certainly putting on weight. He'll be big when he's grown. Broad through the chest and shoulders…"

she trailed off, her gaze skating away from Cooper.

He hunkered in front of her. "Then you agree."

"I have time to make that decision, but his genes are excellent." She tugged the empty bottle from the calf's mouth, its thick pink tongue sweeping out to lap the last droplet of milk that dripped onto her wrist. "I do want to change a few things on this ranch." Her mouth turned down. "PawPaw called—before those calves were killed—and I'm running out of time to prove myself."

"He's on his way home?"

"No, he and Will went even farther inland. The fish up north are teeming, he said." She patted the calf, then watched him scoot off to the far corner of the stall. "I have my work cut out for me," she said, then told Cooper about her talk with Ned. "Before he gets back, I want to digitize the breeding register—can you believe he still keeps it in longhand?— update his accounting system, the inventory as well and, while I'm at it, shift a few attitudes around here."

Cooper held up both hands. "Don't include me."

"I won't," she admitted, "unless you give me reason to. You've been, well, more supportive than I expected, but the last time I looked, your name wasn't on the deed for the NLS."

For a second, he wished they hadn't ridden onto Ransom land after all.

Nell cracked a smile but her eyes remained downcast, and Cooper doubted her comment about him had made her that happy. "Mom went home to Kansas City this morning, so at least I'm not outnumbered right now. I wish I didn't have to beat Jesse in some contest for the NLS, but apparently I do. He's not going to win."

"Nell, I can understand about Jesse. We had a brief skirmish too, and I'm pretty sure he's hiding something. Don't know what it is yet, but why do you keep fighting *me*?"

He almost didn't hear the words. "You mean instead of showing my *softer side*?"

Cooper rose. He stared down at her. "We both want the same thing, don't we? To preserve this ranch? Have it prosper under your management?"

"That's part of it." She didn't wait for him to respond. "We both know why *you're* here.

I won't let you take back Ransom land—
NLS land now—because of a little sweet
talk, or because you've been a big help with
the ranch."

His jaw hardened. "I'm here—right
now—because I'm your foreman. Nell, why
are we arguing about this? We work fine together when you aren't trying to show me
who's boss every five minutes. I understand
I work for you. I believe in you and I'm
trying to help you succeed." He shook his
head. "All you seem to focus on where I'm
concerned—"

"—is your plan to take away my land!
Don't try to pretend you're just another cowpoke helping out. That aw-shucks pose is as
clear as day."

Mad enough to chew nails, he took a step
toward her. "That's amazing. I've never *tried*
to hide anything from you. You've known
from the start what I intend to do, Nell. That
doesn't mean I can't do my job now. Later
on, we'll deal with the rest." Cooper turned
away, then back again. "The other day, I
showed you exactly where I'm coming from.
You walked with me through that house and

I hoped you saw what the place still means to me, what it means to my mother."

"I understand that, Cooper. What I don't understand is why it's so important to you all these years later to make a play for Ransom land when I'm just coming into my own. I'll have a hard enough time convincing PawPaw I can manage this ranch. I don't need you to complicate everything."

"You can fire me. I'll be off this property before morning."

To his surprise, her voice shook. "If I fired you, Jesse would try to take your place. Prove himself the better choice." She lightened her tone. "No, I do appreciate your help. I'll stick with what I have. Thank you for your faith in me."

Cooper reached out to frame Nell's face in his hands. Her chin tilted up and her gaze held his. They'd been dancing around their persistent attraction—at least his—ever since he set foot again on the NLS. A few days ago, he'd walked into his parents' house, and he'd known without a doubt he was home. If only she could share that emotion with him. When she'd put her arms around him for the first time in fourteen years, he'd thought she did. "I'm not your enemy, Nell. Remember that."

He expected her to challenge him, to remind Cooper that because he wanted what she did too they were indeed enemies. Instead, Nell moved a little, closing the short distance still between them, and in the same instant Cooper drew her to him, relishing the sensation of Nell against him.

"I remember lots of things," she whispered. "I don't know if they're good for me." But she didn't move.

With a half smile, Cooper lowered his head and kissed her, soft and light and warm, cautioning himself that this wasn't good for him either, or his plans. But it was exactly what he wanted.

As he went back for another deeper kiss, and Nell responded, her arms around him too, he wondered how much of his job here related to his feelings for her, and not for his former home.

CHAPTER TEN

NELL WORKED EVEN harder than she normally did the next day. No matter how she tried, she couldn't get Cooper's kisses out of her head. She was clearly still attracted to him and, she had to admit, he was more than a temptation—too much for Nell's comfort. But what had she been thinking? Or rather, not thinking?

The remembered feel of his lips on hers seemed to follow her wherever she went, from morning feeding at the barn to a quick check of the herd for further coyote damage and, finally, to the home office, where she discovered Jesse at the wall safe, spinning the combination. Nell stopped dead.

"What are you doing?"

His hand froze. The safe door remained shut. She glanced over at the desk, where the latest month's statement of expenses and profit filled the computer screen. "Why were you trying to open the safe?"

He spun around to face her. "As a matter of fact, I was headed into town—I hear Jack Hancock's a wizard at the new diner and I could use a nice French meal for a change—but I'm a little short. I decided to withdraw a few bucks." He glanced behind him. "Paw-Paw still keep operating funds in this safe?"

Cooper had mentioned his suspicions of Jesse and Nell agreed. "You haven't earned a free lunch. You're already getting room and board here. The NLS runs on a tight margin. If you were doing any real work, I'd say fine, but you're not. If you want to eat, make yourself a sandwich."

"Don't be such a hard nose, Nell."

She didn't think she was. Even with the few chores he'd agreed to take on, Jesse was often missing in action, and whenever something critical came up, say another coyote attack, he was nowhere to be found or quit before he could be of any real use. She couldn't imagine why PawPaw believed he could take over the ranch.

"If you need money, Jesse, you should tap into whatever you made from all those acquisitions." To hear him tell it, he was a multimillionaire, which made her wonder again, as Cooper did, why he wanted the NLS. She still hadn't noticed any sign of his affection for the place.

"I'd only take a couple hundred," he finally said.

A few bucks. "For lunch?"

"No, for a…while. I'm waiting on the payout from my last company, if you must know, and most of my assets are illiquid at the moment. I don't expect you to understand high finance."

"Jesse, this makes no sense. If you're that successful, you must have accounts you can draw from."

"Tied up in investments," he said, avoiding her gaze. "You wouldn't believe the complications I deal with every day. I'm usually on the phone, in meetings, making deals, working more hours than you ever could trying to prove yourself to PawPaw."

She hesitated. "What aren't you telling me? We may not be close, but we are brother and sister. Family. If something's wrong—"

He flinched as if she'd hit him with a cattle prod. "Nothing. Is. Wrong. Get that? My life is not as simple as yours, that's all. If you don't want to open this safe and lend me a bit—"

"That isn't the issue."

"Then what is?" He ran a hand through his hair. "I'm tired of this, Nell. I wish Mom was still here. She'd understand." He sounded like the often-whiny boy he'd once been. Nothing was ever enough for Jesse.

"And I'm sure she'd *lend* you whatever you asked for."

"So would PawPaw."

"If he was here," she said. "I didn't say I wouldn't give you the money. I just wonder why you seem so desperate."

"That's ridiculous. You're the one who keeps grasping at things—the NLS, for sure—when it's obvious you'll never inherit this ranch."

Nell stifled a retort. She stalked over to the wall safe, which was normally hidden behind a portrait of Ferdinand, PawPaw's prize bull. The stud was getting on in years, and soon the ornery animal would have to be retired. Nell meant to replace him—maybe with the rescued calf when he was grown. Her back to Jesse, she twirled the combination lock and the door opened. Nell reached in, counted out several hundred-dollar bills, then turned.

Jesse stood right behind her, and she nearly bumped into him. He peered into the open safe, his gaze intent. "Here," she said, slapping the money into his hand. "Go have lunch. I hear Jack makes a mean coq au vin. Tell him I said hey."

"One of these days, you and I are really going to have it out," Jesse said.

"Not today. I have ranch duties." She shut the safe door, reset the lock, then slipped past him. "I'll enter your withdrawal from the account later."

His gaze bore through her but Jesse said nothing.

Nell could feel his anger like a living thing all the way to the barn, where she needed to double-check the rest of the day's schedule with Cooper (while blocking out any recall of their too-tempting kisses last night and her growing reliance on him). The back of her neck prickled as if Jesse was still watching her. Whatever was going on with him must be bad. Later, she'd change the computer password and the combination on the safe.

Sadly, Nell didn't trust her own brother.

NEITHER DID COOPER. To him, Jesse was trouble on the hoof. Cooper couldn't figure out why his former friend was still on the NLS—why he hadn't given up by now on taking part in the challenge Ned Sutherland had thrown down like a gauntlet before an old-fashioned duel. Nell could hold her own, but Jesse was no rancher and never would be. So what other motive was he hiding? Cooper was still mulling over the subject when Grey Wilson, an old friend who owned another ranch in the area, drove up to the barn.

Scowling, Grey hopped out of his truck without so much as a greeting, then slammed the door. "Finn Donovan says you have coyotes on the NLS."

"Yeah." Cooper leaned on the pitchfork he'd been using to move manure out of a nearby stall. "A pack of them killed one of Nell's cows. She lost two calves as well. We've ridden out several times and possibly wounded one coyote, but he got away."

"I hate coyotes." Grey shoved his black Stetson off his brow. "Last night, Dad and I lost three head. Slaughtered like lambs— and not far from the house. For a while, one of the ranch dogs was missing. He came home this morning with his tail between his legs. I swear he seemed guilty for not doing his job."

Grey's spread was miles from the NLS with the town of Barren in between. "That's some range if it's the same pack."

"I stopped by the Circle H on my way over." The Hunter ranch was next door to Wilson Cattle. "Logan says they had some trouble too the other day. His grandfather's all fired up. He claims he saw 'em circling his herd in broad daylight."

"Sam's bison are tough critters," Cooper pointed out. "I'd imagine they can take care of themselves—one reason Sam switched from cattle years ago."

"He's determined anyway to look for the coyotes tonight. It wasn't enough for him that one of his bison sent him flying into a tree last year and broke his leg. He loves them as if they were children." Grey's frown deepened. "Frankly, I'm worried too. My nephew, Nick, lives more at the Circle H than he does in town, and now that Olivia's set to marry Sawyer, she's there too." He drew a breath. Olivia was Grey's sister, and although they'd been at odds for years, Cooper had heard they were now close again. "Just as bad, my Ava goes tearing around Wilson Cattle on her horse like she's in some Wild West show. What if something happens to her? I don't like this, Cooper."

"I'll do anything I can to help," he said. "You know coyotes rarely attack humans, but Nell doesn't need to lose any more cattle either. As her foreman, I want to end this."

Grey resettled his hat. "On horseback. No sense letting those coyotes know we're coming by using Gators or pickup trucks. The noise alone would scare them off. And the terrain's better for horses."

Cooper straightened. "You'd think somewhere between here and the Circle H or your place there'd be more dead cows. This time of year, calves are even easier pickings, especially the smaller, weaker ones. I need to caution Nell to keep an injured calf she's been caring for in this barn a while longer."

He'd be wise to lock down his feelings for Nell too. After last night he didn't want to ruffle her feathers right now about the ranch. He sure didn't want to hurt her. But after the kisses they'd shared, he also had to keep a lid on those emotions.

"How's the job with Nell otherwise?"

"Touch and go." He hefted the pitchfork.

Grey followed Cooper into the barn, where he laid the tool across a wheelbarrow. He'd finish the job later. Cooper steered the discussion away from him and Nell, and for a few minutes they talked about other topics.

"Olivia?" Grey answered when Cooper asked about her. "Round as a beach ball. Sawyer is betting she'll pop any day. But Nick came late, so I doubt Sawyer's going to win that bet." He grinned, the first since he'd arrived today. "In any case, I'm going to be an uncle again." He added, clearly pleased, "Maybe a daddy too. Shadow and I are trying. Ava will be ten this year, a long gap between. And, of course, her pal Nick already has a baby half sister—so Ava wants one too."

For a second, Cooper experienced a twinge of envy. Once, he and Nell had planned to have half a dozen kids, three of each. She'd named them all. Now, he was afraid to even mention their embrace, let alone delve deeper into their relationship.

But after all she'd kissed him back, so maybe he should test the waters with her again, find out if he was truly the only one who'd felt the old zing between them.

What if they could reach some kind of détente? If he and Nell were together, his problem with the Ransom ranch might be solved… But for now he had to deal with the coyotes.

"Count me in," Cooper said, which made Grey laugh. "I meant about going after the pack, not about babies. I'll trailer my horse over to your place later."

"Once we track them down, we'll cover the NLS too. Sound good?"

"Perfect." Cooper couldn't wait to get in the saddle, ride the range with his longtime friends and maybe resolve the coyote issue too. "Unless the coyotes hit our herd again first." He still couldn't believe it was the same pack. "Seems strange just our three ranches are involved. And I'd expect Fred Miller's outfit to be part of this."

"He hasn't filed a report with Finn. On my way home, I'll stop at his place. He may be lying low after that rustling business."

Grey didn't need to elaborate. Last summer, some of his cattle had been taken. His brother-in-law had turned out to be behind it, but he wasn't the only perpetrator. According to Finn, Miller's nephew had also been part of the gang, and Miller himself had sheltered the stolen herd for them. The third rustler had fled the state, but Finn had helped round up the others.

Grey continued, "Maybe there's been some kind of coyote population explosion this spring and they've spread out to feed themselves."

"If Miller's been hit, I doubt he'd want to talk to Finn again."

"Or me," Grey said. "But there are a few other outfits. I'll ask around."

Cooper said goodbye to the other man, then squared his shoulders. Before he rode out with Grey and the others, he'd have to talk to Nell.

NELL WASN'T PLEASED with Cooper's plan. He stood beside her at the kitchen sink, and she didn't like how near he was either. His proximity only reminded her of their kisses.

She shoved her hands into the soap-filled sink and attacked the pots and pans from dinner. "We should keep trying to locate the pack here. If you're at the Circle H or Wilson Cattle all night, what good will that do the NLS?"

Cooper explained that they'd cover every ranch in time.

She dropped a pan into the water with a plop. "And before you say anything, I won't stay home like a good girl making sandwiches for the vigilante group you've put together. Letting you *men* have all the fun." Wiping her hands on a dish towel, she spun toward him. Cooper merely gazed at her as Nell went on. "You know, in school, some of my friends like Olivia and Shadow wanted nothing more than to be cheerleaders. I wanted to play football."

"Did you make the team?" he asked mildly, his eyes the gray of the fog that often covered the hill this time of year. She'd never noticed before, but they had a darker rim around the irises. Way too attractive.

Nell cleared her throat. "No, of course I didn't get to play. It's a rigged system."

He sighed. "You're a strong person, Nell, but come on. You don't have the bulk, the muscle a linebacker does."

"I could have been a quarterback. I'm smart too," she said.

"I know others have questioned your ability, and especially your authority, but this isn't about who gets to play. It's about finding those coyotes and stopping them from doing worse."

"Losing Elsie and those calves *was* worse." Almost like losing her resolve the other night and letting Cooper kiss her, then kissing him back. They hadn't been friendly, let's-be-pals kisses; they'd ignited a slow fire inside her that wouldn't seem to burn itself out. A small spat about his determination to ride with Grey Wilson and Logan Hunter and the others after the coyotes, leaving her behind, seemed wiser than letting her awareness of him go any further. "A reminder. I don't work for you, Cooper." She rushed on before he could speak. "You work for me—and either you stay home to do whatever I need you to do here or I ride with you." When he merely continued to stare at her, she said, "I'm as good a rider as any man there. Better, even, than some. Finn Donovan's a beginner and he's going, isn't he?"

"Yes. Finn has horses to safeguard—a new one for Annabelle, plus the two Grey gave him—and he's planning to buy a few head of cattle. With his new acreage, his farm is turning into a ranch, which no one ever expected."

"The NLS is vastly bigger, as you know. I'm a landowner too through PawPaw for now," she admitted. "If you don't get my point, I can fire you this minute."

He propped both hands on his hips. The color in his face had changed from the tan acquired working outdoors to a dull red. "You keep threatening to do that. So do it. Right now, or don't say it again."

Moving fast toward him, she forced him to back up against the table behind him. "I'm the boss here." Even to her own ears, she sounded breathless. For a second, she couldn't remember what they were fighting about, or why. Nell was a tall woman, but her gaze fixed on the Adam's apple in his throat. She could see his pulse pounding in his neck.

"Nell."

His low tone of voice nearly undid her. First, she'd had PawPaw to deal with, and

Hadley, then Jesse and now Cooper. Nell took another step, angling her head up to his.

"I dare you," he said in that same throaty tone. His eyes were steady on hers, and his mouth seemed ever closer… Too close now.

Nell tried to catch her breath, their quarrel forgotten in another swirl of memory. Long ago, Cooper had charmed her, wooed her, taken her down into this same slow spiral of attraction. She could no more resist it now than she could then.

"Nell," he said again. "If you'd let me finish what I was trying to say, I would have told you no one is cutting you out. I want you to come along. I'll load Bear on the trailer too."

His words surprised Nell, but all thought was lost when his strong arms came around her and they shared another kiss that seemed to never end.

She didn't want it to, even when he murmured against her lips, "You didn't fire me. That's the end of it."

Nell couldn't agree, but standing in the kitchen wrapped around each other, with the rest of the world far away, for these few moments, she didn't care. This didn't feel like an ending; it felt like a new beginning.

Nell might have to fight everyone else, but Cooper saw her as an equal. Yet, the danger he presented was that very feeling of being understood—and ultimately losing herself to him.

Cooper was dangerous. And after tonight, he was more of a threat to Nell's heart than she'd ever imagined.

CHAPTER ELEVEN

IN THE PITCH-BLACK DARKNESS, the newly formed posse rode across the Circle H, then spilled like a ghostly specter onto the adjoining Wilson Cattle ranch. So far, they hadn't seen or heard the coyotes. The night remained silent, the sky full of stars. Yet, the back of Cooper's neck kept prickling. The predators were somewhere nearby. He could almost smell them.

"Wild-goose chase." Jesse's saddle groaned as he shifted his weight again. He'd insisted on coming along, even riding next to Nell as if he wouldn't let her out of his sight, let her win this part of their competition. He'd been complaining since they loaded the big four-horse trailer at the NLS. "I say we go back and get some sleep. Nothing's happening tonight."

Cooper rode on, keeping pace with Grey, Sawyer, Logan and Finn. Fred Miller had stayed home. Nell came up beside them, and Cooper's mind flashed on an image of her in his arms earlier. He was in a heap of trouble now that had nothing to do with the murdering coyotes.

You didn't fire me, he'd said, but it was their kisses that had stayed with him. Those and the surprised look on her face when he'd reassured her she was part of the group tonight. He shouldn't have let her go on so long believing he would try to ride without her. But, as he'd liked to tease her in the past, Cooper had been unable to resist. Besides, he couldn't get a word in edgewise. Watching Nell bristle had been entertaining…until it had turned into something else.

"Let's fan out," she said. "No sense staying bunched together—unless you boys are just having a fraternity meeting here."

"We are," Grey agreed. "Better fun than your Girls' Night Outs."

"I'm not a member." Nell was quick to correct him. "Besides, how would you know what kind of fun they have? You stay home with Ava."

"Quiet," Cooper said, standing in his stirrups to scan the horizon with a pair of powerful binoculars. "Let's not broadcast our presence." He swept the area again. "Ah. Here we go." He pointed. "Two coyotes slinking through those bushes over there." He spurred his horse into a canter, crossing the field closest to Grey's house. The others followed, a soundless flow of cowboys and their mounts. And one determined cowgirl.

Jesse rode behind. No surprise there. Cooper had only let him come along because he remembered Nell's brother was a fair shot. Years ago, they'd gone hunting together, and it was always Jesse who bagged the most quail, or a rabbit or two. He carried his shotgun now, a birthday gift from Ned Sutherland. The weapon was a piece of art with a hand-tooled wooden stock that had cost Ned plenty, but Cooper doubted it had been fired in a long while.

As he neared the brush on the other side of the field, the two coyotes burst out of the darkness, rustling the foliage, and raced for cover fifty yards away, yipping and barking as they ran. Cooper raised his shotgun to sight them in, but before he could fire he heard a shot ring out. "More!" Jesse shouted and took off after them. Cooper admired his quickness but wondered if Nell's brother would stay on his horse.

"Jesse!" he called, but he didn't respond.

All at once, the whole scene became something from a Western movie, the silhouettes of riders streaming over the land on the sleek shapes of horses, their hides gleaming in the night, hooves pounding the ground like drumbeats. The smell of wild animals in the air, and fear.

Nell kicked Bear into a gallop and surged ahead of the posse. As she streaked past, Grey's horse startled, but with a quick check of the reins, Grey held Big Red to a rocking canter. Logan and Sawyer merely gaped at her, then spread out with Finn in an attempt to flank the coyote pack and surround them.

Cooper could scarcely believe his eyes. Jesse was still in the lead. His next shot hit its target and one of the coyotes fell with an audible thud. Cooper raised his gun, fired— and watched another of the predators stumble off into the darkness, clearly wounded. Then he almost rode right over the carcass of a dead cow.

Cooper heard Grey swear. But shaking his head, he went on with an even more determined look in his eyes, managing to wing another coyote. More shots followed, turning the scene into one of battle. There were many more coyotes than the two he'd first spotted.

Then, to his horror, a human cry split the night.

His heart in his throat, Cooper looked around for Nell. She was suddenly nowhere to be seen. "Nell!"

To his relief, he heard a small voice not far away and spun his horse on its haunches. Cooper covered the distance between them at a gallop, as if his horse was a barrel racer. At the edge of the brush where he'd spied the first two coyotes, Nell was already off her horse and on her knees.

"You hurt?" His blood pounding through his veins, he hoped she'd say the simple words *I'm okay.*

Nell shook her head. Not hurt, but she gestured and Cooper saw Jesse lying on the ground. Her horse, Bear, had been blocking his view of her brother sprawled in a heap, with one arm at a weird angle and blood streaming from his head. He was out cold. Jesse's horse stood a few yards away, head down in the grass, ripping blades with his teeth, his sides heaving. Cooper dismounted quickly.

"That horse'll colic if he keeps eating. Grab him, Nell. I'll see to Jesse."

"No," she said in a tone that brooked no opposition. "He's my brother."

Cooper tried again to gently pull her to her feet, but Nell dug in her boot heels. Jesse lay so still that for an instant Cooper wondered if he were dead. "Come on, let me help, Nell."

In the distance, the remaining coyotes disappeared into the night. They were sure wreaking havoc in the area if, in fact, there was only one pack, and he wished the posse had done more damage.

Cooper stepped around Nell. Despite her resistance, he managed to draw her away from the scene, but she gave him a glare that could kill. He didn't care. He wouldn't have her witness her own brother's demise. Her horse and his were ground-tied nearby, but Cooper steered her toward Jesse's mount.

"Go," he said. "You can hate me later."

"I hate you right now," she said, but her tone didn't have much heat.

Cooper knelt by Jesse. He assessed the other man's arm, knowing it was broken. As a cop in Chicago, Cooper had assessed plenty of such injuries and figured it was a pretty bad break, though he was no doctor like Sawyer, who was now riding across the field to them.

Sawyer slid off his horse. "Is he breathing?"

"Yep, but still unconscious."

Sawyer checked Jesse's vital signs, then the arm as best he could in the middle of a darkened field with no medical supplies on hand. "Compound fracture," he said.

Logan, Grey and Finn approached too, and Grey said, "Let's get him to the house."

Sawyer straightened. "I'd rather not move him. We need an ambulance. Hope they can reach us here."

Finn had his cell phone out and was punching in the number.

Cooper glanced around. Nell was walking Jesse's horse in a big circle, cooling him off and keeping him from eating more grass. The big tracks of tears on her cheeks that she wouldn't want anyone to see appeared silver in the night. When she noticed him gazing at her, she turned aside, the horse's swishing tail like a signal for him to keep back. Cooper went to her anyway.

She still wouldn't look at him. "Is he...?"

"Sawyer's got him. Jesse will be okay," he assured her, hoping that was true. Whether or not she wanted him to, Cooper took the reins from her, handed them off to Logan, then put his arms around her. "I've got you," he said.

NELL COULDN'T SLEEP. The house was too quiet with Jesse in the hospital. She worried about him. She hadn't realized how much she welcomed even his company at night while PawPaw was gone.

And she kept hearing Cooper say *I've got you*. In Grey's field, she'd wanted to preserve her pride and shove Cooper away, but she'd wanted even more to curl deeper into his embrace, to just...let go.

What a horrendous evening, and they hadn't managed to drive off all the coyotes. Nell had no doubt the animals would be on Wilson Cattle land, the Circle H and the NLS again soon. On all three ranches, there'd be more of the herds lost, more of the unique animals Nell loved taken from her.

After leaving Farrier General, she'd spent part of the night in the barn, making sure her little calf was safe and well and still thriving. Counting heads to make sure the ranch dogs and the barn cats were accounted for. Nell hated feeling this...fragile.

Despite her differences with her brother, she loved Jesse too. What was it Cooper had once said? *It's okay to show your softer side, to just...be a woman.* Tonight, she'd certainly done that.

At dawn, while Nell was brewing a pot of coffee in the hope of staying awake during the day, her parents phoned. She'd left them a reassuring voice mail on the way to the hospital last night but, of course, they wanted to hear the full story.

"Jesse will have surgery this morning," she told them. They were already packing for the trip to Barren, and she heard tears in her mother's voice.

"Chasing coyotes again? What was Jesse doing with a gun? He hasn't gone hunting in years."

Nell didn't respond to that. "He'll have the

best orthopedic surgeon, Mom. The break is bad, but they can pin it. And his concussion is mild. I'll be with him. Afterward, he'll be fine here for a while." Not that she looked forward to more of their quarrels.

Her father weighed in. "You should have brought Jesse to a hospital in Kansas City."

"His doctor is from there," she said. "He operates at Farrier General two days a week. Please don't worry. Everything's under control."

Her words reminded her of Cooper. Earlier, she hadn't fired him when she should have, especially after that dare of his, and Nell worried that she'd lost her edge, weeping in his arms like a...like a woman who needed a man to shore up any weakness. Nell hadn't resisted. Tonight, she'd let him take over. He'd seen her at her worst, helpless, and so had Grey, Logan and Sawyer and Finn.

"My children," Mom went on. "I have one son and one daughter, Nell."

"Yes. I realize that."

"Why didn't you leave those animals to Logan Hunter? It was his cattle that were killed."

"This time Grey's too," Nell said. "They

would both have helped me when we lost the cow and calves here. I didn't know then that they were having trouble too."

Her father broke in again. "Nell, this has gone far enough. Your mother's right. I thought we'd left that miserable place behind."

"The NLS to me is hardly miserable." Nell, however, was becoming more upset by the second. Her dad was usually in her corner, his acceptance of her goal often laced with an indulgent smile. He'd never come out before in such solidarity with her mother. Had Nell made the wrong decision tonight? Taking Jesse with them had risked his safety and jeopardized her hopes to inherit the ranch.

Listening to the silence from the other end of the line, and the burble of the coffeemaker's carafe filling up, Nell paced the kitchen.

This was the place where she'd grown up watching her grandmother and her mother cook for the family and the hands. As a baby, she'd sat in a high chair at this table, banged her spoon on the tray. When she fell off her first horse, she'd rushed in to have her scrapes tended and her pride soothed. After

her high school prom, still in her gown, she'd
shared a late night girls' talk with her mom,
the kind of conversation she might have with
Olivia, Shadow or Annabelle and their other
friend Blossom, who was married to Logan.
She'd cried her eyes out here the day Cooper left town. "I'm happier on the NLS than
I'd be anywhere else," she said at last. "You
might as well give up on the notion that I'll
become a city girl. No one was hurt tonight
except Jesse, but he'll be fine. Don't worry."
She told herself the same thing.

Nell stalked across the room to pour a
first mug of coffee before the beep sounded
that it was ready. A flash of guilt ran through
her. Nell could guess how concerned her
mother was, how frightened for her children
she must be, but without kids of her own,
maybe Nell couldn't truly understand.

"I'm sorry, Mom. Dad, tell her. I'm doing
a good job. I don't want to give up here. Yes,
ranch life is tough, and Jesse's accident isn't
the first. It won't be the last. But talk about
miserable," she added. "You'd both feel even
worse with me under your feet in that house
in Mission Hills, mourning what I'd lost."

Her dad's voice gentled. "Nell, I can empathize, even when I never want to set foot on that ranch again. But aren't you taking this too far? It's time," he said, "to let someone else take over the NLS when your grandfather's gone."

Her tone flattened. "You mean Jesse."

"Well, yes. Of course, we worry about him too."

"But you're trying to protect me. Why?"

"Because as a woman you have to be safeguarded, Nell," her dad said. "To be kept from danger more."

Nell saw red. "You realize that's a double standard. Don't you?" She considered herself to be the better, more capable person than Jesse, at least on the ranch. She didn't need protection, but her dad clearly disagreed.

Nell could hear him breathing into the phone.

"You too, Daddy? I thought you respected me. You've known since I was three years old, maybe even before, that I wanted to have the NLS. You know I'll cherish this land, that I'll do right by it. If Jesse wants his share in cash, he can have it. I'll keep this ranch profitable, make it even more so—"

"And in the blink of an eye," her mother said through obvious tears, "you'll be over forty with no husband, no children, *nothing* to show for your life except that old ranch house and a bunch of smelly cows. Is that what you really want, Nell? To work yourself to death for that place and end up alone?"

"I wish you didn't feel that way."

"We both do, sweetheart," her dad put in.

Fuming now, Nell gulped down a swallow of hot coffee. "You mean, let a man do the work. Because he'd obviously find a wife to support him, to bear his kids and raise them while he ran the NLS. No," she said. "I hate to be such a constant disappointment to you. I realize you want grandkids to spoil, Mom. But there's no reason you can't have them."

"You don't have all the time in the world, Nell," her mother said.

"But I do have some. One day, I'll meet someone, marry him. Then you can throw the biggest wedding, the most lavish reception. I won't say a word about the engraved invitations or the party being held at your country club. If Jesse—or any man—can have it all and still do work that makes him happy, why can't I?"

"It's not the same," her mom insisted. "What if you were pregnant and trying to ride all over that godforsaken ranch as if you were still a ten-year-old girl? There are all kinds of accidents that can happen, Nell. It could be you in the hospital just as easily."

Her mom had returned to the topic of losing her children, a hard thing to argue against. It wasn't as if her mother, and her dad, didn't want her to be happy. They just wanted her to be happy according to their view of what that meant. For a moment, she nearly weakened, but there was no way she'd knuckle under.

"I have to go," she said. "Jesse's surgery is scheduled for 9:00 a.m."

"We'll be at the hospital by noon," her father said, a familiar note in his voice. He was going to play the dad card, appealing to her in that affectionate way of his to change her mind. She felt betrayed by his lack of support. He'd been the one member of the family to think she could do the job. "Nell…"

"See you then," she said, and ended the call.

They'd never been this adamant before, but Jesse's broken arm had made their objections worse. Nell couldn't blame them for being troubled about their kids. She had no doubt their next call would be to PawPaw—if they could reach him.

She felt suddenly alone and incompetent. Too bad she *didn't* have it all right now. A darling family of her own, a man who loved her with all his heart and the NLS too. For an instant, an image of Cooper ran through her mind. Tall, handsome, strong again after his injuries in Chicago, a man, she'd learned, who could do the job. At least she had his support, his belief in her. Or was she paying too high a price for her dream? What if she could have what she wanted and her family's support too?

Clearly, considering their antiquated views, most of all PawPaw's, she needed a husband. How would she ever inherit the NLS unless…? What if she beat them at their own game?

The idea began to grow roots in her mind.

Of course, there was one hitch. She wasn't seeing anyone.

And then Nell thought, *I've got you.*

CHAPTER TWELVE

"YESTERDAY YOU WANTED to fire me. Now you want to get *married*?"

"Why not?" Nell asked, hands on her hips.

"A hundred reasons!" Cooper replied, fumbling around for one of them. Her awkward proposal had blindsided him.

She'd knocked on the door just a few minutes ago, and they were still standing on his porch. "Where did you get such a cockeyed notion?"

"It would only be a temporary arrangement."

"No dice," he said, his heart skipping a beat. What did she take him for? A fool? A patsy? "This is quite a switch. In fact, it's crazy, Nell."

Although, he had to admit, the idea held more than a little appeal. He'd once been in love with her, ready to do just what she was proposing—hunt down a justice of the peace, then slip a ring on her finger. Make a forever commitment because he couldn't imagine being bound to anyone else. He'd settled for giving her an emerald chip necklace, which she'd thrown in his face. Their recent kisses showed they both still had feelings for each other, but…

"A few kisses and you decide now we should tie the knot?" He'd more than enjoyed those stolen moments with her, but he shook his head. "One of us has to be clear minded. Obviously, at the moment, that's not you."

Nell's mouth firmed. "Thank you so much. First, my family all but threatens to show up and haul me off the NLS. Then you decide to make light of a very serious proposal."

"Serious? You've got to be kidding. Don't get me wrong," he said, "I like kissing you. I wouldn't object to more of them. But marriage? That's not something you enter into as if it were a fun night at the county fair. I'm talking a lifetime here, not a quick trip to Vegas with some Elvis impersonator to perform a five-minute ceremony."

"I said *temporary*. Why is that crazy? I didn't mean the whole white-dress thing, flowers, and toasts from Jesse and my father, and maybe PawPaw. This would be quick, private…no horde of guests, no fairy lights strung around the yard like when Blossom and Logan got married. No…" she trailed off, her cheeks flushed. "…honeymoon," she finished.

Now he was getting angry. Half the time, she appeared to barely tolerate him. Of course, there were the other times, like when Nell had melted into his arms the night before.

Was this about her sheer worry over Jesse and the ranch? Her brother's surgery had gone well and he was at Farrier General with Nell's parents tonight. Or did this mean, because of their kisses, that she could rely on Cooper? Trust him as she'd begun to trust him as her foreman? "Are you talking a marriage of convenience here?"

Nell's glance fell away. "There'd be no reason for us to share a room. This would be a business arrangement." A few spring peepers were chirping down at the creek and overhead the stars were out. "I've told you what my parents said. Jesse has the same opinion and so does PawPaw. I used to have my dad with me, but he's gone over to the dark side and I—"

"What's in this for me?" Which he knew sounded crass, but he was hurt.

For a moment, she didn't answer. Nell blinked. "You get to keep your job," she finally said.

"Lucky me." The scent of hay from the barn mingled with the sweet night air. Soft light filtered through the bungalow's front window to illuminate Nell's face. "Maybe instead I'll take your advice—go somewhere else in the county and buy acreage there, or even leave the state again. Maybe move to Texas. There's plenty of land there. Buy some longhorns instead of Angus, build a big log house for the wife I get to pick out for myself. It will have antler chandeliers and a master suite, plus six bedrooms for all the kids we'll have."

"Now you're being sarcastic."

"No, seems like a pretty good idea to me."

Her eyes brightened. "But that isn't what you really want."

Ow, Cooper thought, feeling as if she'd torn a piece off his hide. For a second, the scar on his stomach hurt again. She had him there. No one else's land was the land where his soul still resided, the land he'd dreamed about for fourteen years, and she knew it. He'd told her so his first day back, which maybe hadn't been the wisest choice after all. It gave Nell too much power.

He turned away, then back again to face her. Once, he'd thought that if they could only reach some kind of détente their problems would be over. "Nell, let's be straight here. Keeping my job isn't all I have in mind. And why should this be temporary?"

"Because. I need to…appease my parents, my family. What is it *they* want? To see me safely married, thinking about children and, above all, having a strong man's support here on the NLS."

"I can't imagine they'll be wild about the divorce then—the one you must be planning." He paused. "Plus, they're not crazy about me in the first place. Or have you forgotten my fight with Ned—my promise to take back my family's land one day? And his threat to run me off if he ever saw me again?"

"I didn't forget. He'll change his mind," she insisted. "Once we're married, he'll have to accept you, especially if we can't reach him before the, uh, ceremony. He'll come to see it was the best course of action. He'll view us as the team we are, a team with the ranch's success uppermost in our minds."

"And he'll leave the NLS to you." Which was her real plan all along. She must be mentally crossing her fingers. "I don't want any part of this. Marry you just so you can get the ranch? What is this, some grade C Western movie in which the gullible cowboy wants land so bad he enters into a loveless marriage?"

"Well, not exactly... Of course not."

"Yeah? Then what is it? Because I'm perfectly happy to support you as your foreman, but I already said I see marriage as a lifetime thing, a partnership of equals."

With his last words, Nell's expression changed, melted in fact, and Cooper took a slow step toward her, then another until he and Nell stood mere inches apart. The light through the window gilded her cheeks. He noted the fresh uncertainty in her gaze and the dilation of her pupils. She wasn't immune to him. She'd liked their kisses too, though he hesitated to use that to his advantage.

He bent to kiss her but she put a hand against his chest.

"Don't," she said. "We're trying to have a rational discussion."

"I don't feel so rational," he told her.

"Cooper," she began. "This is a business agreement. And I can understand that you might want something out of it for yourself. But not more kisses! Strictly business."

"Okay, here are my *business* terms," he said, cupping her face in both hands. "I'll agree to playing your loving husband all day and working as hard as ever as your foreman. I'll make sure you succeed in any way I can, helping you prove yourself to Ned— and winning out over Jesse. Frankly," he added, "I think the ranch deserves you."

"Cooper, thank you." Her eyes got even softer. "And what else?" she asked, her gaze riveted to his.

"I'd like access to Ransom land whenever I want."

"You have that now."

He explained, "I'd want to work in my off

hours there, fix up the house—get it ready
for my mother."

"But—"

The house doesn't belong to her, he expected to hear, yet she didn't say the words.
"I want to make her wish come true. There's
no telling how much needs to be done on
the house, but I want her to live there." He
remembered the afternoon they'd ridden to
his old home, the rush of emotion that had
come as he stood with her in his old room.
Was Nell remembering that too? "I'll rent it
from you. Fair enough?"

"You don't have to pay me. I can surely
understand how she must feel. If I couldn't
live at the NLS, my heart would break." She
probably didn't realize, but Nell had moved
closer to him and wrapped her arms around
his middle as she had before. "Then we have
a deal? Once PawPaw makes it official that
instead of Jesse I'll inherit the ranch, we
can…"

"Not so fast," he said, his hands still
framing her face. "I mean, maybe we're not
compatible…" He paused while she made
up her mind. To his satisfaction, she didn't

pull away, so they seemed to be on the same wavelength. Just as he'd hoped.

His mouth covered hers, and Nell immediately responded. Cooper kept the kiss easy, testing until she flowed deeper into his embrace, and he felt himself start to smile against her lips. *Okay*, he thought, *there it is. The rest of what I want.* What he'd probably wanted for half his life—why deny it? He wasn't about to tell her that though, and make her think of his offer to Ned. He could wait a while longer.

After another moment of standing close, kissing her again, he finally drew away, his hands slowly slipping from her cheeks to trail along the sides of her throat in a touch as light as a whisper. Her heart was beating as hard as a taiko drum. But then so was his.

"All right." He heard the tremor in his voice. "I guess I'm getting married."

"We are," she corrected him.

Cooper grinned. Nell didn't know how true that was.

HAVING GOTTEN WHAT she wanted, Nell spent part of the next day at the hospital with Jesse. Her parents were there now, so later

that afternoon she went back to the NLS
to do evening chores and go over the day's
events with Cooper.

In the barn, lit by strands of burnished
gold sun that shafted down from the hayloft
and snuck in between the outer boards of the
stalls, they talked about mundane things.
Nell sat on a hay bale, urging her calf to
eat more of the gruel she'd prepared. She
and Cooper were engaged but it was as if
that had never happened. Their most recent
kisses too.

Cooper leaned against a stall door across
the way. "Tomorrow, the boys and I will ride
through the herd again. I doubt we'll see
many more late calves drop but you never
know. You have a good bunch of cattle," he
said, his gaze wandering to the open barn
doors. "Ned should be proud."

Nell focused on the calf. He no longer fit
across her lap but stood, legs splayed, in the
aisle, his head thrust toward her in eager-
ness and pink tongue lolling. A few beads
of porridge ran from his mouth. "No sign of
the coyotes again?"

"Clete thought he heard some over by my
place. Said he could be wrong."

My place. She could only imagine what her grandfather would say about that. About this engagement of hers too. He was probably still angry with her about Hadley Smith and for a moment, Nell wished PawPaw would stay away until after she and Cooper paid a visit to the justice of the peace in town. Which should happen as soon as possible. She was about to say so when he cut off her thoughts.

"Fence on the north boundary needs attention. I'll send someone out first thing in the morning." His gaze slid from the doors at the end of the aisle, quickly over the calf that was slurping up the last of its dinner and skipped past Nell. "Doc Winslow's coming over soon as he can to see to the mare that's gone lame. While he's here, he'll take a look at that older gelding Clete rides. I'm afraid he has the start of some laminitis. I've assigned Clete the new chestnut you bought last month."

Nell decided he must be covering his true emotions with this laundry list of the day's achievements. She felt a twinge of guilt. Maybe she'd come on too strong yesterday. "Good," she said anyway, then rose to put the calf back in his stall. The baby Angus had gotten so trusting, and content, here she wondered if it would be wise to return him to the herd even after the coyote pack was no longer around. Certainly, the orphaned calf would find no protection from another cow as his surrogate mama. By now, he'd be on his own. Should she have tried to stick it out on her own too? "Cooper, if you're having second thoughts about…us, say so. Now."

"A deal's a deal," he said, not looking at her. "I keep my word."

Her spirits plummeted to her boots. Was he reminding her of his vow to regain his land too? What else had she expected? She'd all but strong-armed Cooper into their agreement.

"This won't be an easy thing. With my family around, Jesse coming home…and PawPaw showing up any day, assuming someone can reach him… I mean, they'll certainly try—"

"I know all that. Are *you* trying to weasel out?"

"No, I just—"

"Business, Nell. Remember?"

She hadn't been wrong about his irritation

but, oh, he had an edge about him today; Cooper wasn't happy with the arrangement. "At the hospital, I told my mom and dad we're planning to get married. Be prepared."

She didn't get the last word of warning out before she saw her father's car coming up the drive. It stopped first at the house, then halted by the barn while Nell was still preparing what to say. A door slammed and a second later, he appeared. Nell stiffened. So did Cooper. "Showtime," he said under his breath.

"If we're going to do this, then—"

Nell didn't finish. Her dad marched up to Cooper, drew himself to his full height, which was still inches below Cooper's, then glared at him. "My son is loaded up on pain-killers today, and I'm not in the best mood. I hate to see my children suffer. You tell me why you've decided to marry my daughter."

Cooper's gaze flicked to Nell. "The usual reason," he said.

"After fourteen years of not exchanging so much as an email as far as I know? Then you barge in here, take Hadley's job and all at once you can't wait to stand before a minister and take vows? I don't buy it. I don't trust you," her father went on. "I haven't trusted you since your family moved off this ranch."

"Our ranch," Cooper said.

Nell stepped forward. "Dad, be reasonable." For an instant, she considered lying to him, saying she and Cooper had been in touch over the years. Instead, she mentally made a wish that Cooper wouldn't throw her under the bus now. "We've made our decision. Please, can't you wish us the best?"

"I'll tell you what I wish—that this didn't have the feel of a shotgun wedding." He glanced at Nell. "You're not pregnant, are you?"

"Not unless it was the immaculate conception," Cooper muttered. She could see his eyes change as his anger with her father increased.

Her dad rounded on Nell. "This may be a new day for people your age and such things as tradition don't matter anymore, but on the NLS they still do and at the house your mother is crying, which she's been doing since you informed us of *your decision*. That matters to me, and in this family we still do things the right way," he said, his gaze returning to Cooper. "You didn't answer me. Why do you want to marry Nell?"

Cooper studied her for a long moment before he smiled, his eyes only for Nell. "I've wanted to marry her since I was nineteen years old."

"That would have happened over my dead body," her dad replied. "You were both too young, and once John sold off his land—"

"Not that he had much choice."

"—and you broke Nell's heart, that was the end of it."

"Apparently not," Cooper said. Nell couldn't seem to speak. If he was playing a part, which he must be, he deserved an award for best actor. He moved closer to her, slipped an arm around her shoulders. "We're not too young now, and we want to get married. As soon as possible. It's as simple as that. I believe in doing things the *right way* too."

"In such a rush?" Her dad looked skeptical. "If you think that gives you the *right* to the land your family sold years ago, think again."

"I'm not marrying Nell for that reason. Sir," he added, a muscle ticking in his jaw.

"I'm not going to tell you how our relationship started up again or what we said to each other about making it official—except I proposed and she accepted." He looked down at Nell, who edged even nearer to him, astonished at how easily he told the lie. "All I can say is, I'll care for your daughter with everything in me, and if you love Nell as much as I think you do, you'll give us your blessing."

Her father didn't respond. He stood there in the aisle, in the fading light, assessing Cooper, then Nell with a steady look that seemed to bore through her. She tried to meet his gaze without flinching, but it was still true; they were both lying to him. And this wasn't a movie or a Broadway play. The fate of the NLS was at stake. So was her integrity and Cooper's. Still, her eyes didn't shift at all from her dad.

Maybe Cooper, not Nell, was the better liar. She was sinking into a pool of misery at prolonging this deception when her father spoke again. "Close," he said, "but I'm still not hearing what I need to hear."

Cooper didn't even try to misunderstand. He held Nell's gaze and tightened his hold on her shoulder. Then he bent his head, and just ahead of taking her mouth with his, said, "I still want Nell to be my wife."

The kiss barely touched her lips before they ended it, but Nell had felt the surge of emotion through her whole body. Shaken, she leaned against Cooper. He hadn't used the word *love* but…

"Is this what you really want, Nell?" her dad asked.

"Yes."

"Then I guess you have my blessing," he said. He looked a bit rattled too. "Get ready. Once your mother is used to the idea, she'll want a full-scale blowout. No quick trip to the town hall will please her. And she won't want to see cowboy boots under that fancy white gown, Nell."

She returned his smile, then drifted from Cooper's arms into her dad's and kissed his cheek. "Thank you, Daddy."

Wow. She was reeling. She had her father's blessing, even when she would have to disappoint him all over again, and Cooper's words kept tumbling around inside her, ricocheting like the bullets that had hurt him in Chicago.

What if his words were not another lie? What if they were true?

"ARE WE LATE?" Olivia rushed into Nell's bedroom four days later, at least as fast as her very pregnant bulk would allow. Right behind her came Shadow and Blossom with Annabelle. They wore matching sea-foam-blue dresses, and they'd all had their hair and makeup done.

Nell had drawn the line at that much fuss. After all, this would be a sham wedding. In front of the long mirror, she surveyed the floor-length confection of tiered white silk that her mother had insisted they buy during a flash trip to Kansas City. No lace, which pleased Nell. Fortunately, there'd been no need for alterations either. Like an omen, the secondhand dress had been returned after another wedding failed to take place. But Nell's hair hung straight and sleek, her concession to cosmetics a simple lip gloss, blush and the smoky liner her mom had applied to her eyes.

"Nell, you look…bridal," Annabelle said, blinking.

"Gorgeous. I'm going to cry," Blossom murmured, fanning her face.

Nell felt more like a runaway bride, one foot poised to race off and avoid this whole thing. She would have offered them champagne from the bottle her dad had produced earlier, but only Shadow and Annabelle could drink any and Nell was afraid if she took one sip, she'd fall down the stairs in her high-heeled satin sandals. She settled for saying, "You're all right on time. Thank you for being part of this…day."

Olivia brushed that away. "You're an honorary member of our Girls' Night Out group, even if you don't attend every meeting," she said with an arched brow. And when Nell had informed them she was engaged, there'd been a bigger outcry.

"Why didn't you say something before? How could you keep this huge news from us?" Annabelle had asked, for which Nell had no answer.

From downstairs, she could hear the soft strains of music appropriate to the occasion, and her heart began to flutter. She shot her friends a panicked look. She was trapped.

"You'll be fine," Shadow told her. "Everyone gets nervous."

But what if Cooper got cold feet? Nell was a blink away from doing so herself. She still felt guilty for lying to her parents. Was Cooper there now in the living room with Logan, Grey and Sawyer? And Finn? Nell couldn't believe how fast her mother had pulled this together. As her dad had warned her, Nell's mom had become a whirling dervish of focus. A few minutes ago, she'd hurried down the stairs to make sure everything below was perfect.

"I don't know if I can do this," Nell said, not meaning the same thing her friends had about nerves. She was deceiving everyone she cared about.

"Of course you can." Annabelle straightened Nell's skirt. Shadow handed her the bouquet of white roses. Olivia placed the veil on Nell's head with Blossom's help, making the other women gasp at the effect. "Talk about a beautiful bride."

Nell had more than bridal nerves; she wanted to fly down the steps, stop the music and tell everyone the party was over before it started. Come clean with the people she loved. Let Cooper off the hook. And if her grandfather showed up…

"I saw Jesse on my way upstairs, but is Ned here?" Shadow asked, as they ushered Nell toward the door.

"No," she said, saddened by his absence, even when she knew he wouldn't be at all pleased by what she was about to do, and especially with whom. "Dad left messages, but PawPaw and Will must still be fishing. No one's heard from him."

Maybe she should have waited, thought this through again. Nell hated lying to her parents and Jesse. She even hated being unfair to Cooper. He understood their bargain, had agreed to it, yet…

The music changed. Nell's ear picked up the first notes of Pachelbel's "Canon." As soon as she reached the bottom of the stairs, it would change again. She had no memory of being herded to the top of the flight, of taking that first step and then the others. She scarcely heard "Here Comes the Bride" begin, her heart was pounding so loud.

Years ago, she'd dreamed of this moment, of that first glimpse of Cooper standing at the makeshift altar by the front windows, his face grave, watching his expression the instant he saw her.

Which he did now. And Nell's heart filled with unexpected wonder.

He didn't appear regretful in the least. Looking more handsome than she'd ever seen him, wearing a white shirt, dark suit and a silver tie, he smiled a little. His eyes shone, as if he were saying *I love you.*

As if he really meant it.

Behind bridesmaids Annabelle and Olivia, and matrons of honor Shadow and Blossom, on her father's arm Nell glided into the room full of everyone who mattered to her, except PawPaw, as if she were walking on a cloud.

And, for the sake of the NLS, she told herself, she walked along the makeshift aisle's white silk runner to be married.

CHAPTER THIRTEEN

"I NOW PRONOUNCE you man and wife," the justice of the peace intoned. He glanced at Cooper. "You may kiss your bride."

For an instant, Cooper froze. They were married! He'd sure wanted to hear those words as soon as he saw Nell at the bottom of the stairs in her white dress, her eyes soft and seeking him behind the filmy veil she wore. For a second, he'd choked up. So beautiful, and almost…almost his.

But because he'd been part of the ritual this time, not standing by while one of his friends or family or one of the guys he'd worked with on the force in Chicago got hitched, the traditional service had seemed to carry even more weight than it normally would. He couldn't believe how short their exchange of vows had seemed. With a faint tremor in his hands, he finally framed her cheekbones, lowered his head and joined their mouths in a brief warm kiss, Nell's face lifted to his, as moments before they had been joined in matrimony—for Nell, a temporary state of affairs.

Hours later, he was still trying to wrap his head around the whole event. In the white shirt, his neck itched and the silver tie seemed about to strangle him, or was that due to reality closing in? He hadn't much cared for being one of the two centers of attention, surrounded by Nell's parents, her brother and all of their friends. The only person missing was Ned Sutherland. Just as well for today. Cooper didn't relish having his wedding or the reception disrupted by another furious set-to with Nell's grandfather. Wasn't she afraid he'd snatch the NLS from her just *because* of Cooper? But she hoped she could make Ned see her way.

At dinner, there'd been toasts. A long rambling exposition of Nell's girlhood from her father and his wish that she'd be happy (he'd given Cooper a pointed look). Decent words came from Jesse with his one arm in a cast and a few teasing ones from Grey, then Logan and Sawyer. Finally, as best man, Finn gave the last toast, saying he was more than glad his ex-partner had survived that Chicago ambush to become a happily married man, even though Cooper had beaten him to the altar. And when Nell had danced with her dad in the small square of cleared floor that was normally the den to "My Little Girl," everyone had gone misty-eyed. She'd cut short her first dance with Cooper to return to her guests.

"Where will you honeymoon, sweet-heart?" his mother, who'd flown in from O'Hare last night, had raised her voice to be heard above the noise around them. The party flowed from one room to another inside the ranch house from the kitchen through to the dining room and into the living room, even spreading out the door onto the porch, though it wasn't really warm enough to stay outside. Cooper had finally retreated to the ranch office, where his mom, looking excited by this turn of events, had soon found him. Cooper almost wanted to keep her away from Nell, who didn't seem to share his enthusi-asm for their union.

"No honeymoon," he told his mother.

After a short knock, the door opened again and his bride swept in, her long dress brushing the floor, and his heart kicked over. The veil was gone, no longer softening her eyes. The platinum band he'd put on her finger glimmered in the overhead light. "This time of year we're too busy," she said mildly.

Cooper held her gaze. "We'll plan something for the fall."

Nell frowned. "In the fall, we'll have cattle going to market—"

"Let Jesse manage that—if he's still here by then."

Nell's frown deepened. "Are you trying to…take over already? I make the decisions for the NLS."

"Nell, give it up for one day, will you?" He tilted his head toward his mother. She looked distressed.

"Sorry," Nell muttered to her. "But on a ranch, as you know, the work is 24/7. I'm having a hard time taking a day off."

"Our wedding day," Cooper reminded her.

His mother hated discord. She picked up the topic of a honeymoon again. "A cruise would be lovely." Merry Ransom was a true romantic. Her gray gaze met his. "Barbados, the Pacific Islands, Hawaii…or you could sail through the Panama Canal. I always wanted to do that, but when John's heart failed…"

"I was so sorry to hear that, but I'm not much for boats," Nell murmured. "I'm glad you could be here today, Merry," she said, as if remembering her manners. She turned back to Cooper. "Are you ready to go? Mom's herding everyone into the hall. That's why I hunted you down." Not because she wanted to spend time with her new husband. "Mom says we're supposed to leave first before our guests. Are you ready?"

"We're not going anywhere," he pointed out.

Cooper had suggested a night in Kansas City at a nice hotel, just the two of them having a nightcap on a rooftop deck overlooking the city under the stars. But she'd vetoed that idea too. Despite the luminous expression in her eyes earlier, Nell seemed determined to get this over with, which was making the back of Cooper's neck itch even more. "All right," he said at last. "Who am I to fly in the face of tradition?"

Taking his mother with them, they left the office. In the front hallway, people had gathered, talking and laughing as they edged to-

LEIGH RIKER   213

ward the door, then down the steps to line
both sides of the short sidewalk. In a hail of
rice—not the bird seed people used these
days—they ran, their hands linked, toward
the driveway where, to his surprise, Cooper
found a limousine waiting. He glanced at Nell.

"My father's idea," she said.

"Works for me." So would that hotel, but
Nell was having none of that. She tossed
the bouquet, which landed in Annabelle's
arms, then they drove off toward the ranch
gates. A quick trip into Barren, a circuit of
the main drag in tense silence, then they
headed again to the NLS. By that time, everyone else was gone, including Jesse. To
give the newlyweds privacy, he was staying
the night with Shadow and Grey at Wilson
Cattle. Not that Jesse had been overjoyed by
their impromptu marriage. Eager as always
to leave the ranch, Nell's parents were already on their way to Kansas City. The rest
of his and Nell's friends had left too. Cooper's mom would use the second bedroom
in the foreman's house tonight.

Cooper had promised to take her over to
Ransom land tomorrow, but she claimed
she was in no hurry now that she was here.

"Enjoy your wedding night," she'd said with a kiss for him and another for Nell. "I couldn't be happier to have a new daughter."

Cooper settled her in at the foreman's bungalow. When he returned, the main ranch house was silent. He closed the door behind him, then heard a rustle of fabric and saw Nell standing at the top of the stairs, still in her wedding gown. She glowed white in the darkness, like an angel. "You didn't need to come back."

"And have my mother know—"

"We have an agreement," she said, her eyes wide.

Cooper climbed the steps. "Nell."

Her grip tightened on the railing. "We are not going to share a room or anything else."

"We should have worked this part out before. Jesse will be here tomorrow."

"And I'll find some explanation for him."

His temper flared. He couldn't get the picture of Nell out of his head, coming down these same stairs in her wedding gown with that look of…what? Anticipation? Even… love? As if she wanted their vows to be real. Now she was stonewalling him. "Like what?" he asked.

"You must have known how this would be. I made it clear—"

"I'm not living in the foreman's place while you stay here with your brother and thrash out who's the better person to inherit the NLS." He took a breath. "You asked me to marry you so we could put up a good front for your family, for Ned."

"You married me so you could bring your mother home. That's our bargain." Her lower lip trembled. "I'm sure not getting any closer to a man whose purpose in saying *I do* today is to take half the NLS away from me."

"Well," he said, jaw clenched, "as long as we're clear."

Cooper kept going up the stairs until he and Nell stood eye to eye. She was right. He had agreed to these terms, but he didn't have to like them. As he passed her on the top step, she touched his arm. "Cooper, I don't want to start out this way but…"

He pulled away. "Where am I supposed to sleep?"

Nell gestured at the first room on the right. "The guest room's always made up. There are fresh towels in the en suite bathroom."

He paused at the doorway, then softly shut the door and left her standing in the hall just as she'd looked before the wedding.

Let her think what she would tonight. Tomorrow, he planned to change her mind.

NELL WAS IN the barn the next morning before sunrise. Halfway through feeding horses, she heard a truck roll in, and Hadley Smith got out. Nell tightened her hold on the bucket of water she'd been taking to Bear's stall. "Help you?" she asked in a tone that didn't encourage him.

"Hope so," Hadley said.

"I gave you your last pay. We're square. What do you want?"

His gaze fell. Hadley reached out and she recoiled, but he only took the pail from her, sloshing water on the floor. "Work," he said. "I know you and I have had our differences, but I'm glad to put in as many hours as you can give me. Unemployment's not enough. I've run through the savings I had—"

"I appreciate your problem, but nothing has changed for me."

"Except I hear you've married the new foreman."

"Yes." She glanced toward his truck parked by the open doors. "Now if we're done here, I have stock to feed."

He held up the bucket. "Where do you want this?"

She pointed at Bear's stall. Hadley hung it inside on the hook, then slid the door shut. "Rest of my day's free. I'd be glad to help." He didn't give her the chance to say no. "My wife's having a baby, like I mentioned. We're real short on money. I worked a few days for Grey Wilson stringing fence after I left here. He didn't seem to have any problem with me."

Nell half smiled. "Grey's a soft touch."

"Tell me. He spoils that girl of his, and if he doesn't take a hand, she'll ruin that horse he bought her. But he didn't need an extra man long-term. When I left there, I worked at the Circle H with Sawyer and Logan's horses, then at Fred Miller's—you're prob'ly familiar with his place—"

"Yes, I am. I wish I knew of something more permanent for you but I don't."

"Wouldn't give me a reference if you did, huh?"

Nell backed up against a stall door. "Hadley, let's not make this any harder than it has to be. You and I didn't work out, and my grandfather is still away so, whether or not you've talked to him, I'm making the decisions for the NLS."

"You and Cooper Ransom? Thought maybe he'd moved up the chain now that he's elevated himself from foreman to husband—"

"Yes, I have." Cooper sauntered into the barn. "You have an issue with that?"

Nell certainly did, but to her relief he came down the aisle to them. She could take care of herself, but she welcomed him anyway. This morning, his face didn't have the same hard expression as it had on the stairs last night; maybe he'd decided she was right and they should stick to the agreement they'd made.

His suggestion—or hope?—that they'd share a room last night had surprised her into turning defensive. Nell regretted the cool stance she'd been forced to take. Still, their "wedding day" had been a definite temptation all around.

The mere first sight of him at the living room altar yesterday, all dressed up and looking like any groom seeing his bride, had made her doubt her choice. That focused expression, his pose of devotion, had nearly broken her a hundred times.

But she had to keep her priorities clear, for herself too, and the worst thing would be for her to become romantically involved with Cooper. No matter what she might have wanted years ago, and in spite of the more recent conversations they'd had about that past, their union now was a pretense. Nell needed to remember that.

"No," Hadley finally said. "A man's marriage is his to deal with. I'm just trying to earn a decent living before this baby comes."

Cooper said, "You'd probably want a foreman's job again."

"I would," Hadley agreed. "Pay's better than it is for a hand. I need benefits, and if I'm going to be a family man, I'll take every dime I can get."

Nell almost felt sorry for him. He'd obviously taken responsibility for the child he and Amy were having, and rumor had it they'd put their divorce proceedings on hold, though she didn't think they had reconciled. She liked his wife, a pretty woman with reddish hair and golden brown eyes, if not Hadley. She'd been glad when he left the NLS, even more so when Cooper took his place, but she noted the defeated expression he wore now. She heard it in Hadley's voice when he said, "I shouldn't have lashed out at you like I did before…"

"I'm pleased to hear that. And I'm willing to help you out—if I can." Nell didn't want him getting any ideas about returning to this ranch, or getting a foot in the door, but she had cared about Amy. Now and then, when she'd lived in the foreman's house with Hadley, she and Nell had talked, sitting on the porch steps and sharing the scrumptious brownies Amy baked. Although she didn't seem that happy with ranch life, the long hours and the mediocre pay, Nell remembered how much Amy had wanted a family with Hadley. "Are you two having a girl or a boy?" She couldn't keep from asking.

"Don't know yet," he said. "Amy's having her first ultrasound tomorrow." Apparently sensing he wouldn't get any further with Nell, he started to leave. "When you hear from Ned, tell him I asked about him again."

As his truck started down the drive, Nell breathed a sigh. She didn't regret letting

Hadley go, but at least he didn't seem like such a threat anymore. In fact, he seemed more troubled than anything, which made Nell sad. She understood pride. Life had never been easy for Hadley Smith, and it was no easier now.

"Never expected you to offer help to him," Cooper said.

"I never expected that either."

"Careful, Nell. Or you'll become a *softy* like Grey."

And all at once, last night was between them again. He was reminding her that she was not only a cowgirl but a woman. A married woman now. Nell flushed a little, remembering the long night she'd spent tossing in her lonely bed, missing Cooper's company. Listening for any slight sound along the hall from the guest room by the stairs.

"Don't get your hopes up," she murmured.

"Or are those yours?" Cooper said.

AFTER COUNTING CALVES all day, Cooper rode into the barnyard late that afternoon and saw Jesse trying, one-armed, to muck stalls. Cooper had to hand it to him; Nell's brother was attempting to complete the menial task that any ranch required. Not that he looked any more enthusiastic than he'd been about Cooper marrying his sister.

Jesse had come home early that morning, thumping up the stairs before Cooper was fully awake. With the guest room door closed, he was thankful Jesse hadn't seen him, and by then Nell was already up and at work.

"Where's Clete?" Cooper asked, leading his horse into the barn.

"Went to town. He's picking up the wire you ordered, then stopping at Wilson Cattle. Derek Moran has Clete's saddle." For an instant, Cooper thought Derek—Grey's brother-in-law—had stolen it, but in the past few months, the wayward youth had turned his life around, at least according to Grey. "He's got a real skill with leather. Says Clete's saddle is good as new with the billet straps he put on."

"So you're doing chores for Clete?" Cooper motioned at the cast on his arm. "That bone needs to heal, Jesse. If Sawyer catches you, he'll be mad as an ornery bull. I know he told you to rest and not try any lifting, even with your good arm."

With a grunt, Jesse hefted the pitchfork full of soiled bedding he'd taken from Bear's stall, which was empty. Nell hadn't come home from the day's ride Cooper had hoped they would share; instead, she'd cantered off on her own to monitor more of the herd in a far corner of the NLS. "I don't need doctors' orders. I have to make myself useful or PawPaw will decide I'm not the one to take over this place."

"I'm still not sure why you want to," Cooper said. His presence didn't sit right any more than it had before, and Nell had told him about finding Jesse in the ranch office trying to open the safe. Not the action of a man who'd built then sold half a dozen companies for huge profits.

"Because the rest of my family is right. This isn't woman's work."

"A lot of women and many men, including me, would disagree." He named several area ranches now run by friends of Nell's who'd taken over from their fathers. Like Jesse, their sons had chosen other careers. So what was his real motive for wanting to be a cowboy? The question nagged at him. "You know as well as I do that Nell's a competent manager."

"I'd say you're biased." Jesse tried to toss the bedding into the nearby wheelbarrow but Cooper took the pitchfork from him.

"I'll finish up here. Go take care of that arm."

"Let me do it," Jesse insisted, "and if you think you'll inherit Ransom land right along with Nell, thanks to some hasty ceremony, think again. PawPaw is a shrewd man. He'll see through this *marriage* of yours and drive you off the NLS."

"Not likely," Cooper said, although with Nell pushing him away, the old man might not be fooled about them. But he had to find out why Jesse was still here. "What's your beef, Sutherland?"

"I really have to tell you? I said it before. You're not going to hurt my sister, not while I'm around." He paused. "Though maybe you already have—or Nell wouldn't have been in the barn so early, even for her, throwing feed into Bear's bin as if it was a punching bag. Funny, don't you agree, for the morning after her wedding? No honeymoon, I'm told, and not that much of a celebration, although Mom did try to pull out all the stops with only a few days' warning."

He cradled the arm in the cast, a pinched look on his face that told Cooper Jesse was the one hurting right now. "The whole thing doesn't seem very romantic to me…"

Cooper's pulse pounded. Was the charade with Nell over before it had even begun?

"Maybe Nell couldn't sleep. Too much excitement yesterday. When I woke up, she was gone." That much was true; he wasn't about to let Jesse know he'd slept somewhere else. But if he'd somehow guessed…

Cooper remembered what Hadley had said. "Our relationship is for Nell and me. It's private. You and I were friends long ago so maybe you can just let this be. I mean, since you care for her so much."

"That doesn't mean I think she should have married you or that she can run the NLS." Jesse eyed him up and down. "Since you bring it up, yeah, we were friends," he said, pushing past Cooper. "Don't ask me again why I'm here. Let's say that, along with my parents, I'm looking out for Nell. That, and the fact it'll be me to inherit this ranch. Soon as I do, none of us want to see you again."

CHAPTER FOURTEEN

EVERY TIME SHE saw Hadley, Amy's heart clenched. She loved Hadley Smith, always would, but so far she'd failed miserably at getting him back. Maybe today—when they had their first view of their baby—he'd finally see the light. Amy knew, she just knew deep inside where that tiny being was growing, that she and Hadley were meant to be together.

"You nervous?" he asked, taking her arm to help her out of his truck.

"Some," she said. "I'm happy you could come with me though."

"Quite the day."

Amy wasn't sure what to make of that comment. With a slight frown, Hadley steered her from their parking spot at the curb into what had once been Doc Baxter's clinic on Cottonwood Street. Now, Doc and his wife, Ida, spent much of their time visiting their two sons in different places. In their golden years, they'd finally gotten the chance to do as they pleased, and Doc was no longer the only physician in Barren. After a rocky start while the local people made it plain they preferred Doc, Sawyer McCord had gradually taken over the practice.

He met them just inside the door. "Come right in. My receptionist is out until this afternoon so I'm filling all the slots here for a while." Amy sensed he was trying to put her at ease, which wasn't really possible. They went straight into one of the exam rooms where Sawyer indicated the table covered in white paper, which rustled when she lay down.

Hadley stood near the door. "Are you all right?" Sawyer asked, with a glance in his direction.

"Sure. I've worked enough with livestock to know what this is all about."

Amy blinked. Did he just compare her to a cow? She tried to read his expression but failed when she was normally an expert at reading people's faces.

Sawyer, who would do the procedure without any other staff there, opened a tube of gel, then spread it over Amy's abdomen. He fiddled with the monitor at her eye level. She glued her gaze to it, half afraid to glance at Hadley. She hadn't forgotten his last visit to her apartment. "Now let's get some pictures. See what we've got. Come closer, Hadley."

"Never done this before." He took a step into the room. "Will it hurt the baby?"

"No, perfectly harmless." Sawyer perched on a stool. "You okay, Amy?"

"Fine," she said, a hand over her heart. "Excited." Fearful.

"Well, it's an exciting time all around."

"With Olivia expecting too," Amy said, "you must both be thrilled."

Sawyer waved a wand over her gel-slathered stomach. "Can't wait. Olivia's a pro, of course, because of Nick. I'll be a first-time daddy."

"This...baby doesn't seem quite real," Hadley said. Because of his rough childhood, Amy knew it must be hard for him to wrap his head around being a dad. At least, much to her surprise, he'd agreed to suspend their divorce until after she gave birth.

She could tell he wasn't in the best mood to begin with, and yesterday Hadley had gone to the NLS again, practically begging for a job. He'd come away empty-handed, though he'd promised Amy he'd do whatever it took to support her and the baby. Which always made Amy feel guilty.

"Ah-ha. Here we are." Sawyer had moved the wand again and a blurry image appeared on the monitor screen.

"Looks like a blob to me," Hadley muttered, but he stepped closer to the table.

Sawyer laughed a little. "We don't have the best equipment here, sorry to say." He pointed a finger at the image. "This is the spine with all the vertebrae just as they should be, and here's the head."

"Big," Hadley said.

Wishing she'd come in sooner for this ultrasound, Amy craned her neck for a better view. At first, she hadn't wanted to believe she was pregnant when things between her and Hadley were bad. Then after she'd told him and money remained tight, she'd procrastinated again, afraid to rock the boat. Now, at the end of her first trimester, she said, "I can see its eyes and nose!"

"Is it a boy or a girl?" Hadley asked, as if interested in spite of himself.

The wand moved again. "You both want to know? Or be surprised?"

"I'd like to know." Amy was a knitter; she had all sorts of patterns for cute baby sweaters and caps, and she'd make an even smaller one for right after she delivered to cover her baby's head and keep it warm. "Do you, Hadley?"

He bounced on the balls of his feet. He shoved both hands in his pockets. "I guess, yeah. Which is it, Doc?"

"A boy."

Amy pressed her hand even tighter over her heart. A wave of maternal love rushed through her body. This hadn't been completely real to her either until now. She hoped Hadley could accept the fact, and he'd like having a son. Tears gathered in her eyes. At least they weren't arguing now. "Oh, Hadley," she said, her tone filled with wonder.

But he didn't seem to be expressing the same excitement she was. Why be surprised? Or so disappointed? Maybe he needed more time to get used to the idea.

"I'll give you a copy of the sonogram to take home," Sawyer said, smiling at her from his seat on the stool. He lifted the wand, then paused. "No, wait." He applied more gel, glided over Amy's abdomen again, and Sawyer let out a soft whistle. "Well, look at this. You two ready?" he asked, also taking Hadley in with a glance, Sawyer's eyes warm and a tad moist, as Amy's were. Hadley stood there, frozen, so close now she could hear him breathing. "Just like me and Logan," Sawyer said. "Can't tell if this one is a boy or girl. We'll try again next time, but this much is certain." He grinned at Hadley too. "You're having twins."

"WHAT DO YOU THINK, Mom?" The next morning Cooper fulfilled his promise to his mother. They had ridden over on one of the NLS's Gators to see their former home. The white-clapboard structure had just appeared before them as they topped the ridge.

She clasped her hands together in front of her face like an excited schoolgirl who'd been asked to her first dance. "Cooper, it's exactly the same! I remembered every detail. All the pictures I saved in our albums didn't show it this well, but I had the images in my heart." They neared the house, pulling to a stop at the porch, and Cooper had second thoughts—as he did about his marriage to Nell.

"Needs a coat of paint," he said. "Probably inside too." For a moment, as they climbed the front steps, he held her back. He'd had a structural engineer go through the house and it was sound, but the trash still had to be dealt with. "The interior was a lot different when you lived here, Mom."

"I don't care," she said. "I'm just happy to be home."

Cooper smiled. He could understand that; his visit with Nell had opened up all sorts of memories. He planted a kiss on his mother's cheek. "I knew you would be. I am too."

As they toured the house, his smile kept growing. His mother had always been a positive person. The only times he'd ever seen her cry were when the moving van doors slammed shut on her belongings and headed for Chicago and, years later, the day his father died. "We spent every minute of our marriage in this house—until we had to leave. Thanks to Ned Sutherland." In the dining room, devoid of her own mother's big mahogany table with matching chairs upholstered in a fleur-de-lis print and the enormous sideboard that had also belonged to his grandmother, she faced him. "Thank you for doing this, Cooper. But I can't help wondering what price you've paid."

He led the way back into the hall toward the stairs. "I don't know what you mean." Although he suspected he did, and her next words confirmed that. She always saw through him.

Trailing a hand over the railing with its rich patina from all the years of wear, she preceded him up the steps to the second floor. "I realize you once loved Nell. I remember what that did to you then. I remember the noisy quarrel you had with her grandfather, your vow to reclaim this land. And no wonder you said what you did. You've always loved this ranch, just as your father and I did. No one blamed Nell either for standing by Ned rather than you—as they say, blood is thicker than water—but if you married her now because of me—"

"I married Nell because...I care about her. That hasn't changed." He didn't fool himself that she felt the same way. *Temporary*, she'd said.

"I suspect from the look on her face at the

wedding she cares for you too," his mother said anyway. "If she didn't, I'd be even more concerned. And I'd certainly say so. Yet, she didn't even want a honeymoon, sweetheart. That shows *me* something I'd rather not see."

Cooper shifted his weight. "Mom, we'll handle this, okay?"

She glanced into each bedroom off the upstairs hall, and Cooper remembered being here with Nell in his old room. "Then you're saying I'm right."

"No, I'm saying it's early days yet. We just got married. Don't tell me you and Dad didn't have a first year or so of learning to live with each other. Nell and I have been single for years. We'll get there." If he had his way.

Cooper thought of their first night as a real couple, and Nell with his ring on her finger, remembered the kisses they'd shared not only at the altar but before, and hoped his mother was right that Nell cared too. He only had to convince her to make their marriage a real one, to cement the bond between them, old and new. But then she suspected his motives as Cooper did Jesse's. It wouldn't be easy.

His mom went ahead of Cooper into the master bedroom. "I agree marriage can be a challenge. It's love that makes all the difference." Her face softened as she looked around. "I'll never forget the years I spent here with your father, sleeping in this big front room—which I intend to occupy again—raising you in the house we shared, and I'll surely never forget how losing all this destroyed him. He was never the same."

"He wasn't. But he still had your love, Mom."

"I had his too," she said. "I suppose that's how we survived."

Cooper put his arms around her. "I know you hate being without him. I wish I could have changed that."

She laid her cheek on his shoulder. "You can't. No, I had all the love I needed."

"I'll put this house right again though. I'll make it good for you."

"Cooper, I love you for this, but I hope you've done the best thing, not for me, but for yourself. There's so much water under this bridge—and listen to me, using all these clichés—that making a marriage with Nell will be hard."

"I'm a tough guy," he said.

She lifted her head. "I know that. You were a handful as a boy too." She eased from their embrace. "I adore you. I have from the first minute I found out I was pregnant." Cooper thought that was too much information. "I want you to be as happy as you've made me today. I hope Nell will be too." She went into the hall. "How long before I can move in here?"

"I'll do my best to make it soon."

"We'll do it together," she insisted, then stopped at the top of the stairs. "I have no idea what your relationship with Nell will become, but I can say this much with absolute certainty. She won't let go of the Ransom ranch. Neither will Ned."

"Then we have a hat trick, folks," he said, trying to make light of things because she'd reached the same conclusion Jesse also had. "Ned, her brother, Nell herself... But I'm still going to try."

NELL HUNCHED OVER the computer in the ranch office. She had a crook in her neck from the bad ergonomic posture, but she needed to finish this before she even thought about going to bed—at opposite ends of the hall from Cooper. First, Nell had to upgrade PawPaw's breeding register, and she had to admit Ferdinand, his bull, had done a good job.

The new software had her buffaloed though. She couldn't seem to get past a certain point before the program abruptly shut down for no apparent reason. And Nell feared she'd lost all of her grandfather's data. He wasn't known for backing things up. She reached for the USB stick she'd used, but a rap sounded at the door. "Miss Nell?"

She minimized the page, then glanced up. "What is it?" Clete and Dex edged into the room. Neither man usually asked for advice, especially after working hours, so she assumed they had another complaint.

"Cooper ordered us to clear out the feed room tonight, then disinfect it. He found mice in one of the bins," Clete said, a sharp frown line carved into his forehead.

Dex avoided her gaze. "He wants a cleaning service, he can hire one. Thought you'd like to know. The boys aren't happy either."

Ah. They considered such chores to be women's work. Nell stiffened. This wasn't the first time she'd encountered resistance from PawPaw's men.

"Cooper told you to do it because I asked him to. I saw the mouse this morning. Clean the room, then set some traps. I stand with Cooper, and he stands with me." They had to make a united front with the hands, if not on a more personal basis.

The two men grumbled between themselves. Nell heard something about the wedding and Cooper becoming her lackey. Dex twirled his hat in his hands and glanced at Clete, whose frown deepened. "Never been *asked* to do something like that before. Not when Ned's here."

Clete had been with the NLS far longer than Dex, and he still saw her as a girl to be indulged, even pampered, not as the someday owner of the ranch and his boss. Nell pushed away from the desk. "My grandfather has nothing to do with this. If you both want to keep your jobs, then clean the feed room. I'll check tomorrow morning if it was done."

"Ned don't look over our shoulders all the time," Dex said.

Obviously shored up by his boldness,

Clete chimed in again. "He leaves us to ourselves. He doesn't assign chores we shouldn't be doing in the first place."

Nell used her usual mantra. "Whatever needs to be done, we all pitch in."

Dex said under his breath, "Like some ladies' group at a bake sale."

"Dexter, who do you think you are? Paw-Paw hired you, but he's not here now, and I can fire you in a heartbeat."

"Same as Hadley," he said, the hat spinning again. "Ever since he left, things have been different."

"And they will continue to be different." Nell's eyes must be burning with anger. Clete stared at the wall behind her. Dex nudged him in the side, but the older man stayed silent, torn, she supposed, by his loyalty to her grandfather, his affection for her and the choice he was being forced to make. "If you all have a problem with my being in charge of the NLS—with me as a woman—maybe this isn't the place for you." She shook her head. "I grew up knowing this is a man's world. My mother's only too quick to point that out, and other people agree." Nell didn't mention her dad's recent change of heart. "But that attitude will have to change—starting now."

"Maybe you'll end up with a bunch of cowgirls working for you instead," Dex muttered.

"With all due respect, ma'am, we all like Cooper too," Clete put in, "but if he's just going to do your bidding now that you two are hitched, then we have a real problem. The NLS has run fine for a long time without—"

A shadow loomed in the doorway behind the two cowboys. Cooper stepped into the room, forcing Clete and Dex to move. "That feed room's still a mess. Why isn't it fixed by now?"

"We're having a difference of opinion," Nell admitted, grateful to him for supporting her. He had a natural way with these two and the others, made easier perhaps because he was one of them, male and automatically viewed as being in command. Stronger, more capable, even authoritative. Which made Nell's teeth clench. For her entire life, she'd been pushed aside, relieved of any duty that required more muscle, in their opinion, sheltered by her grandfather. Ever since he'd left the ranch, she'd been fighting for control. She didn't intend to lose the battle now. "Either do as I said or clear out. Both of you."

Clete blinked. "You don't mean that, Miss Nell."

"Yes. I do." She looked at Cooper. "Was there something you needed?"

Heads down, Clete and Dex shuffled past him to the open door like dogs with their tails between their legs. At her question, they both stopped. And Cooper's hard gaze met hers. "Something you need," he answered. "Fred Miller just called. He's lost a cow to those coyotes. Spotted them heading toward the NLS."

"Then we'd better ride," Nell said, rising from her chair. Miller's ranch was the closest to her place. "Who's with me?"

She didn't stop to see whether the two cowhands followed her from the office. To their credit—and perhaps to please Cooper—Clete and Dex were in their saddles right after Nell mounted Bear, then clattered from the barnyard.

The night was jet-black, moonless, with not a star or planet in view. Before the four of them reached the ridge, she heard the familiar howls of the pack. If only she, Cooper and the wranglers could cut them off before another tragedy happened... But Nell drew a sudden sharp breath.

Beside her, Cooper laid a hand on her shoulder. "They've already been here."

He was right. She realized the coyotes' cries were coming from farther off, not closer in, and she was too late. Seeing where Cooper had pointed, she swayed in her saddle. PawPaw pastured Ferdinand here, but the massive animal, his prize bull, hadn't been safe. Apart from the rest of the herd, he'd had no protection in numbers. In the distance, the coyotes had panicked the others, and the cows' gentle lowing had become a generalized bawling amid the sound of rushing hooves as they scattered. She stopped Bear, then dismounted.

"Better not look, Nell," Cooper said, trying to protect her as he had when Jesse was hurt. Clete and Dex had gone silent, their muttering and grumbling halted in the time it had taken to reach the latest scene of bloody slaughter. Cooper swung down from his horse but not in time to keep Nell from ignoring his suggestion.

She couldn't keep from gagging. "I've taken cattle to market with PawPaw. To an... abattoir. I've seen what happens there, but this..."

The bull had been torn apart as a feast for the predators. The two cowboys leaned on their saddle horns, eyes downcast. "Sorry, Miss Nell," Clete murmured. Dex merely nodded.

Tempted to give in to the nausea rolling through her, then to step away and let Cooper take over with the men, she squared her shoulders and took another breath instead. There'd been enough damage done earlier to her position as head of the NLS. If she folded now, she'd never earn their respect. Nell swallowed. "Clete. Dex. Ride over to the barn. Bring the backhoe," she said. "You know what to do."

"Yes, ma'am. Don't you worry. We'll clean up here too." Obviously chastened by the scene, Clete was already angling his new chestnut mare in that direction. Dex rode on his heels, and Nell supposed they couldn't get away from the slain bull fast enough.

For long moments, she and Cooper stood beside the carcass while Nell remembered the loss too of Elsie, the twin calves and those a few other ranchers had lost, tried not to let go of the last of her inner control. In a brittle tone, she finally said, "Good thing Jesse wasn't here. He'd be making noise about all the prime steaks and roasts we'd have."

"Nell." Cooper moved to take her in his arms, as he'd done after Jesse had gotten hurt, but she stepped aside, her eyes avoiding the fallen bull as she gathered up Bear's reins. Her brother, the two rebellious cowboys tonight and even Cooper's new place in her life weren't the only things she would have to face tomorrow.

"How am I going to tell PawPaw?"

CHAPTER FIFTEEN

COOPER SWEPT ANOTHER load of debris from the Ransoms' old living room into a trash can. With a mop, Nell cleaned a path through the dining room and into the kitchen. They'd been working together in silence for over an hour, but his former home didn't look that much better. And that wasn't what had Nell keeping to herself.

The morning after they'd come upon the dead bull, she was still grieving—and worried about her grandfather.

"Did you get hold of Ned?" Cooper asked.

"No. Once he and Will set out to fish, they drop off the end of the earth—I mean that literally. It's not as if those two just dip a line in the creek here, or take advantage of all the fly-fishing to be done in any Western state. The bigger the river, the wilder it is, the better. Oh, and *remote* isn't the word for it."

"He called from some town before. Don't

THE RANCHER'S SECOND CHANCE

they have to stock up on supplies now and then? Bait, whatever?" Cooper leaned on his broom. He had never cared to fish. He didn't understand how a man could spend a whole day—or, in Ned's case, weeks—with his feet planted in the raging current of some far-flung tributary, waiting for a trout to take the hook while communing with his own thoughts. Cooper preferred action. He and Nell had some decisions to make.

She swabbed the entryway to the kitchen. "He doesn't need bait. PawPaw and Will love tying flies almost as much as they like to actually fish. They're artists, he always says."

He added more junk to the pile he'd been making. "Then they might not have to come into town. That what you're saying?"

"Not unless they run out of beans and bacon." Her voice sounded huskier than usual. She swiped the dirty floor with even more force. "I was irritated with them before. Now I don't know whether I'm furious because PawPaw hasn't checked in again or more fearful that he will. I left several messages."

"Nothing else you can do, Nell."

"Except dispose of his prize bull," she said, then cleared her throat. "I'm going to start upstairs while you finish down here. This floor will need another mopping—and then some."

"Mom sure didn't leave all this behind," Cooper said. "From this mess, I assume that over the years, with the house empty, people camped out here."

"Drifters, although they'd have to drift pretty far from the road to even realize the house is here. Maybe temporary cowhands then from the NLS," she agreed. "We hire on for haying every year and there's not enough room in the bunkhouse for all of them. PawPaw keeps track of that."

Cooper set aside his broom. "Or could be there were young lovers who wanted a place to be together." *Like us years ago, only sloppy ones.* His comment, as he expected, was met with more silence, but there were things that had to be said. For all he knew, Ned might suddenly show up without bothering to respond to Nell's messages, and that raised another issue. "I'm going to sleep here tonight. The lights are on now, the water's hooked up again and I can probably find a sleeping bag or bedroll somewhere at the NLS."

Nell leaned her mop against the wall. "With Jesse back from Grey's and in the main house, he'll learn, if he hasn't already, that we're...not really married."

"We are married," Cooper insisted. "I figured if we can get this place clean enough, my mom can move right in." Today, she was in town buying things for the house. "That will free up the foreman's bungalow. I'll talk to Jesse about moving in there, convince him we deserve our privacy—since we couldn't take time for a honeymoon."

"As the rightful heir to the NLS, in his opinion, he won't want to stay in the foreman's house."

"Too bad." He ran a hand over the nape of his neck. "Jesse gets his way too often. He always did."

She frowned. "And what happens when PawPaw does come home? I mean, after he takes a strip off me for losing Ferdinand?" Which to Nell probably meant losing the NLS too.

"Then we'll have another problem, I guess." Cooper hesitated. "Unless you'd like to stop this nonsense about a *marriage of convenience*, or whatever you call it, and try to make whatever this is between us real. I'd be in a stronger position to support you…"

She tensed. "We've been over this."

"Nell, we have to find a solution here, not some halfway measure. Not a deception that neither of us feels comfortable about. If you want to convince your folks, Jesse, my mother and eventually Ned, then let's just go full gas."

Her gaze faltered. "I don't know."

Cooper's patience ran out. "You want to hear me say it? Okay, I will. A lot of years back, we had a thing for each other. Call it what you want. Attraction, connection… Doesn't matter to me." He touched her cheek, stroked one finger down her soft dewy skin. "Love would do it too. I wonder how much has really changed?"

"It doesn't matter. I'm not going there again."

"Nell. I'm not just talking about…wanting to touch you, to hold you," he said. "Because it's more than that. I hoped we'd gotten past the way things ended before, that we're friends again at least and that you can trust me. Not just to do my job but to stand by your side with Clete, and Dex, and everyone else. I don't want to endanger what we have now. I want to help that grow."

"Let me remind you what *hasn't* changed— your determination to have the land we're standing on. I heard what you told PawPaw then. I remember what you promised me the first day I saw you at Finn's house. Are you saying you no longer want your land back?"

Her words confused Cooper. Was she throwing down a challenge? Give up his plan for this house, the land, everything he'd wanted from the moment he didn't have it anymore? That was all he'd *ever* wanted. Yet, he didn't want to hurt her either. As his mom had said, Nell must still feel something for him, and he ached to have her admit it.

"Listen," he told her, "I'm a guy and we don't talk about things like this much. So maybe you think all I want from you is… physical. It's how a lot of men express their emotions, while women go for the emotional side first and the rest follows. But I do want a true relationship with you, Nell. The whole package. All of it."

"I'm not sure I can do that," she murmured. Nell tossed him a despairing look, then pushed past Cooper. She was out on the porch, down the steps and in the saddle before he realized what was happening.

He called after her as she disappeared, headed for the NLS side.

"I'm not giving up, Nell."

On the ranch. Or her.

But for the first time, he wondered: Was making his offer to Ned a good idea anymore? If he was able to get his land—would he lose Nell?

Nell was still breathing hard when she rushed into the kitchen at noon. Jesse was sitting at the table, eating a burger with all the trimmings, and it appeared as if he'd been waiting for her. Nell hoped he couldn't see the flush on her cheeks or the way her heart kept racing as if Cooper's words had chased her home.

I wonder how much has really changed? Maybe this marriage hadn't been a good idea after all, but she'd be darned before she let Cooper see what he obviously wanted to see in her eyes. That should have been flattering—if she wanted the same thing.

Nell told herself she didn't. But had she outsmarted herself? Cooper's plea for a real relationship with all that entailed, including his support, kept repeating in her mind, tempting her. She sank down on a chair across from Jesse.

He didn't waste words. "So you managed to get PawPaw's best bull killed. Nice work, Nell. Makes me look better though," he added.

She'd been expecting this when he had lain in wait for her. "No one got that bull killed except those coyotes." It was time to call Grey and the others about that. "Somehow we need to eliminate the pack."

"I'd certainly help but…" He held up his casted arm.

"But you got yourself hurt trying to cowboy." Nell had actually been surprised at how long he managed to stay on his horse that other night before he flew over its head. "Jesse, why don't you go back to KC? Mom and Dad wanted you to leave with them, and I don't understand why you didn't."

"Yes, you do. I'm not about to tuck tail and run when PawPaw's likely to show up any minute. Then we'll see who gets the NLS."

Nell's spirits drooped even lower. Once her grandfather learned about Ferdinand, she'd have no defenses left, even with Cooper's help. So what had been the point of getting married? Jesse was probably right; PawPaw would leave the ranch to him. That wouldn't help Cooper, and it certainly wouldn't help her.

"What would you do with this place? Even after your arm is healed?"

He set the rest of his burger aside with a sly expression. "Maybe I'll put it on the market. Sell off all these acres and make another profit."

"You can forget that," Nell said, fists clenched. "PawPaw would never agree."

"Once he's gone, he won't know about it."

"Do you care about anyone but yourself, Jesse? There are people who love this ranch, most of all me, and you'd throw it all away?"

He laughed. "For millions of dollars, sure. Farmers and ranchers are always land rich and cash poor. Why keep worrying about the weather, the price of beef cattle, coyotes? You'll get your share, baby sister. Then *you* can move to Kansas City, make Mom and Dad happy."

"And find a good man?" Nell said, her tone brittle. "In case you forgot, I'm already married." Jesse didn't need to know Cooper's plans. She felt hemmed in on all sides now. *I do want a true relationship with you, Nell.* "You saw us take our vows."

"I'm still wondering what that was all about."

"It's about working together, making the NLS even more than it is now."

"Then why is Cooper over at his old house and you're here?"

"He's fixing it up for his mother. If you must know."

"I need to know everything that's going on here," he said, giving Nell a once-over. "Funny thing, you don't look like the blushing bride. A ten-minute ceremony and that's it? Doesn't ring true."

"How we conduct our marriage is our concern. I won't explain myself to you." Cornered, Nell lashed out. "Why don't you buy another business, build *that* up, then sell it rather than the NLS—instead of pretending you're a cattleman, breaking your arm

so you don't have to actually do any work?"
Jesse winced but she couldn't quit now. "You
could add more millions to what you already
have." She put a hand over her still-racing
heart. Fighting for survival. "That's what
doesn't ring true."

Jesse shifted in his chair. His gaze fell
away from hers. "Calm down, Nell."

"No, I won't," she said. "But I don't understand why you're doing this. Why you
wanted cash from the office safe when you
must have money stashed in accounts everywhere? Illiquid? All of it? Why isn't some
available to you? Or were you trying to get
into the safe for some other reason?"

"I needed the money," he said, studying
his plate. "There are no accounts."

Nell gaped at him. "What do you mean?
You're a wealthy entrepreneur. The apple of
Mom's and Dad's eyes."

"Fiction, nothing more. If you want the
truth, I'm in hock up to my eyeballs."

"But, Jesse—"

"There never were half a dozen compa-
nies, only one. It was going to be the next
Google, huge, and I'd have been set for life.
Then, in a blink, it all went sour. When I

finally tried to sell, the valuation was way lower and the only people who wanted to take it off my hands offered me pennies on the dollar." He stared into the distance, not at what must be Nell's shocked gaze. "Then, of course, there are the lawsuits."

"What for?"

"Copyright infringement, for one. Trademark. All kinds of things I don't want to get into right now. Bloodsuckers, all the people I relied on, trusted, my partner among them. He's suing me too. I screwed up, Nell. Fancied myself the next Bill Gates, or Jeff Bezos, or someone, even Steve Jobs in his heyday."

Nell reached out a hand. "Jesse, a few hundred dollars from the ranch safe wasn't going to help that."

"No," he agreed.

But the NLS would, and she and Cooper had been right. Something to hide? Oh, yes. And that made Jesse—her own brother—a dangerous person.

The question was: To help herself, should she tell PawPaw?

"I'LL TALK TO JESSE." In front of the foreman's house, Nell watched Cooper load his mother's bags into his pickup. Today was Merry's moving day, a far happier occasion, Nell guessed, than when his family had left their ranch years ago. "The house isn't done but Mom's over the moon to be spending her first night there. She wants to pick her paint colors for the walls and outside, but live with what's there for a while first," he said, turning to Nell. "You know I'm not glad. About Jesse."

Nell laid the straw hat Merry had bought on top of the bags. She had told Cooper about her discussion with her brother, who was lying low this morning two days later. Cooper had spent the past few nights at the old ranch house, cleaning up and avoiding the NLS's guest bedroom or any proximity to Nell. Did he regret speaking out about their relationship? "What can you possibly say to Jesse?"

"Things you can't," he said. "Jesse has to understand he can't just waltz in, like he thought, and take over. His being basically bankrupt and in hot water legally doesn't get him special treatment." He glanced up. "Here he comes. Why don't you help Mom pack the last of her things? This won't take long."

"Stay out of it," she said, catching his arm.

Cooper shrugged off her touch. "No way. We're a couple, Nell—"

"For a short while," she reminded him, ignoring the fact that she had indeed out-smarted herself. She was no longer sure she'd want that divorce. Nell couldn't deny she'd fallen for Cooper all over again, and she missed the easy camaraderie they'd developed, until their last conversation, while working together. "You have no stake in this."

"So you'd just step back and let Jesse roll over you?" He frowned. "He will, you realize."

"He'll try," she said. "I thought you knew me better than that. I can handle him. Watch me." Whatever her brother had to say, he would inherit the NLS over Nell's dead body. She didn't factor PawPaw into that decision. Not yet. "I don't need any protection, including yours." Especially when she still knew Cooper's ultimate plan for the ranch. Even though he'd pressed her to make their marriage real.

He planted both hands on his hips. "Why can't you just let go for five minutes? Stop being the cowgirl who can do everything, and that includes shutting out any man who tries to help." He had turned aside so Jesse, who was halfway from the house, wouldn't see their heated conversation. "My dad would never have let my mother deal with this situation alone. He would have stood by her, shielded her—"

"Oh, please. Your mom is no shrinking violet."

"Neither are you." He rolled his eyes at the truth of that statement. "There. I said it for you. You both come from pioneer stock, women who crossed the prairies and the mountains in covered wagons. But so do I." He dropped his hands from his hips. "Let me do this, okay? Don't make me say please."

"Cooper."

"Go," he said, his gaze fixed on Jesse behind her, and for once Nell decided to obey. He did have a point. She was too emotionally invested in the situation, and the whole matter made her as sad as it did angry. If Jesse played on their grandfather's sympathy, would that alone get him what he wanted? Nell doubted that. Still, after losing PawPaw's bull and being torn about Jesse, she was in no better position.

But Nell didn't leave. Jesse had touched her shoulder, and she could feel his hand tremble. "What's going on?" he asked.

Cooper ducked into the truck, rearranging the luggage and, she supposed, giving himself time to decide what to say. Nell didn't respond. She hadn't talked to Jesse since the bombshell he'd dropped in the kitchen. Cooper straightened and looked him in the eye. "You still here?" he said. "Thought you'd be in KC, asking your folks for a loan. What kind of man are you, Jesse?"

Her brother glanced at Nell as if to say, *You told him everything? Traitor.* "Who are you to challenge me, Ransom? I'm family. You don't belong here."

"Yeah," he said, "I do." He tilted his head toward Nell, silently asking her to disappear. Instead, she drifted off to the porch where Cooper had left the next stack of boxes for his mother. Merry had shipped them from Chicago before the wedding and her furniture was now on its way; she'd never intended to go back. Nell cocked one ear to hear what Cooper and Jesse were saying. She didn't need protection, but as a more neutral party, Cooper might say things Nell couldn't without seeming petty. "Now the cat's out of the bag about your financial problems, what's next?" he asked Jesse.

"Make sure you never own this ranch with my sister, for one."

Cooper's mouth set. "And I aim to make sure you never take it from her."

"Then I guess we have a standoff as if we're in that old movie *High Noon*. Come on, Cooper," Jesse said, trying a smile, "you know this marriage of yours is nothing but a three-act play. And don't think letting your mother homestead on *Ransom land* again is going to last either. When PawPaw gets here—"

"I imagine things will get interesting. But Ned will never turn over this place to you—even if you are the eldest and male—after what you've done." Hearing Cooper's words, Nell lifted a prayer to the heavens. There was no telling what her grandfather would do.

"I expect he'll take pity on me," Jesse said. "Because I'm the one he favors anyway."

"Don't be that sure. We'll have to leave that to Ned. He may surprise us all—or I may surprise him." Cooper didn't elaborate. "If my marriage to Nell strikes you as some kind of play or movie, it's nothing compared to your act as the would-be owner of this ranch."

Jesse shrugged. "Think what you will."

"What I think is you'd better not upset Nell any more than you have."

"She can take it, believe me." Jesse's gaze wandered toward Nell, who was fussing with Merry's cartons, her pulse throbbing in her throat. "I'm here to stay."

He'd barely finished before Nell heard the sound of an engine. A white car that appeared to be a rental roared up the drive past the barn and straight to the foreman's house. The driver must have seen the three of them gathered by the porch. And Nell's heart raced so fast she feared she might faint.

Things would definitely get interesting now.

PawPaw was home.

CHAPTER SIXTEEN

"WELL, ISN'T THIS some fine kettle of fish?"

"PawPaw, I can explain," Nell said.

After tearing down the drive, Ned had gotten out of his car and ordered Nell into his office. He now stood by the desk, studying the computer screen and shaking his head.

Nell drank in the sight of him. He'd left the NLS looking pale and weaker than he should after months of indoor rehab from his stroke and then the injuries from his tragic accident last fall. But to her relief, he seemed better now, healthier, and the slight droop on one side of his mouth was barely noticeable.

"I'm sorry I had to leave those messages on your phone, but I thought you needed to know. About Ferdinand," she added, omitting the one about her wedding.

He scanned the breeding register. "I raised

that bull from birth. The best I've ever owned. To lose him to a bunch of coyotes—"

"I'll make it up to you, I swear. The little bull calf I want to show you can't take his place, but he has a lot of promise."

"In a few years, maybe." His jaw set. He closed the new program Nell had set up.

"PawPaw, the coyotes didn't just hit our place. The pack has been roaming through a number of local ranches, including Wilson Cattle and the Circle H. Even Finn Donovan, who has a few head of Angus now, drove some off the other night."

Ned waved a hand at the computer. "And what is this? I don't recognize my own breeding register here. What have you done, Nell?"

"Updated everything. If you'd let me demonstrate, you'll see how much better this program is than the old one was, and I've already entered all the data. It was a learning process with some glitches for a while, I admit, but…" She didn't go on. Nell had finally worked those out with the help of some online tech support. Mentioning that wouldn't aid her cause.

He shook his head again. "I leave here for

less than a month. This is what I come home
to—a crisis and everything I've managed
for decades in chaos. You fire my foreman
behind my back. Jesse breaks his arm fall-
ing off a horse. My bull goes down. This
new program and the ranch accounts are
like reading Sanskrit. And maybe worst of
all—" he leveled a look at Nell "—I find you
married to the Ransom boy. It wasn't bad
enough he took Hadley's place? Why don't
you try to explain that?"

For an instant, Nell wished Cooper hadn't
made himself scarce as soon as PawPaw's
car stopped at the foreman's house. After defending her with Jesse, he'd fled to take his
mother to their old ranch house. He wasn't
being a coward, he'd told her. He'd talk to
Ned later, and maybe that was for the best.
Jesse had disappeared too, grinning at her
discomfort over the scene that was sure to
follow. Meaning now.

"Cooper and I…" *have an agreement*, she
wanted to say, but that wouldn't ease her
grandfather's mind. His dark eyes snapped
with a barely repressed temper, as he dragged
a hand through his brown hair streaked again
with gray. Hating herself for evading the

truth, she stumbled over the words. "We've spent a lot of time together this spring and I guess the old feelings we had for each other flared again, you might say." Some of which was true. Most of which was true. "Anyway, we decided to get married."

"In a hurry," he said as her father had. "Why?"

"I, um, we…didn't want to wait. With the spring calves nearly all born now, the first cut of hay ready to harvest before you know it, and then fall will get even busier than summer right up until the holidays…we chose to fit in a short ceremony—"

"Nell, stop spinning tales. You're well aware of what I think of Cooper—" he raised one bushy eyebrow "—probably the same he does of me. The last thing I expected from you was to come home and find you with that *ring* on your finger. Not even an engagement first," he went on, "or a decent interval before the wedding." The color rose in his face until Nell feared he'd have another stroke. "Now he's *foreman* here and I hear Merry's living in that house again, on *my* land! Don't you see what's happening?"

"I do," she said, but she didn't get to elaborate. Or maybe she was no longer that sure herself. If what Cooper had said about them was really true, was it time to change her own attitude? Did she dare to trust him completely like she trusted him as her foreman?

"It's an invasion, if you ask me—which nobody did. The minute Will and I reached town again up there in Canada and I picked up my messages, I knew. Why didn't your parents step in to prevent this? Or Jesse, for that matter?"

"They tried." Her chin went up. "But I'm an adult, capable of making my own choices." Nell felt increasingly desperate. "You might be thankful for what I've done to improve things around here instead of running on as if I'm still ten years old!"

"That's not what I heard from Hadley. His messages were different. He claims the men don't like to take orders from you."

"That was true at first, but since Ferdinand was…killed, they've seen I'm stronger, more capable than they thought. I didn't fall apart that night, PawPaw, though I was certainly tempted to. The scene was so awful."

"Then why do you need Cooper's help? In any way?"

"He's a good foreman. I'm more comfortable with him at the NLS than I ever was with Hadley."

"That's one point," PawPaw said. "Doesn't explain taking him into this family—" He broke off. "I have to wonder though, why you might think that qualifies you to get this ranch when I'm gone." He raked a hand through his hair again, leaving a few strands sticking up as if to show Nell how unsettled he felt.

"I'm sorry you're disappointed in me. And about my personal relationship with Cooper. You shouldn't worry about us, PawPaw." Ranch business, however, was a matter that wouldn't wait. "When you sent Jesse here to keep tabs on me, I needed someone's support. Cooper, not Hadley, has provided that, and if you'll take a closer look at the ranch accounts, you'll see. My improvements are already having an effect on our bottom line—in part because of the work he and I have done together. The two of us, not Jesse."

Having obsessed over the matter, Nell didn't mention her brother's financial woes. She'd decided that would come out soon enough and, ideally, it should come from Jesse, not Nell.

PawPaw headed out the door. "Right now, I'm going to talk turkey with Cooper. He'd better have some answers I want. You and I will speak again later."

As soon as his footsteps faded down the hall, Nell sank onto the desk chair and dropped her head in her hands. Her grandfather didn't believe her.

What had she gotten herself into?

COOPER WAS IN the hall, about to carry his mother's suitcases upstairs when the same white rental car that had raised a cloud of dust at the foreman's bungalow earlier slid to a stop out front. Ned had been away long enough that he hadn't wanted to leave his truck, which Nell was using, in an expensive airport parking lot. Probably too, he'd hoped to surprise everyone when he returned. The driver's door slammed and Ned charged up the steps.

Cooper expected him to start shouting, *What do you think you're doing with my granddaughter?* He'd always been as protective of Nell as Cooper wanted to be in a more enlightened way, and he'd warned her about this very thing. But when Cooper answered the knocks, Ned didn't say a word. Fire all but shooting from his eyes, he raised one fist, then smashed it into Cooper's face.

He reeled back, rubbing his jaw. "What was that for, you old coot?"

"I'm not finished," he said, then hit Cooper with a second blow before he could react, this time to his midsection. He narrowly missed Cooper's scar. "Take that. There's plenty more where it came from, you miserable son of a—" Apparently hearing a commotion from the second floor, he broke off the oath.

"What's happening, Cooper? Who is it?" His mother rushed down the steps. At the bottom, for a second she froze, then seemed to recover. "How dare you assault my son? Get out of my house," she said, her tone deadly quiet. "You did enough damage fourteen years ago."

Cooper wanted to groan. The words could only make things worse, but he held a hand to his stomach. With the wind knocked out of him, he wheezed, "Mom, let us settle this."

"No. I will not." She actually shook a finger in Ned's equally shocked face. If the situation hadn't been dire, and his jaw wasn't throbbing, Cooper might have laughed. In full battle mode, his mom was something to behold. "You can just turn around, get in that car and hightail it down this drive to the NLS. Don't you even think about driving across my land to get there."

"I am on the NLS. This is not your ranch any longer, woman," Ned insisted.

"Don't call me woman."

He ignored that. "It's sure as blazes not your house. I suppose your *son* is to blame for this, but you don't have squatter's rights."

Cooper tried to explain. "Nell agreed to let my mother stay in the house. Ever since I got shot in Chicago, Mom's wanted to live closer to me."

Ned's face got even redder. "My granddaughter is not the head of the NLS, no matter what she might think or want. I'm home now."

"Yes, we can certainly see that," Merry said. She had arched her brow—a sign that had always told Cooper he was in trouble. Thank goodness, she'd leveled it on Nell's grandfather instead. Not that Cooper wasn't guilty too. He'd known this would happen.

"Go ahead," his mother went on, "throw me out of this house again, off *your* land. You always were a bully, Ned Sutherland."

To his utter surprise, Cooper watched the man practically deflate like an old tire that had blown. One second he'd been ready to kill Cooper, the next he was holding up both hands and looking shamefaced. "Now, Merry. Let's be reasonable."

"Why should I? You were never reasonable, not one day in your life."

"Well, I guess you know me well," he said, as if trying to make her smile, but her face remained set, her mouth in a straight line that said, *Don't mess with me.* Cooper would have advised Ned to heed the warning.

Her index finger wagged in the air again. "You hit my boy again and I promise I'll knock you right down those stairs—" she pointed at the porch "—into next Sunday. Do as I said. Get off this property right now and don't come back." She circled to face Cooper. "Do we have a shotgun here?"

"In my truck," he said, the new one he'd bought weeks ago, "but no one's doing any shooting unless it's at that pack of coyotes."

"I'm not afraid of them either," she said. "I'm sure not afraid of *him*."

"Maybe you ought to be," Ned muttered.

But Cooper's mom didn't flinch. "Don't threaten me. Now go."

Ned held his ground. He glanced at Cooper, who had the definite impression he was searching for a safer topic. "Coyotes. That's the other reason I stopped by."

"Stopped by?" his mother echoed. "This was no social call."

With one shoulder to her, Ned's gaze fixed on Cooper. "Before your mother beats me senseless or puts a bunch of shotgun pellets in me, we should discuss the coyotes. I'm on my way next to talk to Logan and Sawyer, then Grey. And I understand his dad is living at their ranch again. He'll help. Might call on Fred Miller too. You and *Nell* have any plan?"

"We've all ridden after them before, Ned. They always slip past us." Cooper broke his stare to look out over the land between the house and where the bull had been slaughtered. He hadn't told his mother, but he worried about her being here alone. "Once I get Mom settled, I'm going to take a night watch out here like Grey did last year when his cattle were being rustled, see if on my own I can turn up those coyotes."

"That's a start, I guess." Ned's agreement sounded grudging.

Like any devoted husband, Cooper said, "I'll call Nell." He reached for his phone. "I probably won't be home all night."

Which solved one problem anyway.

Yet, his jaw aching, Cooper supposed he hadn't done Nell much good.

"No sign of them," Cooper said to Nell and her grandfather the next morning. Nell had led the way on horseback from the barn to the spot where Ferdinand had died, but she and PawPaw hadn't ridden alone to meet Cooper. To her surprise, Hadley Smith came with them. As soon as Cooper rode up, sporting a large bruise on his jaw, his gaze settled on the ex-foreman. She could all but see him thinking, *What is he doing here?*

Nell wondered that too, but her grandfather said he'd explain later. PawPaw's mood wasn't good and she couldn't blame him. Whatever her chances had been to inherit the NLS, they seemed to be slipping lower. At least Jesse hadn't joined them; he was in the stables trying to mend a bridle one-handed.

For a few long moments now, no one spoke. She heard the familiar creak of saddle leather, smelled the scents of cattle and grass on the air. PawPaw's head was bowed, one still-strong forearm laid across his horse's neck.

"Well," he finally said, "no use turning a good piece of pasture into a memorial. What's done is done, sad to say." He glanced at Nell. Did he know she'd buried Elsie and marked the place? PawPaw reined his big roan around toward the barn below, and her spirits fell even deeper down a hole. It was as if the last weeks of her managing the ranch had never happened. He didn't seem to approve of anything she'd done.

Cooper touched the purple bruise on his face. "What's going on here, Ned?" He'd asked the words she had imagined, his horse blocking PawPaw's path. "I know we didn't exactly get on together yesterday but—" He indicated Hadley, who was keeping close to her grandfather. Hadley stared at Cooper as if daring him to say the wrong thing and get fired.

PawPaw said, "I've hired him on again," as if that ended the discussion. It was the most explanation anyone would get. Cooper had a different opinion.

His grip tightened on his reins. "I thought—as foreman—I had the say over staff. With Nell's agreement."

"Not when I'm on this ranch." PawPaw nudged the roan's sides, angling Beauty around Cooper. "Don't assume because you've *married* my granddaughter that gives you the right to take over."

For an instant, Nell expected Cooper to make his offer for the land; she'd been dreading that confrontation even more since PawPaw's rented car had come up the drive. Cooper glanced at her, then away. "I didn't marry Nell to make an end run around you. Are you planning to make Hadley your foreman again?"

PawPaw didn't answer. "Keep that mother of yours away from me" was all he said, then with Hadley riding close behind, they cantered toward the barn.

Nell watched them go. She sent Cooper a distressed look. "He couldn't have made things any clearer. I knew as soon as I led

Bear out of the barn this morning and saw
Hadley. Taking him on again sends the message, doesn't it?"

"Ned's in charge," he agreed. "Nell,
maybe it's time we made things clear too."

"What do you mean?"

"When you fired Hadley and hired me,
that only gave Ned another reason to leave
this ranch to someone else. The dead bull is
one factor but not the chief means for him to
make his decision, and you knew how Ned
felt about me. I sure gave him reason years
ago to hate me. Our marriage was likely the
last straw. Obviously, you haven't swayed
him."

"I'd hoped he would come around. What
does he want most? To see me married,"
she said.

"Even to me?"

"Then what are you saying? I should give
up? Leave the ranch to Jesse?"

"No," he said, "but unless we convince
Ned our marriage is real, he'll keep on sus-
pecting it's not. I realize you married me to
show him and your whole family you had
the kind of traditional relationship they want

for you, but do you want to live that lie any longer?"

Nell's voice shook. "Convince them how?"

"Let's make it real." He edged his horse closer to Bear. Before Nell could move away, Cooper had slipped one hand around the nape of her neck. "I want to be with you, Nell. Heart and soul. I still believe you want to be with me too," he murmured.

Nell couldn't answer. She could admit to herself that she'd fallen for Cooper all over again, and right before PawPaw turned up she'd felt tempted to tell him so, but then he'd complicated matters with his emotional pitch for their relationship, which only made this worse. How to say yes when she'd married him to beat her family at their own game? Now, she'd jeopardized her independence, her yearning to be head of the NLS. No matter what her grandfather wanted, she would not become a wife who leaned on Cooper. And PawPaw had used Hadley Smith to demonstrate his power.

She gently touched Cooper's face. "Who nearly broke your jaw?"

His face fell. That wasn't the response he'd probably wanted from her. "Guess."

Nell stared at him. "PawPaw?"

"Then my mother threatened to shove him down the steps."

She couldn't help but smile. "They never did see eye to eye on most things."

"Losing our ranch, particularly. I know who I'd bet on in a fight."

"Not you, apparently," Nell teased, although as an ex-cop Cooper, she'd bet, could take care of himself. She didn't see any bruises on PawPaw though. "Thank you for not bloodying his nose."

Cooper snorted. "My mother didn't raise me to beat up an old man. So what do you think?" he asked.

She understood what he meant. But go all in with him? Her heart went pitter-patter, and Nell felt winded. She also knew that would be the worst decision she could make after all. Wasn't it? Then Cooper would have power over her too, and she'd be no closer to running the NLS without a man's help.

Still. Her neck tingling from his touch, she turned Bear toward home.

"I think you should put some ice on that jaw."

CHAPTER SEVENTEEN

NELL HAD ATTENDED several Girls' Night Out meetings, but she hadn't been there for a while. Tonight, she welcomed a dose of female companionship—and maybe some advice. This gathering was being held at Wilson Cattle, and Shadow answered the door.

"Wow, this is a surprise!" Shadow pulled her inside as if she feared Nell might turn around and head for home. Instead, she handed Shadow a casserole of cowboy beans with bacon and NLS ground beef.

"A peace offering," Nell said, leaving her hat on the entryway table.

Shadow took a whiff of the rich aroma that wafted from the bowl. "Everyone else is here," Shadow said. She called out, "Hey, everybody! Nell has decided to grace us with her presence."

A round of hearty hugs followed from

Shadow, Blossom, Olivia and Liza, her step-
mother, and Annabelle. Two other women
Nell hadn't expected to find there had come
too. Shadow's sister, Jenna Moran, and
Sherry, who owned the Baby Things shop
on Main Street, stood back a little.

"Your group's even bigger," Nell said, as
they all flowed back into the great room,
where a cheery late-season fire shimmered
on the hearth and, to Nell's surprise, pack-
ages wrapped in pink and blue and yellow
patterned papers with big bows were stacked
on the stone surface.

"If you came to more meetings," a very
pregnant Olivia murmured, "you'd have
heard." She barely paused before adding,
"This is a baby shower, as well as the farewell party I mentioned before we leave for
Kedar. Don't panic and run. The men have
already done that."

Nell's face fell. "Oh. I didn't know. I didn't
bring a gift."

"I accept IOUs," Olivia said, but winked
at her. "Come on, join us. As an old married lady yourself now, you'll fit right in."

Nell had never thought that was true, but
after this morning on the ridge she relished

any event that would take her mind off Cooper. She wondered where he was tonight; if he'd taken another watch for the coyotes, so he wouldn't have to face an awkward trip to the guest room with PawPaw in the house.

After the usual round of predinner drinks and then the meal, coffee and tea were served with various desserts to choose from: Shadow's homemade brownies, Annabelle's luscious-looking crème cake, Liza's blueberry pie, and several plates of cookies that Sherry and Jenna had brought. Again, Nell felt she'd come up short on dessert.

"I don't bake much," she said. "Sorry I didn't bring something."

"Neither did I," Olivia put in, massaging her stomach. "I refuse to gain another pound before this baby comes."

"You brought those delicious beans, Nell, and yourself," Blossom pointed out. "We're glad you're here."

And she did feel welcome. These were people she'd known all her life, longtime friends except for Blossom, who was newer in town, and Liza, who'd married Olivia's father fairly late in his life. They now lived here at Wilson Cattle too, though the talk soon turned to a new ranch house that was being designed by an architect in Barren.

"Privacy has been at a premium," Liza said with a grin. "Grey and Shadow made it clear they'd prefer to be alone. But then so would Everett and I. And our granddaughter Ava's at the age when she plays horrible music every night. No house is big enough for a whole bunch of Wilsons."

Nell flinched. Already the NLS seemed crowded, and PawPaw had been home for less than two days. If Cooper stayed away tonight, she'd be lying awake until dawn— and what would PawPaw think? She had no doubt he'd notice that Cooper was missing.

In the flurry of gift opening that followed, Nell didn't take part. Marriage was not her thing—even a sham one—and babies were alien beings. Yet, an also-unfamiliar twinge of longing ran through her. What if her relationship with Cooper could be real, and they, like Olivia and Grey, were soon expecting a child? That was something she'd also set aside long ago.

"Why so pensive, Nell?"

Annabelle sat beside her on the sofa,

studying her with what seemed to be a compassionate expression.

"You know me," Nell said, shrugging off her insecurities. "I'm more comfortable with cows than people, definitely not babies." That didn't sound good though. She watched Olivia open a big box that contained a fancy baby carrier. The delighted expression on her face said it all. "I mean this is lovely, the gifts and bows…" Nell trailed off, not able to meet Annabelle's eyes.

"Are you and Cooper all right?"

"Fine," she said, trying to brighten her expression. "Why do you ask?"

"You seem…sad. Or is that envious?"

"I'm too busy with the NLS to feel anything." She rolled her eyes. "PawPaw's home now, and while I'm happy he's looking well, he's not that happy with me. That's all. It has nothing to do with Cooper."

"Hmm." Annabelle's face didn't hide her concern.

Nell's pulse lurched. "No, seriously. Why would there be anything wrong? We just got married." She attempted a smile. Could other people—not only PawPaw—see through the pretense? "We haven't had time to quarrel."

"Hmm," Annabelle said again. She leaned closer. "I don't want to pry, but if you remember on your wedding day, we all thought it was pretty sudden. If you need to talk or a shoulder to cry on…"

"Goodness, do I look that bad?"

"Of course not. But you don't have that newly married glow either, so I wondered. And when Cooper came by about the coyotes, Finn says he refused to talk about anything else. It didn't strike him right. He claims Cooper was crazy about you years ago and he certainly still appeared that way at the altar but…"

Nell checked the others in the group. Olivia was trying on the carrier, which bulged out over her stomach. Blossom was helping her figure out the straps. Shadow was urging everyone to take a second helping of dessert—"Please, or we'll have tons left tomorrow"—but Liza hastily said she didn't need more calories. Being almost too slender, Sherry took "just one more cookie," and because Jenna had lost a few pounds during her painful divorce not that long ago, she helped herself to a half slice of pie. Nobody was paying any attention to Nell, and

Annabelle was one of the most caring people she knew.

Nell took a breath. "Can you keep a secret?"

Annabelle frowned. "Sure."

Nell hesitated, then said, "Something's very wrong."

Hoping she was wise to confide in Annabelle, Nell told her everything. The deal she'd made with Cooper that he now wanted to change, her fear of that, then how she'd ruined her chances with PawPaw for the ranch, her own uncertainty that she'd done the best thing after all. "At the time, I thought it was," she finished. "Now it seems I only made things worse." And what if, considering Cooper's goal for his land, she did give him her heart? And he broke it again?

Annabelle pondered for a moment. "These Kansas men can be pretty protective, and your grandfather's far from the only one," she said. "I realize how difficult that is for you, how old-fashioned that can seem. But Finn, who's a much newer cowboy, would sacrifice his life for me—for Emmie too—and I love him so much just knowing that. Logan, and Sawyer, and Grey would do the same for the women they love. I imagine Cooper would too for you." She cleared her throat. "I can also understand why you entered into that agreement with him and what you hope to prove to Ned. But, Nell, I sense that more than that, you're afraid. Of something else."

"You mean, risking my heart."

"Yes," Annabelle said, "and that can be scary, but now and then you have to lose a battle to win the war."

Nell thought of being in Cooper's arms, not for a few moments but throughout the night. "Then instead of maintaining the lie to PawPaw and the rest of my family, you're saying we should…"

She didn't go on. Across the room, Olivia had an odd expression, one hand pressed to her swollen abdomen. "The baby," she said. "I'm in labor."

After they all tended to Olivia, Nell went home without the answer to her question.

COOPER SPENT THE evening at his mother's house. Ned Sutherland sure disagreed that it was hers but Cooper didn't care. Soon enough, the old man would get his offer, and most of the time Ned was full of bluff. Cooper could only hope that in the end her grandfather would agree to sell. After that, Cooper would deal with Nell's reaction.

He hefted one last carton to carry upstairs. From the kitchen came the enticing aroma of his mom's fried chicken. Cooper hoped there'd be dumplings too, and he meant to stay for dinner. She would expect him to. He still wore a smile, the pain of yesterday's punch to his jaw being forgotten, if not his failure to persuade Nell about their relationship, when someone rapped at the front door.

Cooper set the box down. His hand went to his face. It was still sore, and if he didn't miss his guess, the man standing on the porch was Ned Sutherland. Cooper recognized him through the frosted glass panel by the bulky shape of his body and his stance. Cooper stiffened.

"You want company, Mom?" he called. After all, to him too this *was* her house.

"Depends," she said, banging pots around. A cabinet door slammed.

The knock sounded again. The man had no patience. "It's Ned."

"Oh, I definitely want his company." As

Cooper swung the door open, she came out of the kitchen wearing her red-checked apron, cheeks flushed from the heat or high emotion, and wielding a rolling pin.

Ignoring Cooper, Ned stepped inside. "Merry, I need to talk to you."

"Do I want to hear whatever you have to say?" She seemed anything but glad the older man had come. "You take one step toward my boy again and this—" she waved the rolling pin "—will come down on your head, you stubborn fool."

"Mom, I can take care of myself." He sounded like Nell, but did his mother think he was still five years old?

"No need," she said, "when I'm here to defend you. And I haven't forgotten the long history between the Ransoms and the Sutherlands. You're not going to win this range war, Ned. If you've come to kick me out of this house just when I've gotten settled again, you will be sorry."

Ned glanced at Cooper, then his mother. "Can we talk alone?"

"Making myself disappear," Cooper said, retrieving the last carton. He was up the stairs to her bedroom before Ned said another word. If he'd been afraid for her, he would have stayed, put Nell's grandfather in his place, even if that meant another blow to his face—not that he'd give Ned a second chance to hit him—but his mother could hold her own. Just in case though, after he deposited the box in her room, Cooper listened from the hallway. He'd be down those steps in a heartbeat if necessary. Ned Sutherland had better keep a civil tongue.

"I came to apologize," he said from below, making Cooper blink in surprise. "I was out of line the other day."

"You should apologize to Cooper, not me. Did you see his face? The bruises on his stomach are just as bad. What if you'd reinjured his wound? I wanted to weep after you took your fists to him. It's lucky you didn't break his ribs."

Cooper could almost hear the smile in Ned's tone. "You're no weeper."

"No, but I am a mother. A tiger," she went on. "Even a tough cop—former cop—like my son needs someone to look out for him now and then. If you ever—"

"I got your message the first time. I'm not here for a replay. It isn't easy for me to admit

I was wrong, you know." Cooper imagined Ned running a hand through his hair in frustration. "Why don't you just take my apology? Then we can start over."

"Start what?" she asked in a jaundiced tone. "Unless you change your ways, which I seriously doubt will happen, we have nothing more to talk about, certainly nothing to *start*."

Cooper tensed. What was going on here? No wonder Ned had wanted him out of hearing range. Was he trying to put the moves on Cooper's mother? He was old enough to be her father. Cooper took a step toward the top of the stairs.

"And maybe you'll change your mind," Ned said. "Move back one day to Chicago if the mood takes you."

Cooper detected a wistful note in Ned's voice, as if he were testing the waters, finding out whether she meant to stay.

"The last of my family is here," she said. "I expect to end my days on this ranch, not soon of course, and not before I've put this house to rights and enjoyed life a little. I want to see my grandchildren born and raised."

"Is that so?"

"You can take it to the bank, deposit it in my new account with Barney Caldwell. I was surprised he was still there. By now, I'd hoped he'd left town to get away from that mother of his."

"You already opened an account," Ned said, and Cooper could envision him shaking his head. "I never meant to drive you and John away. I hope you knew that."

"No, I did not. But you did what you thought was right then, and so did we. The saddest part, other than losing the ranch, was witnessing what that did to my husband."

"I was sorry to learn he had passed, Merry. Truly, I was. John was one of my best friends before all the trouble began... Cattle prices falling, loans drying up. I was lucky to be able to keep the NLS going then."

"I'm glad you did. You two," she said, clearly remembering better times, "were a couple of stubborn cowboys. He never did make the adjustment to city life or the job he had to take there. In the end, his yearning for the ranch killed him. Cooper is right about that."

She seemed to be leaving something out, but before Cooper could figure out what it might be, Ned went on. "He thinks he's right about my granddaughter too. If you ask me, she has another take entirely on that marriage of theirs. Don't expect it to last. I sure don't see any grandkids on the way."

"Because you don't want it to last," she said. "But let them work it out, Ned."

Cooper knew he should intervene, but he stayed where he was, letting his mother handle her relationship to Ned.

A long silence followed. Then finally, Ned took an audible breath. "You look good, Merry. Younger than ever. You haven't aged a day."

She actually laughed. "You *are* an old fool if you can't recognize the truth." She hesitated another second. "You look pretty good yourself."

"Do I? You heard about my stroke? The accident after that?"

"Yes, and I'm pleased you've recovered from both. You're as…manly as ever."

"You think?" He must have touched his face. "The droop's still there whenever I get too tired—which I hate to admit I do these days—but better than it was. Same goes for my weak hand. Hair's a bit grayer now—"

"And you've been dyeing it," she said, not sounding troubled at all.

"Yeah, but it's hard to stop time. Even climbing on my roan's getting harder than it used to be." Then he laughed too. "Don't tell anybody or those young folks will throw me off the NLS before I'm ready. Nell's a mother hen with me anyway," he finished. "If only she'd been born first..."

"Oh, no, you don't. Just because Jesse's the oldest and a man. Nell is a fearsome woman, strong enough to run your ranch." Cooper's mother paused again. "She loves you, Ned. That counts for a lot."

"We'll see. Things lately have been pretty messed up."

"Don't try to tell me you've never lost a cow or a bull to predators."

"We all have, prob'ly more to come if we don't tend to those coyotes."

"You worry too much."

"I'm also worried," he said, "that you haven't forgiven me for everything, then and even now."

Her tone softened. "You're forgiven. How else can we exist as neighbors?"

Another silence made Cooper wonder what they were doing. Were they overcome by emotion? Had Ned given her a hug? Kissed her? Maybe he should find out. Now. But he didn't take that first step. Cooper heard some murmured words he couldn't catch until Ned asked a question that seemed far too innocent.

"What's that I smell cooking?"

His mom raised her voice so Cooper could hear. "I guess it's your dinner."

AS SHE'D EXPECTED, hours later, Nell couldn't sleep. She'd been wide-awake at nearly midnight when PawPaw finally came in, clumping up the stairs to his bedroom. Where had he been all evening? Her ears alert, she'd listened for Cooper too, but he never came home. She supposed he'd taken that watch for the coyotes again. Or was he staying out because he was angry with her? That mattered more than it once had. Nell turned over, punched her pillow, then gave up.

She wouldn't rest tonight. She wondered about Olivia, who'd gone to the hospital, Annabelle's advice kept playing in her mind and at last Nell flung back the covers. Trying not to wake her grandfather across the hall, she dressed hurriedly, fingers shaking on her shirt buttons. She fumbled to find her jeans, her boots. PawPaw already suspected her relationship with Cooper wasn't on the level, and maybe Cooper, as well as Annabelle, had been right. About her.

In the barn, she quickly saddled Bear. "Sorry, boy. I'm sure you'd rather sleep."

She led him outside, mounted up and, with the moon and her lifelong knowledge of the NLS's terrain as a guide, she headed for the border of Cooper's former land. If he wasn't there, she could turn back.

In the darkness, Bear stopped short. Cooper hadn't made a fire—that would have alerted the coyote pack. His horse stood picketed in a small stand of nearby trees, and Cooper lay covered to his shoulders in a bedroll, one arm behind his head, looking up at the stars.

"I almost rode right over you," she said, leaning on her saddle horn to gaze down at him. "Why didn't you say something?"

Cooper turned his head. "I heard you.

That horse wouldn't step on me. Decided to wait you out."

"Are you that mad at me?" He'd always been stubborn.

"No. Not sulking either. I'm enjoying the great outdoors. Hear that horned owl deep in the woods?" Nell didn't. All she heard were the horses stamping an occasional hoof. "He spooked Domino a while ago, but I couldn't blame him. The owl is out here looking for a mate. The herd's silent though. The coyotes might come this way later. Got your shotgun?"

"I didn't come after the coyotes," she murmured, not certain she wanted to have this conversation after all. "I got worried. And I couldn't sleep, wondering where Pawpaw was so late."

His white teeth gleamed in the night. "He and my mother had dinner. Well, I was there too, but afterward I fetched Domino and camped here."

"Dinner," she said. "I can't even imagine that."

He touched his bruised jaw. "They've made a truce of sorts—partially based, I'd guess, on my mom's expertise with a rolling pin and her excellent fried chicken. The way to a man's heart," he said.

It had been a long time since Nell's grandmother had passed away, and by necessity PawPaw had learned to cook for himself. She led Bear to a sapling near Cooper's horse and tied him to it. He was so well trained he didn't really need any restraint; he'd have stayed ground-tied by his reins until morning, waiting for Nell forever if necessary, but she'd wanted a moment to take in what Cooper had said. Still unable to believe what she'd heard, she walked over to his makeshift bed. "You think they're…?"

"Friends, maybe more in the making. People do change. Even Ned. I'd say that could work for you and me too." His gaze met hers in the dark. "Why'd you really ride out here?" She heard a lighter tone in his voice. "Were you looking for me?"

Nell's courage had deserted her. She, who prided herself on independence, on being as tough as anyone on the NLS, couldn't speak.

His low voice, edging on a rasp, went through her with a zing. "Maybe you thought over what I said before."

"Maybe I did."

He sighed. "Nell, either we make this thing between us real, see where all these feelings take us, or we go on as we have. But that's not going to work much longer," he said, then paused. "What are you so afraid of?"

Nell cleared her throat. Annabelle had seen that too, but she didn't know if she could put this into words. "Fourteen years," she said. "Do you have any idea how hard it was for me to make a choice then? Between this ranch, my family and…the man I loved?"

"The same as it was for me, Nell. Losing you."

Her breath seemed to lock in her lungs. "Cooper, I don't—I'm not sure—I could do that a second time. What if… What if everything goes bad again? I don't want to choose between the NLS and you."

His tone was almost a whisper. "Neither do I."

"Then don't make your offer to PawPaw."

"And do what instead, Nell? Keep on being your foreman—not *moving up* like Hadley said—trying to make up to Ned for things I told him long ago?" He shook his head. "That's no life for me. Neither is playing at this marriage of ours, one without everything a marriage should be. That's not fair to me, and if you're honest, it's not fair to you either. You really want half a life?"

"I want the NLS," she insisted. Then her voice dropped and the words came out shaken. "I don't want to get hurt."

"I don't want to hurt you," he said, "or to get hurt myself. So where does that leave us now?"

She shivered, remembering what Anna-belle had said about a war. "Making excuses for you to stay out all night like we did before? Lying to everyone? Me hoping Paw-Paw doesn't cut me out of his will? No," she said, then tried to find the shreds of the courage she'd lost, deep inside. Her heart threatened to beat out of her chest. Afraid? Yes, but this was her chance to tell him she didn't want a divorce, or rather an annul-ment; that she had fallen for him again, or even loved him still. Maybe it was time for her to take this risk. "It's cold" was all she could think to say. "In July, you could camp out here but, coyotes or not, you're going to freeze by morning. Unless you want me… to stay with you."

Cooper didn't answer. For another too-long minute, he lay there, one arm still behind his head, his gaze steady on hers. "It's your choice." Then he shifted his position and held out a hand.

For one more second, she hesitated. If she joined him now, there would be no going back. She'd be giving Cooper her trust along with everything else. Including her heart. Maybe, in the end, they would hurt each other.

But what other choice was there?

At last, without another word, she took his outstretched hand.

CHAPTER EIGHTEEN

"'MORNING, SUNSHINE."

The low rumble of Cooper's voice slid along her spine like a warm caress. He stood behind her at the kitchen sink, where Nell was rinsing dishes from her breakfast. They'd ridden home just before dawn, surprising her grandfather, who was already in the barn feeding Beauty. PawPaw had raised both eyebrows but refrained from saying anything.

"Mmm," she said as Cooper lowered his head to kiss the nape of her neck. Nell actually shivered, and water sloshed over her hands from the running tap. She'd come up to the house alone while Cooper helped with the morning feeding and she hadn't seen him since.

He'd skipped his usual eggs and bacon. "Are you hungry?"

"Yeah."

"I'll fix you something," she said.

"No, I'll just grab some coffee." He straightened. "You all right?"

"More than." She relished the feel of his arms around her waist, the warm and solid strength of him against her, the knowledge that they'd agreed to make their marriage real, trusting each other with their hearts. "I think we shocked PawPaw though."

"At least we put an end to his wondering about us." He reached around her to shut off the faucet. "Let Jesse do this—and the rest. We're taking the day off."

Her pulse stuttered. "Cooper, you should see the list of chores I made while you were at the barn."

"Don't care. Grey just called from the hospital. Sawyer and Olivia have a new son, born about an hour ago. Let's celebrate."

"Oh, that's lovely. Everyone okay?"

"Healthy and happy. And we've been working hard enough to earn a break."

The idea tempted her, almost as much as he did, but Nell shook her head, her hair sliding against his shoulder. When she gave in, she certainly did it all the way, which should have put her on alert. Maybe risking herself by giving him her trust hadn't been wise, but it was thrilling too. "Have you forgotten? I'm still your boss—even if PawPaw did rehire Hadley Smith."

"He hasn't said I'm out of a job and, yes, I realize you're the boss, but I'm a happy man today—most of all because we spent time last night talking. So—" he turned her around "—get whatever you need. We'll ride Bear and Domino over to check on Mom, then keep going. A nice long day in the sun, not a care in the world, enjoying the land." He paused. "And I have a surprise for you later."

Nell twined her arms around his neck. "If you want me to go with you, maybe you should tell me. I've had enough surprises."

"You drive a hard bargain." Cooper pressed his forehead to hers. "But I'm not doing this alone."

Nell reached for a dish towel hanging by the sink. She wiped her hands, thinking, *This is all kinds of crazy*, at the same instant she was mentally packing a picnic lunch for them to take. "I suppose I could use a few hours off," she admitted.

Maybe it would please PawPaw to know

Nell was spending time with her new husband instead of the cows, in his view behaving like the wife he wanted her to be. He was wrong, of course, that once a woman fell in love she could no longer do her job. How to prove that to him? She had to.

But in the next second, even that fear fled from her mind. Cooper had bent his head to her once more and was kissing Nell until her senses spun.

"Ahem." From behind them, Jesse said, "Pardon me for interrupting."

Cooper raised his head to look straight at her brother. "Just doing what married people do. Since you're so set on running this ranch, we'll leave you and Ned to it for the day. I'm taking Nell for a ride, then out for a fancy dinner."

IT HAD BEEN a long while since Amy and Hadley had eaten a meal together, and she rushed around the small kitchen of her apartment, setting the island counter with cheerful place mats and the stoneware she'd once shared with him at the foreman's house on the NLS. He set their cutlery in the proper positions by the plates, then faced her. "You sure you're up to this? You don't have to fuss."

"I enjoy fussing." *Over you*, she added silently. Maybe if he remembered their good times, as she often did, he'd change his mind about them, but so far Hadley only remembered their quarrels instead.

He hadn't said a word to her about the twins since that day in Sawyer's office. Amy had no clue how *he* felt about having two babies at once, yet his stunned face had seemed to say everything. She hadn't seen him since, and in fact, she'd been shocked when he called earlier to ask if he could stop by. She still didn't know why, but when he asked how she was feeling, she said, "Like the luckiest mother-to-be in this world. That's how."

"I have to admire your positive attitude."

Amy went past him to the range, where a bubbling pot of veal stew sent its rich aroma into the air. Suddenly, the room seemed even tinier than it was. Hadley's presence always sucked the very oxygen from any space, his size and innate power both a comfort to her and a reminder of how small she was. Not that he would ever harm her. Even during their worst arguments about her well-to-do family or Amy's spending habits, he'd rarely raised his voice.

"I'd like to know how you feel about this," she said after taking a breath. "I thought it was a miracle, seeing both of them together inside me. It *is* a miracle, Hadley."

"I didn't say it wasn't…isn't," he added.

"You know all I've ever wanted was to have children with you."

"And you've heard my reasons for not wanting to be a father. We kept having that argument over and over. It's partly why we're divorced now."

Amy almost stamped her foot in frustration. "We're not divorced. We're still married and I'd like to stay that way. Or do you think I tricked you with this pregnancy?"

"No." But his mouth set. "I grew up mostly on my own. Living here and there with foster parents until they decided they didn't want me or I gave them some reason to kick me out. Which I did more than once, stupid kid that I was. When we met, I wasn't good husband material. I never learned how to be." A muscle ticked in his jaw. "And I won't be a good father."

"You're already a father." She fought the urge to brain him with the cooking pot. Instead, she pulled it off the burner so the stew wouldn't overcook. "Like it or not, Hadley." She turned away. "Maybe you should have thought twice—even three times—before you spent that last night with me months ago." Her back to him, she banged a wooden spoon against the side of the pan. "I wasn't here by myself."

"I know that." He blew out a breath. "It happened, okay? I'll take responsibility for my part. Here." When she turned around, he had drawn something from his jeans pocket and handed it to her. "My pay this week from the NLS."

Amy blinked. "You're foreman again?"

"Not yet," he said, "but Ned hired me back, gave me this advance, and it's only a matter of time before he gets rid of Cooper Ransom." He frowned. "*Though* Cooper's sure got Ned's granddaughter under his spell. You should have seen them this morning, riding out side by side, holding hands."

She tucked the money in her pocket. "Really?" Amy loved a good romance.

"I couldn't believe they left Jesse in

charge for the day. He didn't last long before he disappeared into the house. But at least I got the chance to show Ned I'd be the better man as foreman."

"He's already aware of that." Amy knew Nell quite well too. She couldn't imagine her married, really; Nell's sole focus had been the NLS when Amy lived there with Hadley, but Amy never understood Nell's desire to inherit that ranch. She preferred living in town. "If Nell's happy with her new... husband," she nearly choked on the word, "then Ned might change his view about Cooper. Prefer him, I mean, to you. I realize you loved that job, but it could be better for you to move on."

She could tell he didn't appreciate her advice. "Are we going to eat?" he asked, frowning.

With quick, angry motions, she began to dish up the stew, ladling it into two bowls. Because of his background, he was never easy to be with, though Amy understood why. She plunked large chunks of freshly baked sourdough bread onto their plates. "There. Sit. Eat."

"Amy." Another quick expulsion of breath

as he reached out to take her shoulders in his big hands. "I never mean to say the things I do. They just come out of my mouth before I can stop them. They get me in trouble—"

"Yes. They do."

His gaze left hers. Hadley stared at his boots. "I came to give you that money. I want the...kids to have whatever they need, and you too. I'm not as bad as my father, who abandoned everyone."

"And I'm not the weak woman you think you married." She softened her words with a little smile. Of course, the first thing she'd done after he walked in was to invite him for dinner like a pushover. Though she admitted, he was right—they did seem to want different things. "I still love you, Hadley. Do with that as you wish. It's the truth, and some day you'll believe it."

She'd left him speechless.

"I appreciate you asking me to stay," he finally said. "This stew smells good."

Amy sat beside him and picked up her spoon. He'd love their babies when they came. If she'd gotten this far, maybe they'd be together again.

THE BON APPETIT, Jack Hancock's new restaurant in the former Annabelle's Diner, already had a good reputation, and with Jack as head chef, the food lived up to its hype—as unlikely as it had seemed that the higher-end French place would succeed in a town the size of Barren. Jack had pulled out all the stops for Nell and Cooper, yet even his excellent *bœuf* bourguignonne failed to take her mind off other things.

"Feeling guilty?" Cooper asked. He knew Nell too well.

"I've never taken an entire day off before, even when I caught the flu one winter. I bundled up and fed cattle in a snowstorm anyway." She added, "At least I didn't feel the cold. I was burning up inside."

Cooper frowned. "That won't happen again. You could have died out there, Nell, but I'm grateful you didn't." Then his features lightened. "Let's not spoil tonight. More wine?"

Nell shook her head. "One glass was enough." They'd toasted each other, then Olivia and Sawyer's new baby boy. "I can't believe Jack stocks such a pricey French label though. Most people around here don't have that kind of money to spend." She glanced at Cooper. "Have you won the lottery or something?"

He took in the small private room Jack had prepared for them—Annabelle's former office—with a white-clothed table set with fine china and sterling silverware. Ivory candles flickered in the center between them, softening the planes and angles of Cooper's face. "No, but I wanted to give you a nice evening. The day too," he said, reminding Nell of the long ride they'd taken among the herd under a clear blue sky. The grass had smelled sweet in the spring weather, and for those hours together, she had to admit, she'd relaxed as she rarely had an opportunity to do.

"Bear loved our outing too," she told Cooper. "The horses don't get much more time off than I do." Making her point again—to him or to herself?

"That's going to change too," Cooper said, twirling the stem of his wineglass.

Nell's senses, which had been lulled practically to sleep by the fresh air before, and the more recent effects of her wine, went on

full alert. "I hope you don't intend to rene-
gotiate our agreement tonight."

"No, I don't," he said, which reminded
Nell of their night on the ridge and how
she'd held on to him as if they were one
person. "Pretty late for that. Still. It seems to
me we've been doing everything backward."

"I don't understand."

"Years ago, you and I had a teenage
thing, sure, but we are different people now.
Adults," he added. "Finn saw that picture of
us in my apartment in Chicago when I was
laid up in the hospital. You know the one—
us with the ranch behind us. It was taken not
long before I left here."

Nell pressed her lips tight. She remembered that day too, the last before she and
Cooper broke up.

He set his glass down. "Nell, when I came
home after all that time, we got off on the
wrong foot, like two horses that can't figure
out which leg should lead. So I'm switching
leads." Sitting back in his chair, he gestured
at the room, romantically lit. "Last night…
I think we both know what it meant that we
agreed to go all in with this marriage, not
just to prove to your grandfather that it's

for real. Or because you want to take over the NLS."

"But I do—and I will," she insisted. "I'm not about to lose myself in this *arrangement*, even when today was perfect." She'd bet Cooper hadn't changed his mind either. "Let's not quarrel."

"I'm not. I'm saying I want to start over, build on what we already have."

"I'm not sure if we can." Or if she was willing to live in fear of Cooper's offer to her grandfather and her potential loss of the NLS. "I know what you want, but I've worked so hard," she said, "and no man— PawPaw, Jesse or you—will take that away from me."

"Nell, it doesn't have to be that way." He reached for her hand. "Come on, you're right. We don't have to talk about this part now. But I was hoping we could begin again, maybe *date* a little. Things like that."

Her chin went up. "All right. Then first, I've been wondering about some things. Tell me about Chicago. In all those years, you must have had another relationship." Maybe with someone he'd given the emerald necklace to? "Why don't we start there?"

"Not much to tell." Cooper toyed with his empty wineglass. "I never married, you know that. Never got engaged. Came close once, that's all." When Nell stayed silent, he said, "She was another cop. In the mounted division. We rode on weekends together in the park, so it wasn't like I was never on a horse again until now. Sooner rather than later, I realized we had two bonds—horses and being in law enforcement. It wasn't enough for me." He squeezed Nell's hand. "Your turn," he said.

She pulled her fingers from his. "So you never gave that emerald to anyone?"

"No."

Nell swallowed. "And I'm sure this will be hard to believe, but I had a brief crush on Shadow's brother Derek. Well, really on his older brother, and we never dated, but after Jared was killed, I started seeing Derek. He dumped me for Annabelle's cousin."

"Odd choice. I mean Derek, for you. I wouldn't think you and Moran had much in common—not even like me in Chicago with my cop friend. No one else?"

Nell hesitated. "I met a guy at a rodeo once, a stock contractor. PawPaw had sent me to buy a new cutting horse. I came home with a nice gelding—and that new man in my life."

"Your grandfather didn't approve."

"No, he did at first, but after a while, well, a commuting relationship is hard to maintain, and this guy didn't want a rancher for a wife. He was nice enough about it, though I suspect I wasn't, and we still keep in touch now and then…" She didn't finish. "There was no one else? For you?"

"I never met anyone who compared to you," he said, his gaze on his plate.

Nell waited until he looked up. "I never did either, Cooper." It was strangely gratifying to learn he felt the same as she did. About him.

Nell took his hand again. He'd given her his heart then just as Nell had given Cooper hers.

Their conversation turned to simpler things after that, the way Cooper's mother seemed happier now in her old house and his view that, because there'd been no further attacks since Ferdinand died, the coyotes might have left the area. Nell told Cooper of her plans for a barbecue at the NLS to introduce Olivia and Sawyer's new baby to everyone. They finished eating, ordered dessert and laughed together as they hadn't in a long time, and for the rest of the night, Nell didn't worry about the fate of the NLS.

Maybe we can make this work...

CHAPTER NINETEEN

COOPER KNEW NED SUTHERLAND liked a good barbecue, and he'd always loved a party, so combining the two at the NLS to welcome Sawyer and Olivia's new baby had pleased Nell's grandfather. He did not, however, care to man the grill so Cooper took over the task. That meant he couldn't be with Nell, but it gave him some solitary moments while he flipped burgers and hot dogs to remember the past few days with her, which had been *idyllic*—the best word he could come up with to describe the change in their relationship. They'd decided to make most Saturdays date night unless a ranch emergency required them to stick around. He couldn't quite believe his luck.

And yet, with Ned home and no other punches thrown his way, Cooper still felt uneasy. When should he give Ned his offer? Or considering how his feelings for Nell had grown...should he hold off on making the bid for his land? Cooper's mom, who seemed to be having a grand time talking to everybody, urged him to speak to Ned sooner rather than later. But because of Nell he was stalling, afraid to upset their new-found happiness. Still, Cooper sensed he was living on borrowed time.

Across the yard, Olivia and Sawyer were holding court, keeping their newborn son close while explaining the baby's middle name. "I thought it appropriate and fortu-nately Olivia agreed," he heard Sawyer say. "Meet James Khalil McCord." They'd used the name of his partner's son at their clinic in far-off Kedar. "I'm already convinced he'll become a rodeo star," he said now of the baby.

Olivia's eyes gleamed. "Don't test me. I'd hate to become overly protective again as I was with Nick."

Her son, his best friend, Ava, and little Emmie, Annabelle and Finn's daughter, were racing around the yard squirting each other and anyone in their way with water pistols. On such a mild afternoon, no one appeared to mind, but in good humor Grey retaliated, snatching a gun from Nick and spraying him instead. Nell was laughing—until Ava got her right between the eyes. Blossom narrowly escaped being "shot," but she laughed too, her and Logan's baby in her arms, turning just a bit so Daisy didn't get wet.

Having made the rounds as today's host, Ned finally settled at a table next to Cooper's mother. As Cooper checked the meat on the grill, he watched them all with envy. He and Nell weren't even considering a family—or, on her part, even staying together yet as far as he knew—but he had hopes they'd get there...unless he ruined things with his offer to her grandfather.

He looked up. Hadley Smith stood by the grill with two plates in his hands, staring after the kids. "How many?" Cooper asked, trying to keep his voice neutral. He and Smith had been at odds since Ned rehired him. Obviously, Smith wanted his old job, and Cooper supposed Ned agreed, though he hadn't said so yet. Something else that troubled Cooper.

"Two," Hadley said. "Can't believe it my-self."

For a second, Cooper didn't understand. Then he remembered Hadley and his wife were expecting twins! But Cooper had asked about food, not children. After a second, Hadley looked back at him. "Amy's hungry all the time. I need a couple of burgers." His gaze returned to his wife, and Hadley's mouth tightened. He didn't seem to feel the envy Cooper did.

He put the burgers on Hadley's plate. "Salads and drinks over there," he said, pointing with a spatula at the nearby folding tables. "Help yourself."

Hadley hesitated. "If you want, I'll take over the grill. Soon as I deliver these."

Did he not care to eat with his wife? Cooper hadn't seen them together until today, and he thought that was odd. With reddish hair and soft golden-brown eyes, Amy Smith had a nice way about her. One hand frequently pressed to her growing abdomen, she chatted with Cooper's mother and the other women, her gaze often straying to the children running across the lawn. Every time she saw them, her face lit up.

Cooper glanced at Hadley again. "This

is your day off. I'm fine doing the cooking. Enjoy the party."

"I'd like to help. You and Nell have seemed pretty tight lately. I bet she'd want to picnic with you again." His face remained neutral, but Cooper still searched for a hidden meaning to his words.

"What's your agenda?" he asked Hadley. From what he knew of the man, he usually had one. Most of the time that wasn't good for Nell. "Your wife keeps glancing this way. Seems to me you ought to pay her some attention. Sawyer says pregnant women need a lot of tender, loving care."

"I don't have much experience in that area."

Cooper slid the next batch of burgers onto a clean serving platter. The first round of eating seemed to be over, and he and Hadley were alone, but soon people would queue up again for seconds. "Smith, you know what I think?" He didn't give the ex-foreman a chance to answer. "You make things harder for yourself, for others too—" he glanced at Amy "—than they have to be." Which was often true of Nell as well and, right now, maybe Cooper.

Hadley stiffened. "Didn't ask your opinion."

"No charge," Cooper muttered, turning back to the sizzling grill. He slapped more raw NLS beef onto the heated surface. "I realize you and Ned's granddaughter were like oil and water. That happens. I also understand you work for Ned, not her, and certainly not for me. I've noticed the resentment, but that's your business. If you keep doing your job the way you have, we'll be okay. Just don't cross me either is all I'm saying."

"You already said too much."

Across the yard, Grey stood up from the table where he and Shadow were sitting with Logan and Blossom, Sawyer and Olivia with their baby, and Finn with Annabelle.

Grey tapped his knife against his water glass, and everyone stopped eating. "Shadow and I would like to make this occasion even happier," he said, lifting the glass. "A toast to Sawyer, Olivia, big brother Nick and little James. My sister always makes beautiful babies." He paused. "And I'm pleased to announce there'll be a new little Wilson soon. Shadow and I have just told Ava she'll be a big sister. Thanks for keeping our secret for ten whole minutes, honey." People laughed, but then Grey sobered. "We love you, Ava."

The cheers went up. Glasses clinked. Shadow leaned against Grey's shoulder, faint color in her cheeks. Ava joined them, throwing her arms around her dad, then her mom. The others crowded close, backs were slapped and kisses exchanged. More than a few eyes looked wet. When Cooper realized the burgers were about to burn, he snatched them off the heat before any real damage could be done. Then he glanced at Hadley, who was staring at Amy, not the happy couple.

Cooper felt another twitch of envy, but Hadley only stared. And stared.

"You may be right," he said. "You probably are."

With his plate of cooling burgers, Hadley set off across the grass, his long strides determined, to the other table where Cooper's mom was regaling everyone with some story—from his boyhood?—and Amy sat leaning forward as if to be part of the group. One hand cradled her stomach, protecting, already loving the two babies inside her. From her expression, that was plain.

Hadley sat beside her. They spoke a few words, and to Cooper's surprise, he put an arm around her. True, the motion seemed stiff, even awkward, but he'd done it. Making things easier for her? And maybe himself?

Was Cooper wrong—and Hadley had approached him not trying to make trouble but amends? He caught Nell's eye, and she flashed him a thumbs-up, presumably about Grey and Shadow's announcement. But he wasn't thinking of that now.

He wished things could stay that easy with Nell.

He wondered if he should take his own advice and not upset the apple cart with her.

HADLEY DIDN'T PUT his arm around her often, and Amy wondered for the rest of the barbecue why he'd done so today. Whatever the reason, she welcomed his embrace. As the sun began to set and the air started to cool, she shivered.

Hadley was a few feet away, talking with two other ranch hands, but he spotted her chafing her arms and approached the old stump where she was sitting. Most of the folding chairs had been put away and the party guests were leaving, but Hadley had gone to the barn to check on the horses. He was wearing his more familiar expression with Amy, a kind of tolerance, and she saw none of the earlier affection he'd shown.

"Cold? You should have brought a sweater," he said.

"I meant to. I forgot."

He drew her to her feet. "Better go then."

Amy didn't object. She stifled a yawn and looked around the yard where Nell's brother was trying to help take down tables and people were drifting toward their cars and pickup trucks. Ned Sutherland guided Merry Ransom toward the Gator he'd left by the barn, both of them laughing as they climbed in for the short trip over the ridge to her house. Nell and Cooper remained deep in conversation, sitting on the porch steps with mugs of coffee. The nearby grill was empty now, the salads gone and the dessert trays too. The air filled with the sounds of *goodbye, see you soon* and *let's get together more often.*

"My family was like this," Amy told Hadley as they walked to his truck.

"Mine wasn't." She'd also come from money and he hadn't, another barrier between them in his mind. Amy kept wishing she could make things different, but so far she hadn't been able to.

Halfway to the pickup on the gravel drive, they met Blossom and Logan. He was carrying their baby daughter, who slept on his shoulder, and the couple held hands. Amy and Hadley walked several feet apart now; he'd obviously forgotten their brief closeness. Had that been merely for show? She hadn't thought so then. Later, more than once, she'd seen him from a distance watching her, but she couldn't read his expression, except when he'd reacted to Grey and Shadow's news. He'd appeared shell-shocked again, as he had when she told him she was pregnant. She'd probably gotten her hopes up when she shouldn't have.

"Good to see you, Amy," Blossom said. "Let us know when the babies come."

Logan clapped Hadley on the shoulder. "You ready for this?"

Hadley sent them a weak smile but said

nothing. He didn't look at Amy. Calling out a few more goodbyes to people he knew, he steered her to the truck. Hadley opened the passenger door, then helped her in, waiting while she tried to buckle her seat belt. She had trouble with the clasp so he did it for her, and Amy felt the warm brush of his fingers through her cotton dress.

All the way home, he said nothing. Amy tried to make conversation about the day and the people they knew but avoided any mention of Grey and Shadow's coming baby. They had pulled in to a parking space at her apartment complex before he spoke. "You have a good time this afternoon?"

"I did." She paused. "Did you?"

"Talked to Cooper," he said after coming around to help her out of the truck. "Interesting. If he and I weren't in competition for the job, we might get along."

Amy's pulse jumped. "You argued with him?" Cooper was Ned's son-in-law now, which gave him power at the NLS. She no longer expected Hadley to get his job back, but he wouldn't seem to give up the notion. When they lived on the ranch and she'd made a home for them there, growing tomatoes and flowers, baking every Saturday, hanging curtains at the windows, she wouldn't have dared say anything, but she wasn't that person anymore.

"I suggested you move on. Have you found another foreman's position?"

"Don't worry about it."

"I do worry, Hadley. I have to. The babies—"

He sighed. "I said I'd provide for them and I will. You don't need to rub it in."

Not caring if he followed her, Amy marched up the sidewalk into the building. She didn't stop until she'd unlocked her door on the second floor. Her neighbor across the hall was Jenna Moran, Shadow's sister. She would have knocked on her door for support, but Jenna, who'd missed the barbecue to spend the day with her mother, wasn't home. "Thanks for driving me today. Goodnight, Hadley."

He caught the door before she could shut it in his face. "What's got you in a lather? What did I do?"

"It's what you don't do," she said, crossing her arms. "Can you imagine how I felt when almost every woman there today was with a husband or boyfriend who actually cares about them? Grey and Shadow looked so happy. Olivia and Sawyer too. Even the kids have all bonded with each other like one big family."

"Let's not get into that again. I have no family. I don't live in some fantasyland. I leave that to your folks, holed up in that fancy mansion of theirs. Not a care in the world."

"Except they lost their daughter to you, and it's not a mansion." Their house was big, but she guessed to Hadley it was more of an estate.

"If you weren't pregnant—"

"Don't you say one word against our babies—" She broke off, a hand against her stomach. "I love them. If you don't want to be involved, then go. I won't care if I never see you again." She took a step toward the door. "Leave *right now* and don't come back."

"Hey, hold on."

But Amy couldn't stop. "For one minute or two at the NLS, I actually hoped you held me because you wanted to, but I've waited long enough for you to come to your senses. In case you've never figured this out, I'm someone who can take a lot but when I reach my limit, I'm done. Which I am." She sucked in a breath. "With you."

For a long moment, he didn't speak or move. Amy's palms went damp but her mouth dried out. She couldn't swallow much less say another word. She guessed she'd said it all though.

"Are you done talking?" he finally asked.

Amy just nodded, her arms crossed again.

Hadley stepped past her into the apartment and closed the door behind him. He took her in his arms again, as he had at the ranch, then rocked her slowly back and forth. "I've been thinking," he said, "and before you say anything more, I did that before tonight." He held her gaze with his. "I'm moving in," he went on, his voice gathering strength, "with you, and you can't talk me out of it. That's reality. After the babies are born, then we'll decide."

She held her breath. "What does that mean?"

"Maybe I didn't try hard enough. I'm sorry, Amy. Maybe we should try again."

THE PARTY TO welcome Sawyer and Olivia's new baby had been a smashing success.

Nell hummed to herself as she tidied up the kitchen. Suddenly, she heard voices coming through the open window. Men's voices. At first, she assumed they were ranch hands talking, possibly Clete and Dex, who were like conjoined twins, but then she realized it was Cooper and her grandfather.

Her internal radar spinning, Nell switched off the overhead lights.

She set the platter she'd washed and dried on the counter. The sight of Cooper at the grill this afternoon, and the coffee they'd shared side by side on the front steps, their shoulders brushing, his voice low in her ear, vanished from her thoughts.

"I've been meaning to talk to you, Ned," she heard Cooper say. Nell leaned closer to the window as PawPaw answered.

"I figured you were."

"I know what your objections are likely to be, but hear me out."

Nell froze. They stood off to one side, and she hoped they couldn't see her in the dark.

Cooper had made no secret that he intended to reclaim the Ransom ranch, yet for some reason she'd wanted to believe he would never go through with this. The more

time she spent with him, the closer they became, the more she prayed that was true. But
this was what she'd feared since she first met
up with Cooper again at Finn's house. And
hadn't he warned her recently that he'd make
his offer for his former land soon? What else
could he be talking to PawPaw about now?

"When my folks had to abandon their
place," Cooper began, "and watch it become
part of the NLS—"

PawPaw's tone hardened, "I paid good
money for every foot of that ranch."

"And broke my father's heart. My mom's
too, though she's finally gotten her legs
under her again since she's come back." He
paused. "You seem to like her being here
too, I've noticed."

"Never mind that. Pay attention to your
marriage," PawPaw growled. "My girl looks
happy these days and I'm grateful for it, if
that has anything to do with you." He didn't
let Cooper respond. "Don't break *her* heart
again. You hear me? Because if you do—"

"I'll try not to."

"Nell remembers what happened years
ago just like I do," PawPaw said. "The day
some hotheaded kid proved he wanted that

land more than he wanted Nell. Frankly, when I heard you two had married, I was dumbfounded."

"I *was* a kid then, and I apologize for the threats I made and how I handled things, especially with Nell. I've told Nell that too. Can't we put it behind us?"

PawPaw made a scoffing noise, which didn't surprise Nell. "So let me get this straight. Because your mother likes it here—and I can't blame her—I suppose you expect me to roll over now with the NLS. That why you wanted to talk?"

Cooper paused. "My mother is finally happy again. I hope you'll let her stay that way."

Nell's ears perked up even more as Paw-Paw said, "She can live in that house forever if she wants. Nobody else has been using it. Maybe all this time, it was waiting for her."

A moment of silence followed as if the two men were recalling shared memories. Of evening barbecues with both families after a long day of haying in summer, or mustering cattle in the fall. Parties like the one they'd had that afternoon for baby James McCord, though they would have been for her then, or Cooper, or other kids graduating from high school, going off to college, or friends leaving on their honeymoons. Nell remembered funerals too, like the sad day they'd buried her grandmother, wounding her grandfather's soul.

"Were you planning to buy that house from me? Where'd you get that kind of money anyway?"

"My dad invested his money from the original sale of his ranch. He did so wisely, with sound advice, and got good returns over the years. When he passed, I inherited half. Mom has the rest—"

"Let me guess," Nell's grandfather said. "She'd be willing to pool those funds with you." PawPaw rushed on, "I'll be talking to my lawyer about a new estate plan next week. You know my granddaughter wants this spread as bad as she needs to breathe."

"Yes, sir. I do."

"I suppose you also know my view of that. Nell shouldn't work herself to death keeping the NLS going. She should have a family of her own. Then there's Jesse to consider."

Nell heard Cooper's voice tighten. "I disagree about your limited view of Nell, and Jesse comes with his own problems."

To his credit, Cooper didn't explain them. He must know PawPaw would talk to her brother soon as well, but Nell's spirits were sinking by the second. Her grandfather had cut Cooper off several times. When would he make his offer instead of dancing around it? She was leaning hard against the sink, ears straining to hear every word when Cooper said, "Nell's heart and soul are in this ranch. Together, we've kept the NLS profitable for you, and although I admit some of the men didn't care for having a woman in charge at first, they've mostly come around. Maybe it's time you did too."

"You are your mother's son," PawPaw murmured.

"I hope so," Cooper answered.

"Did your father let Merry run that ranch years ago? No, he did not."

"That's not the same thing, Ned. And yes, with Dad gone, Mom is my responsibility. I'll take care of her—as much as she'll let me."

"Nell's no different, though she'd argue she is. She needs a man, children—"

"And I can give that to her." Cooper let out a breath. "But times have changed. Why can't you also respect Nell for what she does, see that she's fully capable of having a good marriage, kids and the work she loves too?"

Nell's spirit warmed. Maybe she'd been wrong about Cooper. He was defending her, or so she thought until he spoke again.

"I want you to know I'll take care of Nell too."

"How, exactly?" PawPaw asked. "By buying back half this ranch? That really why you married Nell?"

"I do have an offer."

"Let me hear it."

CHAPTER TWENTY

NELL'S STOMACH HIT BOTTOM, and she backed away from the window. The blood seemed to chill in her veins. She didn't have to hear the rest.

At first, she'd thought Cooper was sticking up for her, but instead he was like all the other people in her life, particularly the men, who didn't respect or understand her. She'd gone against her better instincts, surrendered herself, and this was what happened when she did. Then he'd said, *I'll take care of her*, as if she were some brainless female, weak and dependent on a man, as if he were the one who should make decisions for her. She didn't need to hear his offer. He would hear from her though.

As she swept from the kitchen, slammed out the back door and pounded down the steps, she trembled. She marched up to Cooper and grabbed his shoulder. Taking him by surprise, Nell managed to swing him around to face her. "How dare you!"

Behind them, PawPaw's boots shifted on the gravel. "Looks like you two should talk," he said, then began walking toward the barn. "You and I will continue this later, Cooper."

Nell waited until they were alone. She glared up at Cooper with angry tears in her eyes. She didn't even try to hide them. Let him know he was breaking her heart all over again, as her grandfather had warned him not to. "I trusted you! And this is how you treat me?"

He held up both hands. "I was only trying to help, Nell."

"How? By acting just like PawPaw and the others with all their talk of protection? You figured you could convince my grandfather that you wanted what was best for me. Well, I know now you don't." She clenched her hands not to lose control and strike him. "You still want *your* land. No matter how many children I might have someday, I could have that with the NLS in my name, not yours. Not half the NLS but all of it!"

His mouth flattened. "Haven't our past weeks together meant anything to you?"

"Don't turn this around on me. I can't believe you'd use your own mother to get what you want."

Cooper swore under his breath. "I did not use her. I'm not using you," he insisted. "Nell, I'm trying—I tried—to support you. I believe in you. Didn't you hear me tell Ned that? Why can't you let go of this too-tough stance of yours for a change? Bend a little? I thought we were getting somewhere. I thought—"

"You could come in, sweep me off my feet and take charge like some...*cowboy*!"

"I am a cowboy," he said, daring a half smile that made her want to deck him after all. "And you know the code we live by. Come on, Nell. I *want* to take care of you. That's what a man does. There's no reason why that doesn't work with your vision too."

She gasped. "Oh, that's a low blow—playing the concerned *husband*. I will not be the *little woman* to your big, tough *man*." Nell pointed at her chest. "I take care of myself, mister."

"Mister?" he echoed, but without the smile now.

"*That's* what's best for me. Is this what

you call *support*? If you thought for one minute I'd hand over this ranch, even part of it, to you to get around my grandfather, because you and I were married, you were wrong. I am not that person. I never was, and I never will be." This time, Nell poked Cooper in the chest with her index finger. "You're no better than PawPaw, you're just not as honest. At least I've known where he was coming from. You were the one person I thought who understood. Who wanted me to succeed. I *trusted* you," she said again, "against every instinct not to—and you betrayed me."

"Nell, wait. Listen. Do you want to hear the offer I was going to make your grandfather?"

"I've been waiting for that since you showed up at Finn's. You made it plain just what your offer would be then." She spun on her heel.

"Nell."

"Sleep at your mother's house tonight," she said over her shoulder. "You and I are finished."

COOPER DIDN'T GO after her. Listening to Nell stalk away, then the slam of the door at the house, he stared at the ground. He'd never meant for this to happen. Maybe he should have spent more time thinking things through before he spoke to Ned but when he'd seen the older man, he'd seized the opportunity. *I'll take care of Nell too*, he'd told her grandfather, possibly the worst words he could have said after all. She hadn't let him explain the sentiment behind them though, and she'd never believe him now. *I take care of myself*, she'd said.

After Ned had prompted him to make his offer, a dozen scenarios had run through Cooper's mind. Him and Nell on the ridge, sharing dinner at Jack's new restaurant, riding together after the coyotes, revisiting their better memories at the old house where his mother now lived again.

And earlier, Cooper had fallen under the spell of all their friends having what he wanted for himself and Nell. But he realized he couldn't have that unless he gave up his dream.

If he went ahead with his original plan to buy back the former Ransom ranch, his marriage to Nell would be over. The new memories they'd made would be nothing but dust.

When Ned asked if he really intended to get his half of the ranch back, Cooper had hesitated, knowing he couldn't go on any longer feeling torn between his two options.

When he'd finally had his chance to make the offer to Ned, he'd waffled, because the cost would prove too high. To Ned he was still that hotheaded kid who'd wanted the land more than he did Nell.

He'd had the chance to show both of them that had changed. And he'd messed up.

Wrestling with his growing sense that he'd lost her completely, Cooper marched toward the barn. He didn't want to go to his mother's, let her see the turmoil inside him as she surely would. A night alone, camped out in the tack room with his saddle for a pillow might be better penance.

"Marital spat?" a voice said from a nearby stall.

Jesse. Cooper looked in to find him brushing Bear as if he wanted to get on Nell's good side by doing her a favor. "No," Cooper said, "a discussion. You're doing pretty well with one arm."

Jesse tugged at Bear's forelock. "I'm not as useless as I seem."

"No one ever said that." A few people had come close though; so had Cooper.

Jesse ducked under the horse's neck, came out of the stall, then shut the door behind him. In the aisle, he faced Cooper. "What do you guess the old man's going to do?" He must have overheard, or somehow learned about, the offer Ned had asked about. Part of it, at least. Like Nell.

"What are *you* going to do?" he asked his old friend.

Jesse shrugged. He had as much at stake as Nell did.

"You make this into some fight with your sister," Cooper said, "you'll lose."

Jesse's face became a blank mask.

Cooper went into the tack room and pulled his saddle off the rack on the wall. "I realize how desperate you must feel." He couldn't forget their talk about Jesse's business failures and his need for money. "But you don't really want this ranch. You never did."

Jesse stood in the tack room doorway. "Now you're a mind reader?"

"No, but we've known each other forever. You've always taken the easy path, but this isn't—won't be—as easy as you want it to be." Cooper glanced over his shoulder. "You'd sell this place, wouldn't you? A second after Ned passed away, as his heir you'd put it on the market and hope for a quick sale."

"The NLS has been in my family for generations. But there comes a time when the only sensible solution to everyone's problems is to get rid of it. You should understand how that goes."

"That wasn't sensible on my father's part. It wasn't my dad's choice. Ned ruined a good friendship fourteen years ago."

"Your loss too."

"Yes, it was."

"So you decided to come back here and marry Nell. You poor b—" He didn't finish. He motioned at the saddle on the floor, the wool blanket Cooper had taken off a tack trunk and tried again. "Looks like you underestimated her tonight. Least I do appreciate what I'm up against. Could be wiser to cut your losses. A second time. If not, then know this—I will fight Nell for the NLS. I'll fight you too."

NELL REFUSED TO give in to tears. For a moment or two after she'd stalked off and left

Cooper, she'd wanted to turn around, to hear his side of things, but her sense of betrayal had kept her walking toward the house. And what was left to say?

Cooper had been her safe haven, her refuge and, yes, the one person who believed in her. Or so she'd thought. But as it turned out, all along, he'd been like her parents, her grandfather. Tomorrow morning, no matter what PawPaw decided, she'd fire Cooper as she'd only threatened to before, and from now on, she'd harden her foolish heart.

In the kitchen, she puttered around, washing the remaining pots and pans from the barbecue, covering a few leftover desserts with plastic wrap. Wishing for a better outcome with Cooper, though she could never forgive him.

She was half surprised her brother hadn't joined the fray earlier. As soon as she'd opened the kitchen door to confront Cooper in the yard, Nell had spied Jesse watching from the doorway of the foreman's bungalow. He'd use the wedge of their argument to better his chances about the NLS. He wouldn't succeed—not while Nell had breath left in her body.

She set the wrapped desserts in the fridge to take to the ranch hands in the morning. Opening the rear door, she put a bag of trash in the can outside, secured the lid against raccoons…and heard a now-familiar, plaintive howl. Then another.

The hairs on the nape of her neck stood up. The usual yips and barks followed. There was no mistaking the eerie sounds and Nell's pulse took off like a rocket. Wrenching the kitchen door open, she yelled, "PawPaw! Coyotes!"

She would have called Cooper but she didn't want to be anywhere near him, and by now he was probably at his mother's. She couldn't say where Jesse might be. She ran to the ranch office and grabbed a shotgun from the rack. Nell borrowed her grandfather's jacket, hanging on a hook by the portrait of Ferdinand that covered the safe, stuffed extra shells into the pockets and pelted through the house, down the back steps and out to the barn.

This time, alone, she would find the pack. Prove she could do the job. Herself.

CHAPTER TWENTY-ONE

COOPER ROLLED OVER in his makeshift bed. Outside the tack room, he heard the sounds of a horse being saddled, but through the narrow window he could see it was still dark. Clete or Dex wouldn't be at work now. He sat up, reached for his boots and stumbled to his feet. Yawning, Cooper stuffed his shirt into his jeans.

In the barn aisle, to his surprise, he found Nell ramming her shotgun into its scabbard. Bear stood hip slung in the cross ties, looking as bleary-eyed as Cooper felt. He called out to her but she didn't hear him at first. "Nell," he said again. She whirled around as if seeing a ghost.

"Where did you come from?"

"Tack room."

She made no comment about that. "Coyotes," she said, checking Bear's girth, his bridle, then leading him past Cooper to the barn doors. The horse was awake now, its ears pricked for the adventure ahead.

"Wait. I'm coming with you."

"I don't want you there. I'll do this."

"You'd risk your safety? Just because we had a fight?"

"It was more than a fight. I'll file for divorce as soon as I take care of this."

Cooper gaped at her. *You and I are finished.* He'd known she was angry with him, hurt, but he couldn't believe Nell would be so reckless as to chase after the pack in the dark on her own. But then she'd always been impulsive and never did like being out of control, relying on anyone, including Ned, Jesse, Hadley Smith or especially…Cooper.

"Nell, I understand you're upset with me. I realize you're determined to prove yourself to Ned, but you misunderstood me before. I do respect you. I know what's important to you. That's important to me too. We can iron things out later. Let me go with you now."

Nell said nothing. Before he could say another word, she was out the door and in the saddle, nudging Bear with her knees from an eager trot into a fast canter. Leaving Cooper in the barn aisle, she clattered off into the darkness.

He let her go but he already had his cell in hand. Juggling the phone and his tack, he saddled his horse while he called the Circle H, where Logan would call Wilson Cattle and Finn. Which was pointless, he realized. None of them could get to the NLS before Nell reached the coyotes.

Cooper swung up into his saddle. It was up to him to save Nell from herself.

NELL RODE FAST, she and Bear racing across the dark grass without even moonlight to see by. But it didn't take them long to reach the slight ridge at the old boundary of the NLS that merged onto Cooper's former ranch.

Of course, she understood how he felt about that, how much he must want to reclaim his heritage for himself, his mother, his children and future generations. He'd cared enough to betray Nell to get what he wanted. Never mind his attempt to soothe her in the barn. They had become enemies again. If she did lose the NLS, she would also lose the very essence of herself. *That won't happen.* She was about to make sure it didn't, and right now Jesse, another rival, must be in the foreman's house in bed, oblivious to what was happening.

And PawPaw hadn't answered her calls. By the time he showed up, if he did, Nell would have finished this. The threat of the coyotes to the herd, to her very being as a rancher, would be ended. She'd already lost far too much tonight.

The lone howl she'd first heard had turned into a chorus. As she topped the hill, Nell saw the pack, nearly a dozen coyotes with a few pups out in the open, milling about, unaware of her presence. Several adults closer up had gathered around a downed calf. Nell struggled not to let the sight overwhelm her. She'd seen what had happened to Elsie and Ferdinand, PawPaw's special bull, but she seemed to be in an even shakier mood tonight and giving in to revulsion wouldn't help. Nothing could help the calf now.

Nell's breath caught in her throat. Was this Elsie's baby? The one she and Cooper had nursed after being injured? When no further coyote attacks had occurred— until now—Nell had finally released it to the herd, strong enough to survive on its

own. Even if it wasn't that calf, every animal mattered. To Jesse, they might be assets
on a balance sheet, but to Nell—and she had
to admit, to Cooper—they were individu-
als, each one unique with personalities all
their own.

She couldn't look at the calf. In that
moment, she didn't want to know. And it
wouldn't change anything; she would still
take out as many coyotes as she could. Their
feast was over.

Behind her in the distance, she heard hoof
beats pounding up the hill, headed for the
flat stretch of land before her that went on
and on to the far horizon.

Nell yanked the shotgun from its sheath,
determined to take out the coyotes before
the sound of the approaching horse scattered
them. She checked the load, then began to
raise it and take aim. From the shelter of
the trees nearby, the panicked sounds of the
herd reached her. Most had scattered, running for their lives, but some were still vis-
ible through a small stand of trees. Without
a clear line of sight, she'd risk killing them
instead.

Nell rode closer. The coyotes were so engrossed in the calf lying on the ground that they didn't seem to notice or smell her until she was right on top of them.

As she approached, a few ran off, but the rest regrouped—and suddenly Nell was surrounded. The snarling of the pack reached fever pitch, lifting the fine hairs on her arms. The one that seemed to be the leader snarled, deep in its throat. Another lunged at Bear, managing to nip his flank. The horse screamed in pain, spun on his hocks and tried to take off, but the pack only closed in more, eyes glowing red in the darkness, about to pull her off her horse, to prey on Bear.

She was alone. The rider she'd heard earlier might not spot her. She'd ridden off, trying to prove she could run the NLS with no one else's help. Instead, she'd put herself in danger, just as Cooper had said. Even worse, she'd risked Bear.

What had she done? *How am I going to get out of this?*

If the pack succeeded in dragging her to the ground, they would try to finish Bear too. At the least, he could be badly injured. For one instant, she considered dismounting to let him race for the barn and try to shoot her way out. Coyotes were capable of reaching a speed of forty miles an hour, but there was a chance Bear could outrun them. Her horse might make it; but he might not. She might make it; then again, she might not.

To prove a point, she'd made a bad decision and trapped them both. If PawPaw had decided she wouldn't inherit the NLS, she might not be around to hear him say it. She wouldn't see him again, wouldn't be able to tell her parents and Jesse that in spite of their differences, even when they didn't believe in her and she couldn't rely on them, she loved them anyway.

She'd never see Cooper again either. In spite of what he'd said tonight, she…loved him too. Maybe she should have listened, opened up to him before tonight, admitted how much his faith in her and their potential future had meant to her.

The milling coyotes kept moving closer, then closer still, until one of them clamped its teeth around the toe of her boot. Nell's pulse skyrocketed. Keeping a tight hold on her reins, she snatched her foot free. Bear was dancing in place, eyes rolled back in his head. Nell could smell the fear rising from his hide, or from her own skin.

"Nell!" a voice called out. "Don't move!"

Cooper had followed her. He galloped flat out to reach them. At his approach, another pair of coyotes disappeared into the trees, making the cows there run out into the open. They thundered off, trying to rejoin the herd before they were caught, but the rest of the coyote pack remained, fixated on Nell and Bear.

"Get down. Low," Cooper shouted. As soon as she managed to duck over the horse's neck, flat against his warm coat, a shot rang out.

The coyote that had bitten her horse fell. A second shot took out the one whose canine teeth had ruined Nell's boot. A third hit the leader of the pack, and as more shots followed, many of the others went down. The rest scattered, yipping and squealing as they ran through the trees, then disappeared. Nell was still in her saddle when Cooper rode up, reined Domino to an abrupt stop, and hauled her off Bear onto his horse and into his arms without Nell ever touching the ground.

"Don't even think about telling me I

shouldn't have come after you." His voice shook. "Do you realize how close *you* came?"

He meant to almost dying or serious injury, but she couldn't say a word. Nell clung to him, her face buried in his broad shoulder, his strong arms around her. Freed of his rider, Bear ran off, hightailing it toward the barn, then seemed to reconsider and came back though he was breathing hard after his own near miss. He hadn't left her either. She felt…humbled. "Oh, Cooper. I knew being impulsive would get me in trouble someday. I nearly got Bear killed."

Cooper didn't comment. He seemed too angry with her—and relieved?—to trust himself not to say something that would only separate them more from each other. Nell deserved that.

Cooper dismounted, leaving her in his saddle, feeling more alone and less capable than she ever had in her life. What had she really proved? After this, PawPaw might take Cooper's offer just so he didn't leave the NLS to Nell. She would still try to fight for the ranch she loved, but she would no longer have a marriage, real or fake, to sustain her. Which, she admitted, it had.

He walked over to the calf, bent down and assessed the carcass.

"Is it Elsie's baby?" she made herself ask.

"No," he said in a grim tone. Cooper rose, came back and swung onto his horse behind her. He gathered Nell to him again, then picked up his reins. Her horse had started to wander off again, not far but enough distance to worry Nell. If the pack returned, he'd be defenseless. Cooper clucked to him. "Come on, Bear. There's a rack of hay waiting for you tonight and a treat. Let's go home, boy," he said. Nell noticed he hadn't included her.

As soon as they reached the barn, Nell found PawPaw waiting. With the adrenaline still pumping through her veins, she dismounted. "I'll see to the horses," Cooper said. Without looking at her, he walked Domino and Bear inside.

That left Nell to face her grandfather. "What happened out there?"

They stood near the open doors, his horse, Beauty, wearing her saddle and tied to a hitching rail. From deep inside the barn, she could hear Cooper unsaddling their mounts, exchanging bridles for halters.

Trying to gather her wits, she gave Paw-Paw a quick report, downplaying the danger she'd faced with Bear. "A good number of the pack were killed," she finished, though Cooper had done all the shooting while Nell had just tried to stay on her horse. She wasn't the hero of this adventure and she wouldn't lie. That had gotten her into trouble before. "The credit goes to Cooper."

At least they'd been alone on the ridge, not with the NLS cowhands to see her in such a vulnerable spot. Her grandfather had obviously been about to ride after her, but before he'd left, she and Cooper had come back. What had seemed to last for hours had ended in those few minutes of terror.

"Then if it wasn't for Cooper," PawPaw said, "you'd have been in bigger trouble."

Yes, but she still had enough pride to stand up for herself. "I took my shotgun. Plenty of ammunition."

"And didn't use it, from what you've said. I should never have gone away."

"PawPaw. I've *tried*. I've done a good job. I did my best—until tonight."

Her grandfather's silence made her feel worse. Would he turn over the NLS instead to Jesse? Though it might help her to get what she wanted, it wasn't her place to reveal to Ned that Jesse planned to sell the ranch because he didn't care about this land. Not like Nell.

With all her heart, she'd hoped to see her name on the plaque above the gateposts by the road. *Nell Sutherland, Proprietor.* She wouldn't give up now.

"PawPaw, I admit I let you down. Give me another chance," she said, willing to beg. "Let me show you I can do this—and do it well."

He ignored that. "Where was your brother tonight?" PawPaw looked around and, as if he had conjured him up, Jesse strolled over from the foreman's bungalow. Her heart sank. He must have noticed the barn lights on and, of course, he couldn't resist getting in on this confrontation.

"I'm here," he said. "Clete ran over with the news that Nell was almost killed by those coyotes. Why didn't someone call me?"

"What could you have done, Jesse?" she asked, motioning at his cast.

"Better than you, apparently. I know how to manage a business—employees, livestock in this case—and that's what the NLS is."

"You don't *have* a business." Nell couldn't keep from saying this after all. The words had popped out of her mouth before she could stop them.

PawPaw glanced from her to Jesse. "Is this true?"

Her brother looked down. "At the moment, I have a few problems."

"Such as?"

With obvious reluctance, her brother reeled off the list: a pending bankruptcy proceeding; lawsuits that, of course, were not his fault but his business partner's; the potential loss of commercial property he owned in Kansas City. "But I'll be on my feet soon. My lawyer's taking care of things."

"That's not what you said earlier." Cooper walked out of the barn still holding a bridle. Its silver trim gleamed in the darkness.

"Tell the truth, Jesse," her grandfather said, his gaze steady on her brother.

"Let me speak first, PawPaw." Nell stepped forward. This wasn't Cooper's battle to win. It wasn't even Jesse's. If she didn't hold her ground now, as she had with Bear on the ridge, she wouldn't deserve to own the NLS. "I can fight coyotes every night if I have to, run this ranch all day long through spring rains and winter blizzards, worry about the herd like you do, treat them as if they were my children. I've ridden with you in the snow to deliver hay to them. I'd protect this land to my last breath," she said, "and my doing a good job, a better job, has nothing to do with my being a woman. Or your granddaughter, for that matter."

"She's right," Cooper said to her surprise. "Nell would have done the same for me tonight as I did for her." He turned to PawPaw. "I understand this is a big decision, Ned, but I hope you'll view Nell's case with all the seriousness *she* deserves," he said. "I've worked with a lot of courageous cops, including Finn Donovan, but I've never seen a braver person—man or woman—than I did tonight when Nell rode out alone to save your herd from those coyotes. I'm sure that, without the slightest hesitation, she'd do it again."

"Cooper," she started to say, overcome

by his support. Even after what she'd said, when she'd made it clear there was nothing left between them.

"One more thing." Ignoring Jesse and Nell, Cooper held PawPaw's gaze. "From the day I came back to Kansas, I've been trying to do right by Nell—just as she has for the NLS. Did I want the land I lost to be mine again? Yes," he admitted, "but I didn't marry her to get it."

PawPaw muttered, "And I didn't steal that land from your father. I bought John's ranch because we were friends and he was in financial difficulty. I paid a fair price so he could get on his feet and start over. For your mother's sake too. I know that meant losing the ranch they loved but the Ransom ranch is preserved as part of the NLS. If our situation had been reversed, John would have helped me. The question is, can you let go of that *promise* you made?" Her grandfather waited, but Cooper didn't respond. "Or will you make that offer you weren't sure about?"

"See, PawPaw?" Jesse said. "That's all he's ever wanted here."

Cooper's eyes met Nell's. Had she heard her grandfather correctly? And Cooper too when he'd said something about the offer he was going to make? What if…?

"Nell," Cooper said. "Jesse is wrong." He took a breath, then faced her grandfather again. "So were you, Ned. Yes, my original plan was to make you an offer for my half of this land, but I'm not making that offer. Why?" He turned back to her, his gaze somber. "Nell, your grandfather, your brother, even your parents may not appreciate this, but I do. You're the most amazing woman I know, the most amazing person, and you're far more important to me than any piece of land ever was or could be again." His voice lowered. "I love you, Nell. No, loving you doesn't even begin to cover it."

He waited a moment but, stunned to the toes of her boots, Nell couldn't seem to say a word. Had he really done that? For her? PawPaw and Jesse didn't speak either. Her brother only cleared his throat, then walked off into the night toward the foreman's house. PawPaw touched Cooper's shoulder before he went up the rise to the main house, and Nell watched Cooper's expression change from one of hope to resignation. With her silence she'd let him down too.

"I've made my choice," he finally said before he walked away. "But if we're going to have a chance, Nell, now I need you to choose *me*."

IN THE BARN, Cooper took Bear from his stall to clean, then disinfect the nasty wound on his left foreleg. Nell's horse stood patiently in the cross ties, occasionally eyeing Cooper as if wondering whether to trust him. Seemed to be a common view just now.

With a soothing touch and soft words, Cooper went about his business, taking comfort in the routine, trying to block out the past few hours. Why hadn't Nell believed him? That if no one else had faith in her, Cooper did?

By tomorrow morning, she'd most likely file for that divorce she'd threatened. The memory of their sweet moments together, the first on the very ridge where the coyotes had attacked tonight, ran through his mind. Other nights too when she'd mourned Elsie, then Ferdinand, and Cooper had comforted her. When they'd shared their feelings. When they'd truly been partners.

He may not have done Nell much good

with her grandfather tonight, but he'd tried.
And failed? His heart thumped as if he had
ridden once more into the thick of things
and found Nell with Bear, surrounded by
the pack.

The horse stamped a hoof. He'd had
enough. "Okay, boy. Time for your treat,"
Cooper said, patting his neck. "Good job,
Bear." He led him to his stall, where, as
usual, the gelding walked in, then faced the
door so Cooper could unsnap the lead rope,
making him almost smile. "You're a smart
one, all right."

Bear had stayed with Nell on the ridge,
even when that had meant getting hurt. If
he'd unseated her instead, then run off, she
could have gotten maimed or worse. That
loss would be even harder to bear than losing his family's ranch years ago.

As he shut the stall door, her grandfather's words came back to him. A challenge.
*I didn't steal from your father. I paid a fair
price for that land. If our situation had been
reversed, John would have helped me.*

He was right. It was time to see his own
truth. To let go of the past, and his resentment, and that promise he'd made. Hoping

to convince Nell of that, to make her believe him, hoping for a second chance, he turned toward the barn doors.

Then he heard boots coming down the aisle. Nell.

Adrenaline surged through him, stronger than in Chicago when he'd faced the ambush and been shot. Once more, his life was on the line.

CHAPTER TWENTY-TWO

NELL WALKED PAST the darkened stalls on either side of the aisle where the NLS horses were slurping water from their buckets, snuffling through the bedding for stray bits of oats and grain. One or two lifted their heads, and from his stall, Bear nickered a greeting.

He didn't hold a grudge about his wound tonight. The familiar sounds, the mingled smells of equine hides and manure made her heart turn over.

All her life she'd hoped to inherit this ranch. She'd believed she would live here forever, growing old as Ned was now, taking comfort to her last days in the horses, cattle, ranch dogs and barn cats that had always been a part of her. But it didn't matter after all that the cowhands, like Clete and Dex, had come to accept her. Or even that PawPaw and her whole family didn't believe in her abilities. She had to find the right words for Cooper.

He was standing in the middle of the aisle, watching her approach, and Nell cleared her throat. Her voice came out even huskier than it normally was anyway.

"Nothing I could say would be enough, but if you hadn't followed me, I don't even want to think what might have happened. Thanks for being there tonight, Cooper." At Bear's stall, she reached a hand through the bars to stroke her gelding's neck, solid and warm.

Cooper stood behind her. "He'll be okay. But if you want, I'll call the vet. Let him examine the wound."

"No, I trust you."

"Do you, Nell?" He didn't wait for her answer. "I can't blame you if you don't. I let the loss of my family's land blind me to the truth. Without Ned's overly generous offer to buy us out, my dad would have lost everything, including any chance for our future. I would never have had the money to make that offer."

"Which you didn't end up making," she murmured.

I need you to choose me, he'd said. From

the start, Cooper had supported her. Then tonight he'd told her he loved her, a public statement with her grandfather and Jesse standing there. He'd said those same words years ago, and she'd believed him then. Yet, for a short while, one small remnant from the past had made her wonder earlier if he'd said them because he still wanted his share of the NLS, as Jesse had implied.

Nell trailed her hand down Bear's broad face and he nuzzled her. "I never wanted you to lose what you love most, Cooper."

His voice held an edge. "Like you do the NLS? All of it?" Cooper hesitated. "Ned and my mom seem to have forged a peace. It's time to end the feud between the Ransoms and the Sutherlands. That includes you and me."

"Because…you love me?" she said.

He turned her toward him. "Yeah, but when I told Ned I'd take care of you—as I will my mother—I didn't mean to undermine you. Demean you. I don't think the way your grandfather does, Nell, or any other man who's ever made you feel less than you are. I do believe in you, and when you rode after those coyotes, my heart nearly stopped. What I was saying to Ned was that we should care for each other. I want to be partners with you in every way. If I didn't care, I would have stayed in the barn tonight with my saddle for a pillow."

Nell's tone softened. "Instead, you saved me."

"Must be a hard pill to swallow," he said, his gaze holding hers.

"Yes," Nell admitted, clearing her throat before she went on, "but maybe I don't need to be so tough—or independent—all the time. I sure wasn't tonight. Even I can accept help—believe it or not—meaning yours when necessary." She paused. "Maybe I don't always have to prove something, even to PawPaw."

"True, and as my mom once said, now and then I need someone to look out for me. And so do you, Nell. We each bring something different, special, to whatever it is we can have," he said, his eyes darker, gentler. "We need each other for different things."

"You're saying I'm not just a cowgirl. I'm a woman too."

"Yeah, and I'm a man." He started to smile. "I'm also a cowboy, as you pointed out. That's where I belong in this world and so do you." He sobered. "I don't think Ned was happy to hear the truth from Jesse tonight." Cooper reached out to tuck a strand of Nell's hair behind her ear. "Together, maybe we can still convince him to leave the NLS to you. It doesn't matter to me now that my family's ranch may never be mine— or that everything would be in your name— as long as we're together."

With tears in her eyes, Nell framed his face in her hands. "Whatever my grandfather decides, if we don't have a scrap of land between us, we'll have each other. I love you, Cooper," she said. "I choose *you*."

"That's all I need." Cooper drew Nell closer, took her hands. Then, his gaze on hers, he bent his head to kiss her. In the stall, Bear shook himself and blew out a breath as if in approval. After a moment, Nell and Cooper drew apart, a few inches anyway. He gazed down at her. "Does this mean you're not going to fire me?"

And Nell said, "Never."

NELL WOKE THE next morning to the sound of someone's fist pounding at her door. "Nelly, get up! Throw some clothes on and meet me downstairs."

"PawPaw," she said with a groan, rolling over to check the time on her cell phone. It was after nine o'clock! And Cooper wasn't beside her.

Sunshine streamed in through the open windows and the sweet smell of clover drifted from the yard below. Nell swept hair from her eyes. She'd never slept this late before, though she and Cooper hadn't stopped talking until dawn.

Nell's hand went to her throat. The emerald necklace Cooper had given her last night—or rather regifted her—nestled in there.

She and Cooper had all sorts of new plans for their future, not all of which involved the NLS. Nell wasn't quite sure how she felt about that yet, but having been summoned by PawPaw, she guessed she would soon find out. Nell only wished Cooper was with her now. Instead, she would have to do this alone.

In the kitchen, her grandfather had his back turned. At the coffee maker, he poured her a cup without glancing behind him, then plopped two sugars into the steaming brew and added a generous portion of cream. He held out his arm and Nell took the mug. "Thanks, PawPaw."

"Don't thank me," he said, "until you hear what I have to say."

Nell took a sip and burned the tip of her tongue but didn't notice the sting of pain. For one long moment, she wanted to drag this out, not to have the actual words sink into her and close the last door on her life-long goal to run the NLS.

I've picked Jesse, he might say, but she'd be okay with that now, she told herself, with only a twinge of regret. She had Cooper.

His arms crossed over his chest, PawPaw leaned against the counter. He sipped his coffee, his gaze fixed on her over the rim of his cup. "I've spoken with Jesse," he said at last, and Nell thought, *Here it comes.*

"I'm surprised he was up this early," she murmured, unable to resist.

"He's not, far as I know. I imagine he's still snoring in the foreman's house. We talked last night."

From the barn, through the window screen, she heard the usual everyday sounds of men working, probably Cooper among them, a horse whinnying from the corral, the clang of the metal gate to the pasture being opened. Again, she wished Cooper was here with her. Nell's nerves were beginning to shred.

"Just tell me, PawPaw." After he did, she'd make her final pitch, as she and Cooper had planned.

"Jesse's decided to go back to KC. He'll leave by noon, he said."

"But…" Did he mean he was going home to pack the rest of his things? Move to the NLS?

"Why didn't you tell me he had financial troubles before?"

"Because that was Jesse's responsibility, not mine. It wasn't my place to tattle on him. Load the dice," she added.

"Integrity," he said. "I like that." Her grandfather frowned. "Jesse didn't have the same scruples. He ticked off everything he could think of that you've ever done wrong from the time you were kids, including the more recent loss of that calf, Elsie, and poor Ferdinand," he said. "He threw in Bear last night too, of course, a couple of issues between you and Clete, then Hadley. Not to mention the breeding register you set up.

Even the new combination for the safe. You shut him out, he said."

Her mouth set. "I realize I acted recklessly last night, PawPaw, but I've made some progress with Clete and Dex. You may not appreciate the changes I made while you were away, and you know how bad I feel about your bull—"

"Don't back down now, Nell."

She blinked and held her breath.

"Jesse's not the right person to run this ranch," he said.

"Do you mean— But you've always thought I needed a husband and children more than I needed to pull calves or pick the cow to breed to your best bull."

"I still hope you'll have a family. But I'm not going to turn the NLS over for those reasons. Even an old man like me can see a different way of doing things." He paused. "After Jesse and I spoke, I couldn't overlook his money problems or his lying. I spent hours in the office last night figuring out that new breeding program. I do like it, Nell. Spreadsheets aren't something I've used before, and they're mostly a puzzle to me, but they are better at keeping track of things. I figure you can handle those too." He smiled. "I guess that's that."

Her heart was beating loud in her ears. "What?"

"When I'm ready, the NLS will go to you," he said. "Jesse will get his carve out, and regular payments as one of my heirs to help with his finances, which you'll administer, but the deed will be in your name."

Nell's ears buzzed and, for an instant, she feared she'd pass out. For a second, she couldn't speak. She'd been mostly enthusiastic about the tentative plans she and Cooper had made last night, but now she would never have to leave the NLS, and neither would he, although her dreams of the ranch had changed. Cooper had given everything for her. If she didn't have him—if she wasn't loved—what else would she really have? This had to be right for him too…

"No," she said at last. "Both our names should be on that deed—mine and Cooper's."

"You trust him that much?"

"Yes. I do," Nell said. "Though knowing Cooper, I'm sure he'll insist on paying for his half. That would be the Ransom ranch."

"Which would give him a stake in this," he said.

"An equal share. We're partners in marriage. We should also be partners in the NLS."

"You sure that's okay with you?"

"Oh, PawPaw." He wasn't saying no. She flung her arms around her grandfather's neck and held on tight. "Yes! I'm okay with that." She couldn't hold the tears at bay. "You had to ask?"

"Now, now." He patted her back. "Nell, honey. You know I love you, but I guess that got in my way, and I couldn't see just how strong you are. I thought—wrongly—that being a woman made you vulnerable, that you needed someone else to do the heavy lifting. I realize now that was old-fashioned," he said. "I can change, Nell. So can your mother and father, even Jesse, once we set them straight. Anyway, Merry Ransom is already working on me. Gave me quite a talking to about my sexist attitude. So has Cooper." That didn't seem to bother Paw-Paw. "I shouldn't have listened to your uncle Will, but I never meant to undermine you. You'll knock this family of ours out with all the good you do here on this ranch."

"Then the old feud is finally over," she managed.

"Well, Merry may have had some say," he admitted.

"And in my children with Cooper, the Sutherlands and the Ransoms will be one. Having a few grandkids ought to soften up Mom and Dad, though she won't care for my riding and roping while I'm expecting." Nell drew back. "PawPaw, are you really courting Cooper's mother?"

He clamped his mouth shut, then couldn't help a smile. "It's time," he said, without elaborating on whether he meant Merry or the feud itself.

Then before Nell could respond, Paw-Paw glanced behind her and someone's hand lightly touched her shoulder. She hadn't heard the door open, but it was Cooper. He'd come to help her out here after all.

"Doing okay, Mrs. Ransom?"

"Doing fine," she murmured.

PawPaw studied Nell then Cooper. "But there is one more thing before I sign new papers for this estate. You sure you made the right choice?" He had a twinkle in his keen eyes. "Getting hitched to this Ransom boy? I heard what *he* said. Do you love him, Nell?"

"I do," she said without hesitation, as if she and Cooper were saying their vows again.

"That's all I needed to hear." PawPaw began to smile. He took their hands and joined them then added his on top. "From both of you," he said. "When Cooper told me last night how much he still loves you, I knew—even before I spoke with Jesse—*I* was making the right choice too."

Savoring the moment, Nell kissed her grandfather's cheek then Cooper's. She had the ranch she had always cherished, and Cooper would have his land again. *Their* land, she thought.

In the end, it was love that had ended the old range war.

She held Cooper's gaze. "I've loved him all my life," she said to PawPaw.

But then her grandfather already knew that too.

* * * * *

Don't miss the next book in the Kansas Cowboys miniseries, available Winter 2019!

Get 4 FREE REWARDS!

We'll send you 2 FREE Books plus 2 FREE Mystery Gifts.

Love Inspired® books feature contemporary inspirational romances with Christian characters facing the challenges of life and love.

FREE Value Over **$20**

THE FORTUNES OF TEXAS COLLECTION!

18 FREE BOOKS in all!

Treat yourself to the rich legacy of the Fortune and Mendoza clans in this remarkable 50-book collection. This collection is packed with cowboys, tycoons and Texas-sized romances!